To Kathy

Griffin Academy
A LitRPG Progression Fantasy

Knights of War
Book 1

Travis Dean

For Atania!

Copyright © 2024 by Travis Dean

All rights reserved.

No part of this book may be reproduced in any form or by any electronic or mechanical means, including information storage and retrieval systems, without written permission from the author, except for the use of brief quotations in a book review.

Contents

Prologue..1
Chapter 1..15
Chapter 2..36
Chapter 3..55
Chapter 4..72
Chapter 5..84
Interlude 1..102
Chapter 6..104
Chapter 7..121
Chapter 8..137
Chapter 9..150
Interlude 2..164
Chapter 10..167
Chapter 11..184
Chapter 12..198
Chapter 13..209
Interlude 3..227
Chapter 14..229
Chapter 15..244
Chapter 16..261
Chapter 17..275
Chapter 18..285
Chapter 19..297
Interlude 4..310
Chapter 20..313
Chapter 21..327
Interlude 5..343
Chapter 22..346
Chapter 23..357
Chapter 24..366

About the Author 382
Check This Out ! 383

Prologue

The tent's flaps blew inward, and a young man stumbled in, wheezing as he spoke. "Sir, they're attacking again!"

Nils rubbed his bloodshot eyes, placed his locket down on the table, and ran a hand through his thinning hair. Grabbing the arms of the chair, he forced himself to his feet. "Then we go again, Leverett. How many?"

"Our report puts it at two wyverns, sir, with ground support from thirty or so others. Mostly drake and basilisk from what I understand, though there are rumored to be other monstrosities. Another orc warband has joined them in the last hours, too."

Overwhelming numbers, but they had known as much. Nils turned to Giana. "Any word from the academy?"

"Not good news, sir," his second in command replied. "Just the adolescent griffins left, and they're barely able to get off the ground."

Nils nodded, a look of grim determination on his face. "Then it's just us. Grab the others. We go. Now."

Giana gave a nod of acceptance, turned, and headed out of the tent, swiftly followed by the young messenger.

Nils picked up the locket again, opening it to see the drawing of his wife and young son. The boy had been a baby when he'd left, and now, he was approaching his third year. He sighed and tucked the locket away. Wearily, he made his way across the tent and picked up his battered golden helmet, its left wing having been torn away after his previous day's evasive maneuver came too close to the claw.

Slipping the helmet on, he turned and strode toward the exit, grabbing his bow and quiver before pushing through the flaps of the tent.

The sun had barely started to rise, and the few rays that filtered through the forest canopy cast the camp in a soft, ethereal glow. The semi-structured chaos of firepits and tents spread through the stomped undergrowth.

The makeshift camp was currently located a few miles away from the battlelines, situated under the dense canopy of the Greater Helerean Forest. It wouldn't do for the wyverns to discover them where they rested, so all effort had been made to keep them well-hidden.

This dawn, however, was abuzz with activity without any effort to hide the plumes of smoke, as what was left of Atania's famed Griffin corps raced to prepare for their last stand.

Nils sighed. *Eight.* Eight riders. There had been well over a hundred when the incursion began, but as they had carved through seemingly unending hordes of orcs, basilisks, drakes, and wyverns they had lost many of their own. The griffins were powerful, and the bond between them and their riders turned the fusion of that beast and mage into units capable of plowing through forces far superior in numbers. Far superior, but not infinite.

Now, these seven and Nils were all that remained between senseless slaughter and Atania, their homes. He strode across the camp, assuming the stoic face of a confident warrior to hide the fatigue that wore him down. It wouldn't do for the soldiers to see him struggle. The riders were the last hope of Atania, and even if they were to die today, he would feed that hope until his last breath.

It wasn't easy to keep his face stern and back straight. They had been forced to ration the health potions these past couple of days, and Nils had gone without to set an example. Now, though, every step reminded him of the collection of cuts and bruises that threatened to pull him under.

A soft chuff brought a smile to his face as he noticed Astraeus gently butting the gate of the enclosure. The hands had been in and prepared her, and she was itching to take into the air despite carrying a tapestry of barely patched up wounds similar to his own. "I wish I was as keen as you, girl," he told her, running his hand down her feathered neck as she lowered her head in greeting. "This could be our last time."

Astraeus chirped and shook her head, seeming to sense from Nils' body language and tone that he needed her encouragement, today more than ever.

Nils patted her back, glad for her company. He doubted he'd have made it through this far, or this long, without his bonded griffin.

Opening the gate, Nils led her back across the camp. The others were there, now seated on griffinback. Seven griffins pawed at the sodden turf, claws idly tearing through thick roots, main feathers standing to attention. Both beasts and riders were eager to be back in the air, defending their land.

Although Nils was a firm believer in his bow, all griffin knights wielded lances first and foremost, ahead of any backup weapon. He'd always been a natural with a ranged weapon. Add on his wind magic and the fact he was in the air, it had made him an absolute nightmare for the enemy to deal with. If a wyvern made it close enough for him to need a sword, the chances were he was already done for.

"This isn't a time for speeches," he told those gathered before him. "We've been here. We've fought. We've bled. Many of our number have died. You all know what's at stake. You know our duty, and this might be the last day we get to carry it out, so anything I tell you now won't make the slightest bit of difference between success and failure. Just search deep within yourselves. Find that extra something. They may wound us. They may even kill some of us. But they will not defeat the Griffin Knights of Atania!"

The riders roared grim approval, their faces dark with that special fury of warriors knowing they were about to charge against impossible odds. The faces of soldiers whose only worry was whether or not they dragged in a big enough entourage to join them in the afterlife. Nils grinned at them. Best men and women he could've hoped for.

His smile softened as he directed it to Astraeus, and she lowered herself to the ground. Slipping his left foot into the strap, he pulled himself up and onto her back, feeling her power between his knees. All griffin riders rode bareback, with just the foot straps and their legs keeping them secure. With a flex of his knees, Astraeus rose to her full height, towering over the others at nearly ten feet tall.

With a nod to those before him, Nils turned. Together with his trusted friend, he led the Griffin Knights of Atania into battle.

The griffins tucked their shoulders in unison, bringing chills down his spine with the display of gigantic muscles beneath their feathers. Galloping on clawed paws and talons, they picked up speed down the grassy slope, aiming for the end of the tree line near the churning river below.

Once they were close enough for Nils to spot something break the water, the group lifted into the air. Turning slightly to fly around it, he gestured to the others that they'd be heading northward once again, and then they flew back toward the distant orange gloom of the frontlines burning on the horizon.

Ground blurred beneath them. Wind howled in their ears. They reached the battle in moments, every beating wing devouring long stretches of grassland below.

A frontline of darkly armored beasts, creatures, and tribal warbands of orc roared ahead of them like some unholy tide of war. They rode on, slowly accelerating, lances lowering, and met the opposing forces with a cry of griffin and man that drowned out the clamor of their opponent.

Power and spells were unleashed. Entire groups of orcs were decimated, explosions of elemental forces reducing them to blood and bone.

Griffins swirled up and dove in for another hit, clearing another small field in the enemy horde. In perfect sync with their bonded riders, the griffins tore enemies apart with their claws and ripped throats out with their beaks whenever their mage wasn't hurling out destruction.

But the horde stretched in from here to the valley and the mountains beyond, seemingly endless.

Lances plunged through armor, swords rendered assailants in two, and huge war hammers crushed bodies to pulp as arrows burst through eyeballs, piercing the brains beyond. Hundreds lay dead in the aftermath of their initial charges.

But the battle was turning. The griffins and their riders still worked as one, linked in a way that allowed them to preempt their attacks in fluid brutality, but the sheer volume of the tide of steel and claw rolling their way was like a force of nature.

They lost Sabastian, Aiken, and Laslo in the blink of an eye. Nils hadn't seen the Darkbrand brothers in minutes either. He made Astraeus cry out a command to fly up and rose high with Giana at his side. His second in command was cradling a huge dark stain on her side as she rocked on the back of Flameborn, breathing heavily.

The human and elven army below rebuffed most of the land-borne attackers. Somehow, they managed to hold the line against a legion of beings many times their strength. No magic or griffin helped them stay brave. No, those mad bastards held on through sheer grit and refusal to submit against any might.

Humbling though the display was, Nils had no time to bask in the awe of fellow man. They'd lost the three riders when half of the team had to drop down to rest their wings and skirmish on the ground. Though the combination of a lance, weapon, magic, beak, and four claws could deliver an unbelievable amount of death at great speeds, it had only bought them seconds of life against these numbers.

Sabastian had been the first to go, run through by an orc chieftain, diving from the back of a huge eight-legged basilisk. He'd hurled out magical fire as he'd gone down, leaving a charred orc corpse next to him as he expired. Aiken had swiftly followed, his griffin, Waterore, dragged to the ground by a drake, another then finishing him off. Nils had almost looked away as he saw his man torn limb from limb, but he owed these riders everything.

They *would* prevail. They had to prevail.

Laslo had remained in the air at their side, firing off lightning magic that tore holes in wyvern wing after wyvern wing as the beasts tried to swarm him. Unfortunately, firing off [Lightning Charge] after [Lightning Charge] emptied his core of mana to the point he couldn't keep his seat. He plummeted to the ground, Farstriker unable to save him after being grasped in a wyvern's claws.

Nils, Giana, and Andor had since managed to slay the first wyvern, riddling its body with arrows to slow it down and allow Astraeus to claw through its neck as small payback for Laslo. However, the second, and larger, wyvern refused to expire despite the burns that marked it body and the eight arrows that pierced its neck.

It swooped in again as the trio formulated the best plan of attack. Nils had reserved as much of his mana as possible for this, but the others were low, barely able to cast a flame between them.

Andor flew left to distract the beast, and Giana headed low, casting a small flame onto her arrow as she went to shoot at the belly of the wyvern. Nils flew right, keeping his distance as he gathered his mana. He pulled one of his last arrows from his quiver, nocked it, and poured a torrent of air mana into it to enchant [Gale Force] onto the arrow.

Nils then nudged Astraeus onward with the smallest gesture. The griffin changed its course, as if reading his mind through the slightest change in his posture. The scales of the great wyvern caught the low rays of sunlight and gleamed with burnt gold and emerald. It banked hard as though sensing their plan, snatching Andor and his mount in its maw and twisting away before Giana could release her flaming arrow. Nils grimaced and dove after the beast, chasing it as it spiraled over the battlefield.

Nils scanned the battlefield as he flew, his eyes widening as he finally spotted Silus and Salep Darkbrand. The brothers fought side-by-side, their griffins lost somewhere amid the melee. The army repelled the orcs with mad bravery. The brothers had taken on the task of finishing off the last of the drakes, and it was proving quite the task. The last drake standing was drenched in wounds and covered in weapons and still fought with brutal ferocity.

Silus, the older of the two by a year, wielded his earth magic to open deep pits, herding the beast into their desired location. Salep, the younger yet taller of the two brothers, flooded the ground, utilizing [Water Burst] to create bog-like areas and prevent its escape.

Having finally cornered the beast, the brothers unsheathed their longswords and hedged their way forward.

Silus paused, maintaining eye contact with the beast while speaking to Salep. motioning with his arm to direct his brother.

Salep sidestepped a bisected basilisk corpse to head left and flank their opponent.

The drake snarled and swiveled its head erratically from left to right, trying to watch both brothers as they closed in.

As Silus paused, presumably to pull forth a lethal strike, his brother screamed. Silus spun and froze. A titanic underground-dwelling wyrm had erupted from the dark, blood-covered ground to grasp Salep and pull him under.

They've got wyrms? Nils realized, his gut lurching with horror. They hadn't accounted for this. The ground forces were going to be decimated!

Scrambling across the ground after his brother, Silus dropped to his knees, clawing clumps of mud away as he vainly tried to save his sibling.

As he put his hands to his face and screamed, Nils saw Silus' mistake before he did. A growl thundered, and claws shot up from the earth, straight through armor and flesh. Teeth clamped down on his head, and Silus joined his brother in death.

Nils muttered a prayer to the brothers under his breath and tensed with his knees. Astraeus pulled up slightly, waiting for Giana and Flameborn to join them. It wouldn't do to take any risks now. Not when their resources were depleted and the enemy had brought unexpected reinforcements. If they fell, so would the ground army. In a way, the two riders were all that remained between entire warbands of orcs and the lands of Atania. Countless lives--friends, family, and neighbors--counted on them.

We must prevail. Nils squeezed the locket under his shirt. The fire in his chest found fuel to blaze once more.

Giana continued to hold her bow, the arrow still magically lit as she pulled up alongside him.

"Mana?" he asked.

"My core feels almost empty," she replied, confirming what he already saw from her exhaustion.

"OK. I've only got a couple of arrows left. So, I'm going to fire both imbued with [Gale Force], buffeting the remaining wyvern while I swing around to the left. If you can head low and then throw as much fire behind an attack as possible, it'll focus on you as it regains its bearing. Then I'll throw everything at it. I've got enough mana left to hopefully take it out for good."

Pausing briefly for Giana to nod in acknowledgment, Nils leaned forward. He ran a hand through Astraeus's mane and whispered, "Let's go, girl. One final time."

Astraeus chirped, tossed her head, and flew on. Nils nocked both arrows and called on [Gale Force] as they closed in.

He found a line of sight, when the beast tossed Andor's mangled corpse to the ground, and released the arrows. They screamed through the clouds as two comets trailing wind mana, punching through the wyvern's neck and wing, causing it to spin out of the skies.

As the wyvern struggled to right itself, Giana closed in. She called on [Flame Throw] but the spell aborted half-way through casting and whiffed as her mana core ran empty. She cried out, smoke billowing from her hand. The wyvern saw its chance and shot forward on pierced wing. It chased Giana across the skies. Exhausted, Flameborn's ability to evade its clutches decreased with every turn and drop, the griffin desperately trying to keep the pair alive.

Nils knew time was running out. With no arrows left, his only option was one final casting to take the beast down. An all or nothing spell.

Drawing on his core, Nils pulled on the entire store of mana his core had produced and spread it through his body. It felt like his veins went cold with wind as the mana suffused his body in preparation to cast [Wind Vortex].

As Flameborn twisted and turned, coming back under Nils, the wyvern noticed Astraeus and changed its line of attack. Nils cooed softly for his griffin to wait and continued to draw on his ever-dwindling mana reserves. His fingers were numbing, sensation leaving his extremities.

It flew straight at them, matching Astraeus on a collision course. Neither the griffin nor man made a sound. She trusted him and tucked her wings to accelerate towards the larger beast.

Astraeus dodged to the side. The wyvern's claws flew out, catching the griffin across the chest and gouging a deep cut. Nils cursed and turned them around. They waited for the monster to come back to finish them off.

Mana continued to spread from Nils' core. Winds began to churn around him as the sheer density of mana in his body bent the elemental forces around him. Pure white of arctic winds glowed in his eyes.

"Soon," he promised to the dead, "soon, I will send it to join you." The wyvern's eyes locked on Nils, its pupils thinning. It surged back toward them, sprinting across the skies. It reared its hind end, massive claws open to grab Nils and his griffin.

Nils drew in a deep, icy breath. His body was fully saturated with every last drop of his remaining mana. Calmly, he raised his hand towards the wyvern falling upon them and released [Wind Vortex].

Air bent under his will. The sky collapsed into a screaming chaos of blade-sharp winds and slammed into the wyvern. The wyvern's shriek of pain was drowned out by the deafening roars of the gale. The vortex, larger than anything he had ever created, pulled the beast from flight and hurled it toward the ground as if it were a paper toy. The wyvern plummeted down, spiraling out of control into the enemy ranks. When the vortex dissipated, only a bloody crater remained with chunks of orc and wyvern spread around it. Sighing in relief, Nils closed in on Giana, a soft smile teasing the corners of his mouth.

It had cost them almost everything, but they'd defeated the enemy's aerial threats. Now, they could join in to support the ground army and help turn the tide. The army could deal with the stragglers that remained. The wyrm was likely gone, but without having to watch out for wyverns, they could take it down if it remained.

As Astraeus hovered in the air, Nils let emotions shudder his breath as he clutched the locket. They had prevailed. He'd kept his wife and young child safe. Every kill had been for them.

The cost had been dear, every victory paid in close friends and irreplaceable comrades. An unreasonable cost, perhaps, but if they didn't pay it, who would? He looked across at Giana to see how she was taking it, but the look that met his gaze wasn't one of relief. Sheer terror stared back at him, just as a huge shadow spread across the ground below.

As Nils turned in the air, a scream came from somewhere.

It can't be...

With no mana and no arrows remaining to defend them, and blood continuing to pour from the wound in Astraeus's chest, a huge burst of flame was all it took to consume the last two Griffin Knights of Atania.

Chapter One

"Close the fuckin' shutters, Jadyn!"

I laughed and turned to see Brom retreat deeper under his woolen blanket.

"How's the head? And you do realize it's almost noon, right?" I asked, straining to keep a straight face as I thought about the previous evening's festivities.

"Feels like a damn ox kicked me," came the mumbled reply from my stocky, brown-haired friend.

Shaking my head, I left the shutters open and headed over to grab some clothes to throw on. We had drunk well into the small hours last night, and although Brom was feeling the worst for it, I had never felt better. We were going to be joining our bonded griffins in the air for the first time today, and not even a hangover could dampen my mood.

I reached my closet still smiling and pulled the worn wooden door open to begin my search. I needed something, anything, that didn't smell like an alehouse. It wasn't going to be easy. Eventually, I discovered a clean linen shirt and dark pants under some haphazardly discarded garments. I pulled them on and headed over to the washbasin to splash some water on my face. Showering would have to wait until after the lesson.

"Are you up yet?" I hollered over my shoulder, taking the mumbled grunt in response as confirmation that he wasn't.

Filling a cup with water, I tiptoed over to his bed, pulled back the cover, and doused his head. He roared in disapproval and threw more than a few choice words at me as I fled.

Laughing, I tossed him a parting, "Catch you in the lesson, buddy," and headed out into the hallway.

Acknowledging a couple of other male fourth-year students with a nod in passing, I headed down the grey stone hallway toward the large dormitory door that would take me out into the central courtyard.

As I lifted the metal latch and pushed open the black wooden door, I noticed that the usual chill of early morning was long gone, replaced by a gentle autumnal warmth. Another good reason to be up and about after breakfast. I couldn't abide the cold mornings and was already dreading the approaching winter months.

I was born and raised south of the academy, in the small fishing town of Farrenport. It was about as far south as one could go in Atania without becoming one with the raging seas beyond. The summers there were stifling, bordering on the fires of hell, but the winters were pleasantly mild. I would choose hot summer over cold winter any day.

I stepped out, the gravel path crunching under my feet. Many of the academy's granite buildings faced this central courtyard, with a few exceptions lying down past the gardens and the stables hiding behind the dormitories.

I scanned the courtyard as I strolled, smiling when I noticed a certain lone figure heading down towards the arena. I'd spent the past three years admiring that exact view — the raven-black hair, the long, athletic legs in those skintight pants, the perfect curvy ass swaying with her steps, and those tight undershirts with nothing underneath.

"Sienna, wait up!" I called, jogging to catch up.

She paused and turned, and I swore she must have used a little of her magic because of the way her hair billowed out. She offered me the sort of smile that made my legs turn to jelly.

"Hey, Jadyn," she said, voice soft, her gaze focused intently on my brown eyes. I hoped it was because she was afraid of me catching her looking me up and down.

"Hey, we really missed you last night. I wish you'd joined us," I told her earnestly as I slipped my arm around her shoulders and gave her a light squeeze.

At five-ten, she was a good four inches shorter than me. She rested her head on my shoulder briefly before laughing gently and shaking her head. We'd been close since we met. The attraction had been instant and intense, but somehow, we'd ended up having some kind of silent agreement that we'd take things slow — a hug here, a hand held there.

We'd talked briefly about our plans while skirting the big griffin in the kitchen, how we were both driven to be the best we could be, and I hoped we could do that together. Sadly, that meant we didn't often have the time to try take things further, but we'd get there eventually.

"I heard you had quite the night without me. How is Brom anyway?" she asked, brushing a stray strand of hair behind her ear.

"Same as always after drinking too much. Left him hiding under the covers. There's no way he'll make the start of class."

She chuckled knowingly, and we strolled on, the route taking us through the academy gardens. A winding gravel path led us past small trees, bushes, and floral borders, a few late-flowering plants still providing bright colors in contrast to the browning leaves of fall that had recently started to dot the ground.

A small, apologetic sigh left her lips. "I really wish I could have been there."

"Me, too," I replied. "I always have a better time when you're there."

She slipped her hand into mine, pulling me onward. "I'll make sure I get there for the next time."

"You promise?"

"For you, Jadyn, of course." She squeezed my hand meaningfully.

I got charmed all over again and smiled a dumb smile, lost in her deep blue eyes. Just because we were taking things slow, making sure we knew what we wanted and fitted it in our lives, it didn't lessen my attraction to her one bit.

"How are you feeling about today?" she asked. "Feeling any party fatigue?"

"A bit, but not much anymore. I'm excited," I admitted, feeling the jitters as my thoughts went to today's big event. "For as long as I've known I had magic, all I've been able to think about is being a griffin knight."

It wasn't just about the power and trust of being bonded to your griffin, though I did want to feel it. It was about what the riders stood for. About what they meant to the people relying on them. About becoming the kind of hero that young Jadyn had once seen fly and land amidst a group of kids in gleaming armor to let them play with his steed. If he could inspire even one person, give just one person a fraction of what that rider had gifted him, he would be content.

She knew my story and nodded in understanding, letting me continue.

"It's... now that it's here, today, it feels weird. Like we're in a dream that's not supposed to be here yet. Does that sound strange?"

She shook her head, making an understanding sound.

"Look." I lifted my trembling hand. "Even my fingers are jittering with excitement."

She gave me one of her cutest giggles and showed her own hand, the one that wasn't holding mine. It shook, too. "It's been going around," she said. "Though, I seem to have found a cure."

The other hand slipped around mine, too, and the way she held them went a couple steps past 'just friends handholding'. The way we stood put her perky breasts right in view if I looked her way, pert nipples reminding me of just how thin that black fabric was.

Thankfully, she let go. A brief walk in quiet followed, with both of our faces hot-red and our minds busy keeping the pent-up wants in check.

Class today was one I'd been looking forward to the whole summer. Finally, we'd begin practicing our aerial maneuvers. We'd been learning the moves on paper for what like forever, waiting for our griffins to reach the age where we could join them in the skies.

Now, the time to ride was finally at hand, and not even the fact it would be old Algernon teaching the class could dampen my enthusiasm. He wasn't even particularly strict. The issue was his voice.

He had a tendency to drone on for hours in that monotonous baritone. To make matters worse, I'd hardly slept, so staying awake would be an even greater challenge than normal.

Reaching the practice arena, I paused briefly to take it all in. At the bottom of the gardens, a short distance from the lake, stood the imposing stone structure that had served as the training ground of trainee griffin riders for centuries. A huge stone archway led into a large oval-shaped grass field, surrounded by several rows of wooden seating.

The academy didn't believe in spectator sports as a part of learning, so it was seldom that crowds entered the arena for anything other than graduation. Stone walls rose a good twenty feet beyond the seats, leading to the open sky above. The ability to be able to fight in any weather was particularly important – as Algernon repeatedly told us.

As we entered through the archway, Sienna gave my arm a light parting squeeze and ran over to join Elandra and Fitmigar.

If you looked up dark and beautiful in any book, I was convinced you'd see a picture of Elandra. She was a touch shorter than Sienna, held a symmetrical beauty in her face that really captivated you, and those lips... Her dark brown hair matched the color of her eyes and cascaded down past her shoulders.

Elandra was super playful, always throwing comments out at me, teasing. To be honest, I was completely confused about where she-me-and-us really stood. Was she interested? I was, of course, but then I did have a really nice thing going with Sienna. But then, to complicate things, she also sometimes teased about us so... To summarize, I was confused, and I'd accepted that state of confusion as the norm.

Not that it stopped me from fantasizing about the what ifs. Especially in moments like these where both girls' rears stood facing my way, fabric squeezing into their asses, leaving tiny holes in their thigh-gaps.

I shook my head, clearing my thoughts. It was dangerously easy to get lost in daydreams when Sienna and Elandra were together.

Fitmigar Ironmantle, on the other hand, was around four feet tall and your typical adolescent female dwarf. She had long blonde hair, braided down to her waist, and she was feisty enough to storm right over and clock me if she caught me checking out her friends.

She'd also been there with Brom and me last night at the alehouse. In fact, Brom's attempt to keep up with her drinking was the reason he still wasn't here – and the reason I had to toss him over my shoulder and carry him back to the boys' dorm.

It didn't matter how many times I thought he'd learned his lesson, Brom could never back down from a drinking challenge – despite never once coming out on top. He couldn't be called a bad loser because he seldom even remembered the events the next day.

Turning away, I headed over to join Sars and Mallen.

Sars was a Darkbrand, and after Brom, he was probably my closest male friend here. He was academy royalty really. An eighth-generation griffin rider, he was the most well-spoken of us all and something of a study fanatic, often sweeping his light-brown hair across in a side parting to complete the look. Coming from such a long line of griffin riders, he never missed a chance to share tales about his family's adventures.

His brothers had left the academy before we arrived to fight in the Griffin Army. He would not shut up about their exploits and how amazing and powerful and absolutely awesome they were whenever he'd had more than half a drink.

In contrast, Mallen, his dark brown hair pulled back into a ponytail that ended halfway down his back, was tall, stern, and very, very elven, though he'd certainly lightened up a little since we'd first met. Still, there was no hiding his elvish roots – and believe me, he tried, though none of us really knew why. He'd even forgone choosing any type of bow or sword when we selected our weapons, opting for a war hammer that somehow just worked.

Mallen had also once revealed to me in confidence that he'd never even wanted to enroll in the academy. It was a complicated matter, and I didn't want to pry, but I hoped that our friendship went someway to making it more bearable for him.

"Fellas," I greeted them, clasping arms and nodding at each in turn. "All ready for today?"

"Like you would not believe. I was made for this," Sars replied. He was the keenest of anyone to be one step closer to graduating at the end of next year and joining the army.

"Can't say my excitement is as high," Mallen admitted. Inclining his head toward Sars, he added, "Not after spending the whole of breakfast with Sars having some form of griffin fanatic meltdown."

Sars laughed and punched his friend in the shoulder. "It is not my fault you do not get excited about anything."

As Mallen went to respond, a loud, spluttering cough pulled our attention away. Algernon was here, and he wasn't about to wait for us to finish catching up before beginning class. Ambling back and forth before us, the grey-haired septuagenarian waited until we were all paying attention before stopping. He straightened up slightly and addressed us.

"Good morning, students. I do hope you are all fully rested because today is the start of…"

Trying to be as discrete as possible, I glanced around but saw no sign of Brom. He'd likely sneak in at some point, and I doubted Algernon would notice. For the lightweight, tardy drunk that Brom often was, he utilized his shadow magic better than anyone. It had got him out of more than one scrape where anyone else would have been caught red-handed.

With the entire class, even Mallen, itching to get to our griffins and into the air, Algernon did his best to delay us longer than usual. I tried as hard as I could to follow for the first thirty minutes, maintaining my concentration even when Brom appeared, bumped my elbow, and winked, but I was only human. I soon drifted off into daydreaming of soaring through the skies, imagining us bolting through clouds and wandering through the mountains to the north.

Eventually, Algernon finished up, and turning toward the stalls in the corner of the arena, he beckoned us all to follow. There were forty students present today, and we all chatted away as we trailed behind the elderly instructor shuffling his way across the ground, kicking up dirt as he went.

Making my way past the first few stall doors, I stopped as I heard a low chirp. I'd recognize that tone anywhere. Unlatching the wooden door, I smiled broadly as I hurried in to greet Hestia. She rose from the straw-covered ground, her light-brown eyes sparkling.

I felt the hardness of her bill as she lowered her head to gently nibble at my ear. Hestia was the largest of the griffins amongst the fourth years, standing at nearly nine feet tall, and she was the only one with feathers all the way down her back, giving her a darker brown appearance than the others.

I ran a hand down her neck through her soft feathers and patted her gently, feeling the bulging muscles beneath her skin. She had chosen me back in the first year, and we had grown together, learning to fight alongside each other as our skills progressed. Today would be the first time we took to the air as one, and it marked an exciting new chapter in our bond.

I nodded my head a fraction, and she lowered herself to the ground. Circling to her left-hand side, running my hand along her flank, I stepped into her riding strap and pulled myself up and over. Slipping my right foot in and tensing my knees, I gave her the signal to rise.

I couldn't help but grin as I sat atop her, my heart thudding a couple beats too fast. Finally, we would be flying!

From the moment Wendia had adopted me, she loved to tell me stories of the great griffin riders of the past: Grendol Weirstack, Hlo the Swift, even tales of the great Bloodblade, Aeric, riding on the only blood-red griffin, Morgart. Of course, back then I was unaware of the magical core growing inside me, but it hadn't stopped me from dreaming of becoming one and playing griffin riders all day as a kid. She had tried to prepare me for the worst, offering alternative hopes and dreams, but I'd had none of it. Maybe I'd always known on some level that I would become one? Or maybe I'd just been a crazy idiot as a kid. Likely both.

I paused for a moment in contemplation. Wendia had passed just a few short months before I started my first year at the academy, succumbing after a short illness. I hoped she would have been proud of the young man I had become.

Still, sitting there, I felt like that kid all over again. "OK. Let's head on out and show them what we can do, girl."

Hestia chuffed in return and trotted out into the arena as I shifted on her back, finding that sweet spot where I'd feel secure when we took to the air.

We were the first ones out, but the others soon joined us, pawing at the turf and feathers standing proud.

Almost every griffin and rider was as keen as us to begin the next stage of our training.

The next few hours were spent running through the first couple of maneuvers that we'd gone over in class that summer. Some pairs had more success than others as the griffins initially struggled to bear the extra weight in low flight. We'd practiced sending them up with loads on their back prior to this lesson, but carrying a moving rider, even one without their weapons, proved a whole new challenge.

Hestia and I had no such trouble. It was likely due to her increased size, but as soon as her back paws left the ground, I felt like we had found where we belonged. We swooped and twisted through the maneuvers seemingly without effort. Air rushed past my face as each powerful beat of her wings drove us forward. My grin didn't loosen up for a second, and it was hard to not keep whooping in delirium!

We still needed the breaks, unfortunately, resting up before rising again each time. However, long after the others were back down on the arena floor and tending to their tired griffins in the stalls, Hestia and I were still flying through the maneuvers, relishing the sensation of freedom and power. Not once during all my trips up did I forget to think of the fact that I was finally doing it. I was flying on the back of my bonded griffin, the ground below racing past as we sped by. It was my dream come true, and the reality was so much more that I could ever have imagined. And I had imagined it a lot.

When we eventually landed for the final time, it was to whoops and hollering from my friends. They had remained to wait for us, the other students long since having headed off to a late lunch.

Hestia held her head regally, appearing to love the adulation as I slipped off her back, landing softly on the ground and mocking a bow.

Brom was the first to come over and pat me on the back, but the others soon crowded around, bursting to gush over our achievements and stumbles, but mainly to gush over how it'd feel to fly, even for just a few wing-beats. I recalled seeing Fitmigar crashing through some of the old wooden arena seating after she turned far too late into a corner, and the less said about Brom causing Algernon to dive to the ground to avoid being wing-clipped the better.

We had all had a blast, even while crashing into things, but the elderly instructor had decided to call it a day before we could destroy the entire arena. He had hobbled out through the archway and toward the gardens a short while ago.

After returning Hestia to her stall, and slipping her a double portion of fresh meat, I joined the others. We headed back through the lush gardens and toward the lunch hall, all of us smiling and giggling like fools. The lesson had gone better than I could ever have hoped and left me full of strange, elated energy.

As we approached the hall, the gravel kicking up under our feet, I paused as a hand briefly grazed across my back and then down. I turned to see Sienna and Elandra glancing at each other, both barely able to keep a straight face.

I grinned in response, draping an arm around each girl as I led them inside.

At lunch, we secured one of the large wooden tables near the windows looking out over a small fountain. The conversation continued to revolve around the previous lesson. "Worth the wait?" I asked, looking around the table.

"Too fucking right," Brom immediately replied. "Did you feel that power?"

"The feel of who knows how many pounds of pure griffin muscle beneath me?" I asked. It was hard to miss that feeling of being untouchable with such a beast.

"It is something else," Sars added, a huge smile breaking out. "Everything the books said and more. See, this is why I have been preaching to you about their greatness. Now you know none of it was exaggerated!"

"Some of it was probably exaggerated," Mallen said dryly.

"I've never felt so close to Dawnquill," Sienna said, smiling softly and gazing at me in that way she had that got me all confused. "It felt like we were one... Does it make sense?"

Everyone nodded and mumbled in agreement. It made perfect sense.

"Right," I said, "it's like our bonds have deepened somehow. There were times when I felt Hestia nudge me in return, almost knowing our next move before I told her."

"It certainly felt good to have something big and strong between my legs," Elandra added, leaning forward with a playfully silly wink, almost making me choke on my lunch.

She had a special knack for wording her flirt in a way that I could take either way, if it was flirt. Part of me was convinced she liked me. The other part just assumed she was messing. Both parts hoped it was the first.

"Was good," Fitmigar joined in. She didn't waste words, and if Fitmigar spoke you tended to listen. Unless she was 15 ales to the wind, of course.

Even Mallen appeared happy, despite his comment. The elf fidgeted as he spoke, "I always thought about it logically, how griffins allow us to chase down enemies and release devastating attacks from the air. But now I've felt that connection, that bond, stronger than ever before... well, it's more than about becoming powerful, isn't it?"

I smiled. We'd all been taken aback by the thrill of joining with our bonded griffins in the air. Sure, we would have to be ready to use that bond to fight once we graduated next year, but for now, we could be students a little longer and enjoy the pure joy of being a rider.

Lunch over, we returned to the arena to be met by our dwarven casting teacher, Therbel. He was slightly taller than Fitmigar at around four-four, and he'd gone short with his hair, at least for a dwarf, apparently at the expense of a blond beard that dropped to his waist.

With the risk of injury high, we alternated between mock altercations and working alone against wooden, stone, and metal targets. Today was one of the latter. Splitting up into magic types, I left my close friends behind and joined the five other fourth-year fire mages.

Each student at the academy had a magic affinity. It was something that appeared in only a small percentage of the kingdom's population, and if you studied the students, you'd notice very few elves and dwarfs alongside the predominantly human adolescents.

You might even think that magic was more prevalent in humans, but it wasn't the case at all. Rather, the elves and dwarfs kept themselves to themselves for the most part, only sending a few chosen children to learn at the academy each year as part of a centuries-old accord.

One of the fire mages, Helstrom, was dwarven. The other four—three boys and a ruddy-faced, bespeckled girl—were human like me. I enjoyed their company, for the most part, particularly a large red-haired lad called Rammy, but there was always an underlying competitiveness that I had no time for from the others. I turned up, did my best to train and push myself, and left it at that. It didn't do me any favors to try show off in front of my classmates. At least, not usually.

Helstrom went first, burning through an extra target with his [Fire Burst]. He'd managed to increase the area of the flames significantly. I ran through the options in my mind in preparation for taking on the singed wooden training dummy that one of Therbel's assistants set up for me.

Mana was generated naturally within our cores. This began at birth, but I hadn't noticed mine until much later due to a complete lack of awareness—and no one with the experience to guide me. The cores expanded naturally with age, but training also boosted the level of mana by increasing the core's density.

Spells were created by trying to shape mana manually into them -- an incredibly difficult and time-consuming process. Even with constant practice, it took time for initial spell impressions to solidify enough that they appeared in our system and became reliable enough to cast.

The ability to muster enough control to form a [Spell] typically emerged between fourteen and fifteen years of age and resulted in the academy welcoming you in as first years. Now, in our fourth year, we were all nineteen or a few months away, and our cores were over double the size and density of fresh first years.

I'd worked diligently in my time here, and I had practiced enough to engrave three [Spells] into my core that I could trust to work as I wanted. A couple of students only had one—Charn and Bernolir came to mind—but they had what felt like ultimate mastery of that particular spell, and then there was Lana with a dozen.

Lana was one of the more accomplished students, and she had the most spells—a little fact she reminded of us constantly. The redheaded girl thought she was better than everyone and seemed to have been born to compete. Naturally, we did not get along.

I was content to become the best I could be. She didn't know how to get along with someone who neither wanted to compete, nor fawned over her prowess.

As I dismissed using [Fire Burst], Het removed her glasses, paused, and cast [Fireball] at her target. A ball of fire roughly 3 inches in diameter flew across the space and struck the dummy in the left shoulder, leaving a small scorch mark but little more. I smiled in understanding and offered a shrug of commiseration.

Deciding to practice my third spell, which I had solidified more recently than the others, I reached within and pulled mana from my core and into my hand, naturally allowing it to flow and take the shape of the spell I had trained. Lowering myself to a knee, I placed my palm toward the ground and released my hold on the spell. Mana surged out of me, coalescing into a fiery figure no more than six inches in height. It hopped off my hand and strolled purposely across the arena floor toward the dummy, dust puffing up under its tiny steps.

Chuckles erupted from beside me, but I paid them no heed as I continued to pull on my mana stores and feed it into the spell. The figure grew in height with each step it took. By the time it reached the dummy, it stood at knee height, fiery hands resting at its waist. Defiant.

I inhaled deeply, and the fire elemental bent its knees before leaping. Pivoting in midair, the elemental surged with a bright blaze of flames and burned its way through the dummy's chest, leaving a smoldering hole in its wake.

Oohs and aahs came from the spectating fire mages.

Satisfied with how far I'd come with [Fire Elemental], I mocked a bow. The others, for the most part, congratulated me.

Het looked more pissed than anything, shooting me a disapproving glare over the top of her glasses, but when I promised to talk them all through my approach she softened somewhat.

With class soon over, I joined my friends from their respective sections. When Elandra joined us, I suddenly found myself jealous of the other water mages. Water dripped from her long brown hair, and her shirt was glued to her like paint, accentuating her breasts as they strained against the material. Nipples stood up hard against her shirt.

She noticed me looking and winked, leaning forward as if to gift me a better view.

"Like what you see, Jadyn?" She grinned ear to ear, wiggling her tits a little to push them up. "Bet you wish you could grab a feel, huh?"

I refused to immediately look away, lifting a single eyebrow and smiling before eventually turning and joining the others.

Chapter Two

Freezing cold water rather startled me from dreams of drenched water mages and raven-haired wind mages with the bluest eyes.

"What the…?"

Sitting up, I scanned the room to see Brom's back briefly, shoulders bouncing in laughter, before the door closed behind him. He did owe me for the other morning, so I couldn't really complain. Amazing how much of a morning person he could be when he hadn't drunk himself stupid the night before.

I threw the covers off me, shook my head, and dropped my feet off the bed. Padding across the aged wooden floor, I freshened up at the washbasin before throwing on a set of clothes suitable for today's lessons.

Checking the sun's position through the room's narrow window, I smiled as I realized I hadn't slept through breakfast—something my growling stomach appreciated. Breakfast was also always the best time to catch up on any news, so I headed out the door, down the hallway, and out into the morning beyond. A horribly chilly morning, I swiftly discovered.

I jogged across the courtyard, shivering from the cold by the time I entered the food hall. Brom was taking a seat next to Elandra, Sars, and Mallen at our usual table, and Sienna and Fitmigar were still plating their meals. I hurried over, narrowly avoiding a collision with a couple of first years as they headed out.

"Morning," I greeted with a smile as I reached the line and peered past to check out the contents of the chafing dishes beyond. Eggs, sausage, ham, and tomatoes. Yes, please.

The girls both turned, Sienna happier to see me than her short dwarven friend, though I always found it hard to gauge just how happy Fitmigar was on any given day.

"Sars has news, Jadyn. From the border. If you can stop gawking at Sienna here for long enough, best you grab some food and come join us, huh," Fitmigar told me, shaking her head in mock annoyance. At least, I assumed it was in jest. She'd clocked me once before for far less.

I winked at Sienna before nodding to the four-foot-tall earth mage alongside her in understanding. "I'll be right over."

I might have been suitably chastised, but that didn't stop me from admiring Sienna's firm body as she headed over to join the others, her tight-fitting shirt and pants leaving nothing to the imagination. She threw back a little glance, met my eye, and added a little extra sway to her walk.

Keen to hear the latest from the war with the orcs, I threw a mix of hot food onto my plate, grabbed a steaming mug of coffee, and joined the others at the table. Luckily, it was Sars with the news today. Brom would have started without me, enjoying any look of confusion on my part as I tried to get up to speed.

Pulling out a rickety wooden chair and dropping down next to Elandra and opposite Mallen, I smiled at the others. Sars shifted from side to side, sweeping his hair across, a serious expression on his face.

I straightened up. This looked important. If the news wasn't good…

"Go on then," I encouraged.

"This may get heavy," he warned.

"It's fine," I said. "We're all here to become warriors."

Agreements were murmured and nodded around the table.

He leaned forward and scanned us from right to left before clearing his throat and beginning.

"I was on my way back from the library last night when I caught the end of a conversation between old Algernon and Dean Hallow."

We leaned in as he lowered his voice.

"Apparently, word came late last night that we have taken further heavy losses."

"Oh no..."

"Silus and Salep okay?" I asked immediately.

"From what I understand," he confirmed, offering me a weak smile. "But, it is looking bad. Griffin forces are down to almost single figures after another few wyverns appeared and decimated the ranks."

"What about the fifth years that headed up a few months ago?" Mallen asked, the elf's expression equally grave.

"One or two left at best. Nils Leandeos is still heading up the force, but he cannot work miracles. The fifth-years were not ready—we could all see that—but they had no choice."

"You think we'll be joining them?" Brom asked, lines of worrying etched on his normally jovial face.

"That is what they were discussing," Sars explained. "The dean thinks it is only a matter of time, but Algernon was telling him we are too green. He wants to give us longer to get used to fighting in the air."

"I'm inclined to agree with him," Sienna said, a tremble of nerves in her voice. "The thought of facing off against a marauding army keeps me up at night."

I placed my hand on top of hers and gave it what I hoped was a reassuring squeeze.

She smiled back at me, appreciating the gesture.

"All we can do is keep training," I said. "We all know that, likely before too long, we're going to be needed. The best we can do is learn all we can to give ourselves the best chance of success when we do travel north."

I'd spent many a night thinking over this war. Huge numbers had already lost their lives to protect those unable to defend themselves. The young, the elderly…

Still, I would give my life without question to do the same. I'd been born with a gift and given the chance to cultivate it. Living up to the legends of griffin riders and protecting the people was my duty. There were moments when I imagined myself growing old, perhaps joining Sienna on that farm she often spoke of working when we moved on from our time with the griffin forces, but if my life was lost, that was just the way it had to be. I didn't fear death, not as much as I worried about what would happen to those I'd leave behind.

I looked around my friends. The weight of Sars' news had brought everyone into deep contemplation. I needed to improve and grow stronger. I needed to keep my friends alive in the battles ahead.

From the looks of determination on my friends' faces, they thought the same.

We finished our meals in subdued silence. War was coming, no doubt about that, but now it seemed we likely wouldn't have a chance to finish the fifth year of our studies here at the academy, let alone graduate, before duty called.

Galen's classes on the art of combat were one of the highlights of the week for me. However, after the news Sars had overheard, I found my usual light bounce as I headed into the lesson replaced by a purposeful stride. As with our recent flight and casting classes, the entire year group was present.

Unlike our open-air lessons, combat class took place in a series of high-beamed, grey stone halls with thatched roofs. We passed through a set of large double oak doors that led into an initial square hall that ran around three hundred feet across. An extended weapons rack lined the right-hand side, and a series of chalk-marked circles were mapped out the dirt floor for one-on-one and two-on-two matchups.

There were two open archways at the far end of the hall, the right of which led to the archery range, the left to the jousting hall. There were temporary griffin stables at the end of there, tacked on almost like they'd forgotten the need when they'd originally built the structures hundreds of years previous.

"Today, we'll be splitting up," the tall elven teacher explained. "Lances, you'll be the only ones on griffinback, so head over to the stalls and then on to the practice jousting arena where young Mirek is waiting for you. Bows, you'll be with Thom here." Galen paused and pointed to his red-haired human assistant. "Melee weapons, you'll be with me."

I nudged Brom and whispered, "Bit strange, right? We don't normally split up straight away. Think there's something going on?"

My stocky shadow mage friend just shrugged. "Does it matter?"

"Guess not," I replied, heading over to the rack to select a weapon. "Perhaps I'm just looking for something that's not there after the news we just received."

Like most of the students here, I'd spent my first two years trying out as many different weapons as I could. I'd even tried out a bow, thinking maybe I had a knack for ranged weaponry, but the less said about that the better. Last year, I'd finally settled on dual scimitars, and if Galen's praise was a good yardstick, I'd come on leaps and bounds since making the choice.

Pulling a pair of wooden scimitars from the rack, I nodded at Brom, and we headed across the hall to find a suitable circle.

"Before you start, and yes, I'm talking to you, in particular, young Brom, there'll be no magic used in here today as we will be focusing on martial skill," came Galen's voice, and I noticed my friend visibly deflate. "There may be times when you exhaust your mana in battle, and you need to be prepared for this eventuality."

If we were ever to take on real-life assailants, Brom would wield a fine pair of obsidian daggers, four more kept in a bandolier across his back, but for the purposes of today's class, he juggled a single wooden pair. As griffin riders, magic would always be our front line of assault, but backups weapons beyond our lances remained important in case we lost our mounts or ran out of mana as the teacher suggested.

We both knew I had the upper hand, and Brom, I was sure, had looked forward to utilizing [Shadow Cloak] to even the odds and move in close, maybe even [Shadow Blade] to even out the reach advantage I currently possessed. Unfortunately for him, it seemed a certain elf instructor was on my side today.

"You want me to just start with one?" I asked, trying to cheer him up a little.

"No, you're good, Jadyn," he replied, puffing out his chest. "I've got you here regardless."

I'd barely stopped laughing before he was moving, feigning left and then rolling right, trying to get in close to bypass my longer reach.

Anticipating his trickery, I slid my foot right and backed off, maintaining the distance between us as he effortlessly spun a dagger between his fingers, his eyes locked on my stance as he searched for an opening.

We'd done this dance plenty of times before, and this was only going to go one of two ways. Either I created an opening for him and lulled him in or I went after him.

Brom was your typical shadow mage, outside of the fact he was the least serious person I'd ever met. He worked best when he could put his increased stealth to use, and the fact he couldn't get in and out unnoticed against me here would frustrate him. He had patience in abundance, his ability to be stealthy required it, but I could just come at him head-on.

If I had a weakness, it was a tendency to relax sometimes and get lost in my thoughts a little too easily. I blamed the training. I just couldn't always get my brain to focus on something that I knew wasn't life and death. I was improving, but it only took a wooden dagger bouncing hilt-first off my shoulder to make me realize I still had a way to go.

"Ha! I told you I had you, man!"

Right. It's time to knock that shit-eating grin off his face.

With Brom down to a single short weapon, I took my chance and lunged, closing him down, utilizing the longer reach of my swords. He kept backing away, evading my blades. I threw in a couple of quick combinations before I came in high and right, my curved wooden sword aiming for his clavicle.

Dropping low beneath a slash, he lost sight of one of my blades. That was all the advantage I needed to change the strike's angle and knock his remaining dagger across the dirt-packed ground. I followed up with a leg sweep that left him on his back and wheezing.

"Oof!"

I smiled and placed a sword to his neck. "Yield?"

"Yield," he begrudgingly agreed.

I bent over and took his hand, lifting him back to his feet.

"Well fought, brother," I told him. "Almost had me for a second."

Brom laughed and shook his head. "We both know that's not true."

"Again?"

"Sure," he replied, his bravado returning. "That was just a warm-up. You'd better watch out now."

With a smile on my face, I tossed one of my swords out of the circle and beckoned him on.

A quick spar later, and it was Mallen looking up at me from the ground this time, the elf's wooden war hammer lying across the hall. "Fine. I yield."

"You're really improving," I told my elven friend, keen to let him know how far he'd come.

"I think so, too. It's really starting to feel like an extension of my arm now. Well, when it's not been kicked across the room that is," he added, walking with me as we headed over to pick it up.

I nodded in agreement. There was no denying that Mallen was perhaps the finest shot with a bow in the entire year, with the exception of maybe Sienna, despite his insistence to use another weapon post-graduation. Several of us had brought it up in the past, but it proved a touchy subject, so we'd all learned to leave it be. If Mallen ever got to the point where he wanted to share his reasons with us, he'd do just that. For now, a war hammer it would be.

Our blond-haired elven instructor took that opportunity to clear his throat and get our attention.

"Great work today, all of you. I know some of you find it hard without your magic to aid you, but none of you have embarrassed yourselves, so give each other a pat on the back and go and get some food in those bellies. Report back here in an hour's time for some dueling in partnership with your griffins."

The other students filed out in small groups. Once Sienna returned from the range and Sars and Fitmigar joined from the jousting hall, we took our leave, too.

We arrived in the food hall and swiftly selected from the choices on offer. We were due back shortly for more lessons, but I was still keen to learn how the others had got on.

"How was the range today?" I asked Sienna as I dropped down next to her, my leg brushing hers.

She met my eyes and smiled. "It went well. I can't get that news out of my head, and I thought it might affect my shooting, but if anything, it focused me more than ever."

"I found that, too," I admitted. "You think we'll get called up soon?"

"I can't stop thinking about the possibility," she replied, eyes looking away in thought. "Part of me is nervous, but more of me almost wants to be there. We have such an opportunity to make a difference. It's where we belong, isn't it?"

"I agree," I said. "I can't help feeling we could be helping more."

Once we'd all finished, we headed back across the courtyard to the main combat halls. The lance-wielders rejoined their griffins, still roaming within the jousting hall. Now they would be riding at each other, attempting to strike with softened weapons. Mirek would make a competition of it, usually sourcing a prize of some sort for the victor.

The ranged weapon wielders joined us melee students in retrieving our griffins from the stalls at the end of the jousting hall. Froom and his team had brought them down during lunch.

I smiled at Sienna and wished her good luck as she disappeared into the archery range. The targets from before had been removed and the area opened for one-on-one duels. Sienna and Dawnquill pretty much always came out on top, and she looked confident as she headed off.

With the melee weapon wielders making up the majority of the class, we took the biggest room again. Everyone stood off to the side as Galen looked on, deep in thought as he considered the best matchups.

I'd sparred with Brom and Mallen earlier in class. Galen took that into consideration as he paired me up with Helstrom first off, the dwarf smiling as he twirled one of his twin wooden axes in the palm of his hand. As he strode over to climb onto his grey-feathered griffin, Mossrik, I noticed he was discretely wearing another two axes strapped to his back, under his shirt.

That's new, I thought, glad I hadn't missed the detail.

We'd fought a few times before, and he'd more often than not found himself weaponless at the conclusion, so it was good to see that he was adapting and trying something new, even if it made my own job harder.

Taking hold of Hestia's straps, I pulled myself up and onto her back, nodding first at Helstrom, then at Galen. The elf combat instructor raised his right hand, pausing, and then dropping it to signal the start of our duel.

Mossrik appeared cautious, eyeing his larger stablemate and weaving from left to right, looking for a good opening. If they behaved anything like they normally did, they'd look to be as elusive as possible. Helstrom was no fool and knew that up close and personal we'd dominate them through power alone.

Hestia was itching to charge in, so I let her. Spreading her wings, she darted forward, nipping at Mossrik's left wing. The grey griffin tucked it in and spun to evade. Hestia continued to alternate between nipping and striking out with a paw, forcing the smaller griffin to dodge repeatedly as we maintained the pressure. The pace of our assault quickened as we worked them from side to side, chasing them around the arena.

In a desperate attempt to buy distance, Mossrik leapt into the air, opening his wings to glide across the space. Hestia turned with them, chasing them down and funneling them back, keeping them on the defensive. Mossrik, feinted to the right, then surprised us by lunging in as Helstrom threw an axe at me.

I tugged on Hestia's straps, and she pulled into an evasive spin. The axe spun above my face and away, close enough for a breeze to buffet my cheek.

Knowing Helstrom normally struggled to contain himself once he thought he had an advantage, I nudged Hestia's flank. She swept to the left, avoiding the onrushing grey griffin.

As they charged past us, I flicked the wooden dagger I had kept hidden in my sleeve out. It struck Helstrom between the shoulder blades, pointed end first.

"First blood!" I shouted, laughing as he scowled at me.

"We're not done yet!" the dwarf replied, Mossrik spinning back around, this time warier about rushing in. Helstrom threw a second axe, which Hestia batted away dismissively. The dwarf thought he could surprise me by throwing his third axe immediately after, but I was ready and blocked it in front of my face with a flick of my sword.

The dwarf nodded, appreciating that I'd seen through his attempt at sneaking in extra weaponry.

Time to end this, I thought, closing in and discreetly slipping my feet from the straps. There was no better time to try out the latest move I'd been working on privately with my fighting partner.

We dodged left, then zagged right. I prepared to commit to the attack, and I noticed Galen signal from the edge of the room, Brom edging onto the floor on Shadowtail, carrying a sword over his usual dagger, maybe to recreate the scenario if he could call upon [Shadow Blade].

Seriously? Another?

I reacted faster than Helstrom, nudging Hestia to remove herself from being flanked by the two assailants. At least, I assumed Brom was coming against me. Better to be safe than sorry.

The pace picked up now. Three griffins darted and dodged swipes from paws, claws retracted. Three riders exchanged blows above them, seeking advantage over one another.

Hestia caught Shadowtail's wing with a forceful strike from her own, and as Brom's griffin spun, I managed to whip out my arm, knocking his sword loose and eliciting a shout of frustration.

He leaned over, grasping after it. I tried to finish him off, but an axe whistled across in front of my face. Only Hestia's evasive maneuver had kept me safe. Brom had to lean heavily on his steed to dodge it, too. Unfortunately for Brom, that opened him up for my attack. Hestia's tail flicked out as he evaded the axe, whip-like, striking him in the chest and sending him flying from Shadowtail's back and onto the floor.

"That's you out already, Brom!" Galen shouted from the side of the room, barely suppressing a chuckle.

My stocky friend growled in annoyance and headed back to the side as I spun back toward my initial target.

"OK, girl. You ready?" I whispered.

She chirped in confirmation, lowering her head and coming at Helstrom head-on. He was out of axes. This was our time to defeat them and win the three-way duel.

As we closed in, Mossrik backed away, rapidly moving left and right as he tried to prevent us from getting close. However, nothing could stop us now as we worked as one. My weight shifted from side to side effortlessly as Hestia twisted and turned, closing in, each powerful stride bringing us closer.

As Mossrik tried one final desperate attempt to evade capture, I slid my feet free again, brought them up onto Hestia's back, and pushed off, flinging myself through the air to the right as my griffin bore left.

Helstrom's eyes widened as I flew. Both swords struck him in the chest and knocked him from his seat.

I slid across Mossrik's back, landing in a roll and coming up to a knee. If I'd turned for a moment to look at those spectating I'd have never seen the wooden arrow flying towards me from the archway to the range beyond. A quick flick of my right wrist sent one of my wooden swords up, and I knocked the arrow off course less than two feet from my face.

I grinned as I noticed Sienna stood there, one hand on her hip, shaking her head in disbelief.

"Nice block," she said, walking over and throwing me a water bottle. "Here's your reward."

"Appreciate it," I said, catching the bottle.

"Victory to Jadyn and Hestia!" Galen roared, and a round of applause sprang up as I headed across to the side, ready to watch the others compete. Maybe I'd learn some new moves. *You never know, right?*

Lana was up next, and the redhead looked at me dismissively as she strode past. Maybe I wouldn't watch too closely after all.

Once the melee duels were over, Galen dismissed us all, nodding in respect to me as I passed.

After walking our griffins back up to the main stables, the rest of the afternoon consisted of potion-making with Madame Summerstone, a middle-aged, blonde-haired human lady with a propensity to wear bright flowers in her hair, even through the colder winter months. No one knew where all the flowers came from.

When I first started at the academy, I was somewhat mystified why a griffin rider needed to know such things. Then, on the first ever lecture, Madame Summerstone explained some old war statistics about how often riders went without support staff and convinced me on the spot. Caught away from others and out of health potions, our ability to collect ingredients and work alone or in small groups could be the difference between life and death.

The potions workshop was situated east of the dorm rooms, immediately to the right. Rather than crossing the gravel courtyard, we headed down the right-hand side of the main academy hall to an annex stuck near the rear.

Potion-making was not high on my list of skills, but we'd been working in pairs for a while now, and I'd lucked out being paired with Sars. He knew pretty much all there was to know when it came to health potions, anti-flame potions, and the like.

Today, we'd been tasked with creating smoke bombs, and we worked as a pair, selecting and mixing ingredients in precise quantities.

My luck appeared boundless as I also found myself seated near to Sienna and Elandra.

As Sars and I discussed whether adding a potent stench to our potion would increase its effectiveness, Sienna leaned across to me.

"Hey, Jadyn," she whispered, "I hate coming here straight from the combat halls. I feel all hot and sweaty still. Sorry for asking, but can you tell me if I smell?"

I raised an eyebrow and leaned in close, inhaling deeply. I studied the way her shirt clung to her, outlining every curve of her body. A sweet, musky scent that reminded me of hot summer days in flower-filled meadows hit me, and my breath shuddered with the exhale.

"Well?" she asked, her breath warm against my face.

I struggled to compose myself and attempted to be as gentlemanly as I could manage. "All good," I told her, easing away and hoping she wouldn't notice the telltale sign that I'd found her scent alluring.

"You'd tell me, right?" she asked again.

"Of course. I'll happily check again after you've showered if you like?" I said, smiling.

She laughed and placed her hand on mine. "I bet you would."

"Always happy to help," I said, loving the feel of her hand on mine. "In fact, how about we all meet up later at the alehouse?"

"If you're going, Jadyn, I'll be there," Elandra said from the other side of Sienna, leaning across and winking.

"Sounds like a great idea," Sienna added, gently squeezing my hand before slowly trailing hers away.

Damn…

As we finished up the lesson a short while later, after discovering in part that it wasn't wise to add anything potent-smelling to your smoke bomb, a second-year student burst in, wheezing and bending double, struggling to catch his breath.

"Have you all heard? The dean wants everyone in the main hall. Now!"

Chapter Three

The mood was solemn as we made our way across the courtyard and into the main academy hall. We all held out the vain hope that we'd been summoned to receive good news, but recent events had taken a certain trajectory.

Fucking orcs.

Sars stumbled as he walked, an almost glazed expression on his face. Striding over, I threw an arm around my friend's shoulders, and we walked on together.

Maybe they are just going to cover what Sars overheard, I thought, hoping against all hope that I was right.

The younger students had already filled the chamber and were seated at the front by the time we entered the hall. With no final-year students, there was still plenty of room. We gathered to the left of the wooden pews lining the front half of the wall, opting to stand.

The main academy hall was a huge stone structure with a high-vaulted ceiling. Despite being one of the largest buildings on the academy grounds, we seldom used it outside the formal events and announcements like today's. The hall also housed some of the administrative offices at the rear.

Dean Hallow, our short and balding head of the academy, took that moment to signal someone at the entrance to close the doors, and then he lifted a hand, and the room went quiet.

"I expect you are all wondering why I called you all here," Hallow began, and a murmur rose in the hall as he slid his spectacles back up to the bridge of his nose.

The dean lifted a hand again, and the noise abated.

"I'm afraid it's not good news. We have received word in the last hour from the border that catastrophe has struck, and our griffin riders are no more."

Gasps of surprise spread throughout the hall.

My eyes darted to Sars. He collapsed to his knees, burying his face in his hands. Uncontrollable sobs wrecked out of him as I knelt beside him.

"Brothers. My broth..." His voice died mid-word.

I clutched his shoulder. Mallen rubbed the other one. The rest of our friends stood uncomfortably, both uncertain how to console him and anxious to hear the rest of the news.

The dean continued briefly, filling the room in on recent events at the northern border. I trusted in Brom to bring me up to speed later. Sars needed support right now.

I struggled to find the right words for a while before I accepted that there really weren't any. Instead, I placed my hand on his back and waited until he was ready to talk. I couldn't imagine what he was going through, but I knew he'd needed us there.

Before I knew it, the first three years were streaming past us. My friends and the other fourth years remained in place.

I turned to Brom as he leaned in to whisper, "The dean's asked us to stay on."

I nodded and rose, gently encouraging Sars to join me. He reluctantly agreed and wiped his tear-stained cheeks as he got to his feet.

Satisfied that the others had all left, all it took was a brief nod and the entrance doors were sealed once again. The dean then beckoned us all to the front.

"Take a seat, all of you. You're going to want to be ready for this."

Forty students complied as one, all shuffling along and dropping into a seat before the dean spoke again.

"I'm sure you all probably realize already, but that wasn't all we heard back from our forces at the border."

A soft hand grasped mine. I looked to my side to see Sienna, wide-eyed, staring back at me. We all knew where this might be going.

"The head of our forces, Commander Flint, has sent a request for your immediate presence at the northern border to aid in the ongoing battle. Rumors abound that in addition to the drakes and basilisks, and several wyverns that have been taken down, a wyrm has also been spotted alongside the main orc army."

Seldom had forty students remained so quiet. I noticed more than a few fearful looks around me.

Was it wrong that something akin to eagerness flared inside me at that point? If we were the next line in the defense of our kingdom, I was damn sure we'd be there to put a stop to this war once and for all. I would not allow monsters to rampage across Atania. Not my Atania. I would die fighting and drag a thousand of those bastards down with me before letting them take a single step into the villages. I met Hallow's eye, and we exchanged nods of understanding.

"Now, Commander Flint is fully aware that we have only just begun aerial classes with you all." Hallow paused, ran a hand over his balding scalp, and exhaled. "So, with that in mind, he is mindful of how long it will take you all to reach them."

I glanced at Sienna again, and she gave me a soft smile. Scanning the others, even Sars had a look of firm acceptance on his face as he pulled the hem of his shirt down and brushed the creases out before sweeping his hair across again.

"So... organize your belongings, sharpen your weapons, and prepare. You leave in three days' time. The journey will be a little under a week, but here at the academy, we are all fully confident you can do this. Atania needs you."

Reality hit us. Glancing around, I saw many blank faces, some of my fellow students not sure how to react.

Dean Hallow turned and strode away, gesturing to his assistant, Rivers, a young Beastkin, to fill us all in on the more minute details.

"I don't think I can do this," Brom muttered.

I threw an arm around my best friend's shoulder. "You absolutely can," I told him. "Do you remember how you felt when you took Shadowtail into the air today? How powerful we are and can be going forward."

"But we're not ready," he replied.

"We're as ready as we get to be. We have a few days, and then we'll use the journey, too. Those orcs won't know what hit them."

Brom smiled, nodded, and puffed his chest out. "Fuckin' right, man."

I patted his back. "We've got this, buddy."

A good half-hour passed before we left the hall, the details all passed on. We'd be leaving three mornings from now, traveling by ground on griffinback to the northern border. We were taking Algernon and Galen with us, our lessons continuing on the road. Mirek and Thom would also be accompanying us, and Madame Summerstone would likely send one of her assistants to help source what was needed to create any additional potions as we traveled.

There were no guards to spare for the journey, so we would be responsible for our own safety. We couldn't very well take on marauding orc forces after being babysat the entire way there anyway. I was glad, actually. We'd likely get some action on our journey to make sure we weren't quite as green when we arrived.

The countryside between the academy and the northern border was mostly verdant farmland of rolling fields and cozy homesteads, with a few smaller towns and villages populating the route. This time of the year with the heat of summer gone, farmers would be out plowing the fields and planting winter-growing crops like onions, beans, and cabbages.

Our route wouldn't take us through any of the larger cities, and most of the villages were off the main track, but we'd pass through a town, maybe two, on the way. My geographical knowledge north of the academy wasn't great, but I remembered the first town would be Riverhaven, the hometown of Charn.

Charn was a sandy-haired wind mage, with a voice that could stop an army. He only had the one spell – [Ballad Boost] – but it could send his voice across miles, allowing him to use his songs as a huge area of effect spell that could boost his allies or hinder his enemies.

Although the orc forces still hadn't made progress into the country, there would still be plenty of dangers along the way with bison, wolves, and bears abundant, particularly near the forested areas.

As we closed in on the border, the ground would become hillier, leading toward the mountainous region that the orcish forces attacked from. The only mountains in Atania were toward the northwestern coast, due west of where we would be fighting. They were home to the dwarves, but they had yet to join in this war, choosing to stay in the mountains for reasons that remained their own.

I placed another round of ales onto the table and dropped back into my chair. We'd already arranged before hearing the earlier news to have a drink together at the Wandering Molerat that evening. After the heavy stuff dropped on us, we had decided to continue ahead with our plans. We all needed to relax and toast the fallen. We'd expected Sars to be reluctant, but he'd agreed, saying it would have been what Silus and Salep would have wanted.

The Molerat was a long, narrow building, constructed from a mix of local stone and hardwood. The bar was situated about halfway back on the left-hand side, while the rest of the space was filled with square and rectangular wooden tables, each seating four or six patrons. We often pushed a few together if we visited in a large group.

The room was lit by several log fires, stationed in the corners and down the right-hand side. Sconces dotted the walls in areas that would have otherwise fallen into shadow. Still, the light was fairly low.

The villagers tended to take the far end of the alehouse and not mix with the students. There was seldom trouble as it didn't pay for us to get involved.

We were enrolled in a military academy, so fighting with the locals wouldn't go down well with the instructors.

"So... how's everyone feeling about joining the war?" I asked before taking a sip of ale, clanking my tankard back down as I noticed I was starting to feel the ale's effects. The Molerat wasn't known for having weak ale...

"Can't say I'm surprised," Fitmigar admitted. "Since they took the fifth years early. Only a matter of time."

"Agreed," Sars replied. "Silus's letters spoke of the worsening situation, so I have been preparing more than ever."

"And that's saying something," Mallen said, gently nudging his friend's shoulder. "There have been mornings I've woken up and not been sure if you've headed out early or just not returned to your bed."

Sars shrugged and mumbled, "Best to be prepared."

"Absolutely," I agreed. "We've got quite the journey to the border, too. Five or six days of travel, at the very least."

"We'll be safe, though, right?" Sienna said, placing her hand gently on my leg.

"Of course," I assured her. "Who would be stupid enough to mess with forty griffin knights traveling together?"

"Knights?" Brom asked.

"If we're joining the fight, we'll be leaving our student positions behind. No more privates and the like. There'll still be a hierarchy, of course, but trust me when I say that we'll ALL be knights."

"Too fuckin' right," Brom replied, slurring slightly.

Eventually, the conversation eased, and we fell into companionable silence as we all took a moment to remember the fallen. Sars stood and raised his tankard in a toast. We decided soon after that it was time to head back.

A soft touch on my hand gave me pause as I went to leave. One imploring look from Sienna's beautiful blue eyes was all it took for me to sit back down.

"We'll catch you all up in a bit," I told the others, ignoring Brom's stupid grin before he pulled the alehouse door closed behind him.

Sienna leaned over and placed her head on my shoulder, sighing contently. "Do you really think we'll be okay?" she asked.

"Of course," I told her. "There's seldom been seven griffin riders as tight-knit as us. I don't think there's a challenge anywhere that we can't meet head-on."

"And the orcs? The beasts?"

"They don't know what's coming for them," I said. I did worry, I'd be a fool not to—death was always a possibility, for me and my friends—but I refused to allow fear to hold me down.

She turned her head and kissed me lightly on the cheek. "How about we get out of here. I've got something I need to show you."

Unsure where this was heading, I agreed and helped her to her feet.

Trees lined the route back from the Molerat to dorms. Beyond them, the dark fields waved quietly with the nightly breeze. The sound of our breathing and footsteps were occasionally joined by the hoot of an owl or small animals rustling in the underbrush.

As we walked, Sienna slipped her hand into mine. A grin crossed her lips as I gave it a squeeze.

"So, what's this thing you want to show me?" I asked.

"You'll see," she teased, leading me back toward the academy.

She didn't elaborate, only squeezing my hand a little tighter.

My thoughts began racing. Even without light to see the details in Sienna's silhouette, my mind's eye was caught exploring the memory of her curves. I felt our hands grow clammy despite the chill.

Five minutes of tension passed without a word. The academy's buildings came into view. Instead of heading back into the courtyard, she pulled me left, past the food hall and around toward the shower block. At this hour there was no light from within. Maintaining my cool, I looked at her with an eyebrow raised.

She stopped, grinned, and slid a hand into her pocket, her face lighting up when she pulled out a wrought iron key.

"Care to join me?"

"In the shower?"

"In the shower." She let her gaze dip to take me in. A blush rose to warm her cheeks.

My breath shuddered. Three years of games and tippy-toeing around the topic, waiting for the perfect time. Was it now? Maybe it was the alcohol in my veins, but I didn't care at this point. This needed to happen.

"You bet," I said, pulling her close and running my lips across hers.

She laughed and pushed me away.

"Wait until we get inside," she whispered and turned to the lock, twisting the key to the right and pulling the door open.

She giggled softly when she glanced back at me, her eyebrows rising as she scanned down my body in the dim light and noticed that my anatomy had betrayed me.

Sienna bit her lips, grabbed my hand, and tugged me inside, pulling the door closed behind us.

"Are you—" I started before she was against me, pulling me in and slipping her tongue into my mouth, cutting off any thoughts that I might have had about her being unsure.

I'd had a few rumbles in the hay since I'd arrived at the academy—once quite literally with a farmer's daughter—but they'd been quick flings without attachment.

Running my hand through Sienna's hair, I pulled her closer, allowing myself to finally give in to my desires. Her smell filled my head. I slid my hand down her back, relishing the feel of her athletic body, before finally cupping her perfect ass for the first time.

She made a small moan-like sound, and a groan escaped me. Perfect didn't cut it. Her ass was divine.

"Are you sure you want to do this?" I asked.

"I can't wait any longer, Jadyn," she replied. "We head off to war soon, so who knows if this opportunity will ever come again. If this is gonna happen, it needs to be now."

"Aren't you worried that this might change things between us?"

"I've never been surer of anything in my life. I've waited long enough. I've fantasized about this for so long."

I grinned. *It wasn't just me.*

She pulled away and smiled, leading me away from the doors and into the showers beyond, easing my belt loose as she went.

"It wouldn't do to get these wet," she said, running her hands around my waist before easing my pants down.

I nodded and grinned as my hands flew to her shirt, the lower buttons flying loose as I gave up halfway down and pulled her shirt apart, exposing her perfect tits beneath and emitting a growl of pleasure.

Stepping back and pulling my own shirt over my head, I dropped everything I wore to the floor as Sienna teased at her own skintight pants before sliding them to the ground, keeping eye contact with me throughout.

She reached for my hand and dragged me underneath the showers. She leaned her breasts against my lower chest and pressed against me, while her hand snaked around my back to start the water cascading down upon us. I could feel the rapid pulsing of her heart through the mounds squished against me and feel the heat radiating from her sex. My own arousal hardened against her smooth thigh.

Hesitant, our hands explored each other. As the water warmed, I couldn't take it anymore. I spun us around, allowing it to run down her face, her raven-black hair falling just across her blue eyes. I lifted a hand and brushed the strands aside as I looked into those eyes and kissed her again, hungrily. Her small hands hugged me closer. Slipping my hand lower, I teased at her breast, running my fingers around her areola and across her nipple, eliciting a soft moan in response.

She smiled as she took hold of my cock and slowly caressed back and forth, guiding me closer to her pussy. My tip pressed against her mound, and I was just about to grab her ass, pin her against the wall, and fill her up. Sensing my need, Sienna pulled away, shook her head, and said, "Not yet, Jadyn. I've got big plans for you."

I huffed in frustration.

She giggled. Sienna had some impressive self-control, considering how wet and hot I'd felt her between the legs. She turned us again, my back now up against the wall, and lowered herself to her knees. A big grin split her face as she looked up at me. "Well, aren't you the big boy…"

"Guilty as charged," I replied, slipping my hands into her hair and pulling her head forward. I was pretty sure she'd never been with anyone else, at least not during our time at the academy, so I prayed she'd know what she was doing.

Turned out I needn't have worried. Far from it.

"I've imagined taking you in my mouth so many times…"

The words sent a pulse of something beastly through me. "You've imagined?"

"And used my fingers to practice."

Fuck.

"To do this..." Her tongue flicked out, running across the head of my cock, then down and slowly, teasingly, back up. Her lips enclosed the tip, and I pulled her head closer as she ran her lips up and down my length, wetting my cock with saliva and shower water. Not once did she break eye contact with me until I threw my head back, unable to control myself. Her fingers cupped my balls, teasing as her mouth brought me ever closer to the edge.

Keen to see just how much of me she could take, I pulled her closer until she made a harsh gagging sound as my tip pushed against the back of her throat. Rather than discourage her, it seemed to spur her on. She gulped down more and more of me, spit running from the side of her mouth as she gagged on my length.

I was close to spurting my load down her throat and pulled back and lifted her to her feet, eliciting a sound of surprise. I spun us again, forcing her against the wall.

"Yesss..." she slurred, grinding her ass against my cock.

Under the steaming water, I slid a finger up her thigh and between her soaking lips, teasing the folds before adding a second finger and plunging in deeper.

She moaned, her eyes rolling back as I continued to thrust my fingers in and out. She gasped as I brought her close to orgasm, my hand accelerating. She dug her fingers into my back, pulling me closer.

"I need you inside me. All of it, Jadyn," she urged. "Now!"

I was in no position to deny her, so I lifted her off the floor, lowering her onto me slowly at first, the head of my cock slipping inside her tight pussy. Her inner walls spasmed against me as I lifted and lowered her, again and again, each time inching deeper.

She moaned in my ear as I quickened my pace, continuing to thrust into her. Her breathing grew ever more rapid as I brought her closer and closer to orgasm.

She screamed as she came. Her body arching as she bucked against me. I couldn't wait any longer. Heat built within me, but as I went to lift her away, committed to spurting across those perfect tits, she growled and pulled me tighter.

"I've waited so long for this, you're not going to deny me now. I want to feel your cum inside me, filling me, dripping down my legs. Now, fuck me harder, Jadyn."

"Yes, ma'am," I replied, driving into her, again and again, until hot spurts of cum flooded out of me, pulsing inside her as she came again, a pink flush rising in her cheeks as she screamed in ecstasy.

Once we'd showered clean, dried off, and dressed, we sat in the corner of the entryway. Her head rested contently on my shoulder.

"Do you think it can work?" she asked, running her hand over mine.

"How do you mean?"

"We'll be leaving soon. Now's not the time to have you worrying about me when you've other things to concentrate on. We'll be Griffin Knights. We'll both need to be more than just Sienna and Jadyn."

"I've worried about you all before this. Nothing's going to change that now, even when we're knights," I told her, squeezing her tighter against me.

"Don't get me wrong, I want it to happen again. A lot. But, I'd hate it if I stopped you from doing what you need to do."

"Me being yours and you being mine doesn't change that."

"All mine?" she asked.

"Yeah?"

"Hmm..." She hummed, suddenly mischievous.

"Okay. What?"

"Nothing. I thought you knew there was more possible. Besides, I know a certain other girl who'll be pretty pissed at me if I keep you all to myself."

"Madame Summerstone?" I joked and received a punch to the shoulder in response.

"Idiot."

Chapter Four

A loud cough woke me. I pried my eyes open to find Brom sitting on the edge of my bed, a grin tugging at the corners of his mouth.

"Well, handsome?"

"Well, what?" I asked, sitting up and rubbing the sleep from my eyes.

"You know full well what, Jadyn. Got anything to tell me?"

"Nothing you need worry yourself with." I laughed and jumped off the bed, heading over to the washbasin and ignoring the deluge of questions that followed.

Shaking water off my face, I turned to my friend. "Look, buddy. A gentleman never kisses and tells."

"Nothing? Not even a token description of that glorious chest, man?" Brom implored, a mock frown etched on his face. "That tight ass?"

"Not for you, no. Get your mind back out of your pants, and let's get off to breakfast."

"Ha. I didn't really care anyway," he said with a light laugh, heading off without me and easing the door shut behind him.

I finished getting ready, feeling better than ever, and took the hallway to outside. Crossing the courtyard, I found everyone bar Sars already seated at the table eating. Grabbing some food and a hot tea, I dropped down next to Mallen and smiled around the table. My gaze lingered on Sienna across from me a moment longer than the others.

Hers lingered on mine. Her smile was unusually happy, which got a strange pride buzzing in my chest.

The topic at breakfast was our planned departure from the academy two days hence.

"No classes today, then," Mallen said. "There's a note up outside Dean Hallow's office, and then he's had Rivers going around telling anyone who'll listen the same information on the off-chance they missed the note."

"Something to look forward to," Brom mumbled.

Brom wasn't a fan of Rivers, though he struggled to tell us why. I also got a bit of a weird vibe off the relatively young five-foot-tall Beastkin, but I usually put that down to him being the only one of his race I'd ever met.

No one knew all that much about him. He'd simply turned up a few years back at the dean's side, and now his brown-furred face and small, pointed ears were a common sighting on the academy grounds. He helped around and even doubled as a substitute when teachers fell ill. He'd likely be in high demand in the classroom once we headed north with a few of our instructors in tow.

Beastkin were the least common of the four races of Atania and seldom seen this far south, hailing from Eilerin Island, just across the narrow Eilerin Sea. The summer heat didn't tend to agree with them—at least, that was what I'd been led to believe—so it was highly likely Brom also had never met another.

"So, what's the plan then?" Sienna asked, discreetly running a foot up the inside of my leg as she spoke, out of sight of the others.

I coughed and shook my head to clear my thoughts. "I guess it's just going to be packing, sorting our weapons, getting the griffins ready, and then saying our goodbyes?"

"Sounds about right," Brom agreed. "And then the Molerat tomorrow night?"

"Ha!" Fitmigar laughed, "I'll see you there, you stocky fool. Figure we have time for one more drinking challenge before we go. If you're man enough, of course."

Brom laughed. "You're going down, Fit."

Fitmigar sighed, leaned toward Brom, and said, "Call me 'Fit' again, Brom, and I'll run you through with a rusty blade after drinking you under the table. How about that?"

Brom stopped laughing, and a quizzical look crossed his face. "Not really, right?"

Fitmigar stood and left the table, dropping her plate off en route.

"Right?" he shouted after her.

She merely shrugged as she walked away.

While our friends bickered, Sienna's foot had continued to travel up my leg to my groin, massaging me through my pants as I struggled to concentrate.

I shot her a surprised stare. This was bold. Way bolder than I'd have thought of Sienna, even considering yesterday's events.

She returned an innocent look.

"Right, I'm all done. Catch you all in the courtyard shortly," Mallen said, rising from the table.

"Hold up, Mallen. I'm all done, too," Sienna added, looking at me and winking before jumping up from the table and following him out.

Hang on. The foot's still there…

It moved left and right, faster and faster, my pants becoming ever tighter.

My gaze shot across the table to see Elandria smiling back at me, barely suppressing a laugh. She pulled her foot back, grabbed her plate, and headed out after the others, parting with a quick, "Catch you later, Jadyn!"

I couldn't get a proper grasp on Elandra. Her comments and actions screamed that she wanted me, but then I always second-guessed it all. Did she just enjoy openly flirting? But then Sienna had said she knew someone else that wanted me. That must be Elandra, right?

With Brom now all finished up, too, he turned to me, interrupting my confused thoughts. "Ready to go?"

I coughed and glanced anywhere but down. "Think I'm just gonna need a few more minutes, buddy."

Packing up was always going to be a breeze for me to complete. I'd arrived at the academy gates with little more than the clothes on my back, and although my wardrobe had grown somewhat in the three-odd years, I still owned far less than most students here. I liked to be presentable, but I preferred to spend money elsewhere or just didn't spend it at all.

My bags all packed, I left Brom to his mountain of belongings and headed down to the combat halls. The weapons rack held wooden training equipment, but a storage section beyond the archery range held our actual weapons.

Venturing into the main combat hall and failing to spot Galen, I wandered onto the range, and then the small jousting arena. Eventually, I found spotting Mirek as he finished up with Sars' griffin, Ralartis.

"I don't suppose you can let me into the weapons storage can you, Mirek?" I asked the tall, brown-haired lad.

He was around my age, and both his mother and father had been students at the academy. Mirek, however, was not magical, and so his family had requested he pick up work looking after the griffins here as a way of keeping the family tradition alive.

"Sure can, Jadyn. Just give me a couple of minutes to find the key."

I nodded and took a seat against the wall. Hestia was up in the main stables behind the dormitories, otherwise I'd have spent my time with her.

A few minutes passed before Mirek returned clasping a key in his right hand. "All good, Jadyn."

I hopped to my feet and followed the stable hand out. He'd taught a few classes, teaching those with lances after receiving tuition at home from a young age, but I still never really thought of him as a teacher. I guessed it was an age thing.

Walking back out into the main combat hall, I followed Mirek as he turned left and headed past the range to the weapons storage. As I walked, I couldn't help but notice how great I felt. Physically speaking, I felt fresh and full of energy like I could run for hours. I shrugged it off and went to collect my swords.

Mirek stood holding the storage door open to let me in. Magical sconces lined the wall, casting the room in a pleasant pale light that gleamed off the countless weapons on the wall. Bypassing the first two rows, set aside for lances and ranged weaponry, I took the third row.

To the right were the war hammers, brutal with the huge steel heads on dark wood handles, all rigid and balanced. To the left were swords, rapiers, longswords, and claymores. The end of the aisle held more pole arms, war scythes, poleaxes, lucernes, and even a trident. The light reflected off the sharpened metal edges and polished surfaces.

I passed two other sets of scimitars before I located mine. They hung in their dark brown sheaths that matched Hestia's feathers, only the griffinbill pommels visible.

Collecting them and my short dagger with matching handle, I returned to the doors and nodded my thanks to Mirek. He locked the doors behind me.

On my way back toward my room, Dean Hallow's words lingered in my mind. I decided to head left around the courtyard and cut between the main academy hall and the dormitories. Taking a path to the left of the main stables, I soon found myself standing before the smithy, the clanging of metal on metal signifying that Tad was present. I might as well get this sorted today, too.

The academy's resident blacksmith was a broad-shouldered muscular mountain of a man. I had spent the first year giving him a wide berth after hearing stories passed down from the older students. When I eventually did get to know the man, I found him to be a wonderful font of knowledge and skill.

Many an hour I had spent listening to Tad talk of the great weapons of the past. Indeed, it had been on the smith's suggestions that I'd tried the scimitars in the first place. He'd even created them for me when I'd commissioned him, designing them after watching me alongside Hestia.

That was where most of my money had gone.

"Tad?" I called, raising my voice to be heard over the ringing of metal.

The banging stopped. I heard heavy footsteps before the huge, bearded man poked his head through the doorway.

"Ho, Jadyn! Well met, my friend. I assume you are here about Orcgrinder and Dragonkiller?"

I laughed and shook my head. "For the last time, Tad. I refuse to name my swords. No number of ridiculous name suggestions is going to make me change my mind."

"Pah. Suit yourself, young one. But don't blame me when heroic tales sung of you years from now mention you winning glorious battles with the pathetically monikered scimitar one and scimitar two."

"I'll settle for them having songs to sing about me in the first place," I admitted. "What they choose to do after that is just how it is."

Tad guffawed loudly and threw out a meaty palm, clasping my arm and pulling me inside. "Let's get you sorted then before I have to deal with the real warriors."

Stepping inside, I skirted around a few partially worked sections of metal before joining Tad at the whetstone toward the rear. Slipping both swords from their sheaths, my breath caught as the light from the smithy fires reflected off the deeply curved Atanian-steel blades. I'd selected them for the perfect balance I felt as I wielded them, but there was no denying their beauty.

As Tad poured some oil and then set to work with the whetstone, I took a seat opposite and brought him up to speed on all I had heard from the front lines. Tad had been quite the warrior back in his younger years, but a serious leg injury had forced him away from the battles. Stories were all he had now to help recall the glory days.

I watched Tad as he worked, moving the blades back and forth, his motions fluid as he tilted the blades at an angle and pushed forward and left in a sweeping motion. While he tended to one blade, he passed the other to me to wipe away any residual oil from the whetstone.

The job complete, Tad wiped both blades down with a dry cloth, removing any residue or metal shavings that had sneaked past my amateur eye. The last thing I needed in battle was to unsheathe a rusting blade, so I appreciated his diligence.

"Appreciate your help, Tad," I told him as I grasped his forearm and nodded.

"Anytime, Jadyn. You have a special future ahead of you. I'll look forward to telling the students years from now how I created those weapons of yours."

I laughed. "Then I'd better make it so. Can't leave you with no tales to tell."

With that, I turned and headed back through the smithy, once again dodging the various half-finished projects that littered the sides and floor. Passing Brom and a couple of other students on the way out, I nodded, patted my friend on the back, and headed on to visit with Hestia.

Still full of energy, I ran the entire way to the stables, almost colliding with Froom on arrival as he exited one of the stalls.

"Ah, apologies, Master Froom!" I told the middle-aged head of the stables.

He shook his head but smiled in understanding. "The exuberance of youth, hey, young Jadyn."

"Something like that," I called back over my shoulder, barely slowing down.

The griffins all had their own stall up at the main stables. Then there was a huge paddock out the rear that they resided in when not at our side elsewhere in the academy grounds.

I skidded to a stop outside Hestia's stall, flicking up the latch and heading inside. I was immediately greeted by soft chirps and a nuzzling beak.

"Hey, girl," I said, running my hand through her brown neck feathers as she stayed seated on the ground.

Froom and his stable hands would be working through all the third-year griffins tomorrow, so although she looked as regal as ever, her feathers and fur needed a caring hand. Normally, I'd get stuck in and do it myself, but I knew the stable team wanted to say their own goodbyes, so I refrained.

Sitting down next to her after propping my weapons against the door, I leaned back against her body and smiled. She lifted a wing to wrap around me in our own personal greeting.

If it were any other day this would be where I'd have snuck in the world's comfiest griffin nap. However, I still felt strangely awake and alert, so I took the moment to visually cycle through my castings, imagining how we could best utilize each together both in the skies and on the ground.

[Fire Burst] was a powerful short-range area-of-effect spell, whereas [Fireball] was long range but weaker. I'd been training it up, though, and its power was rising, the size of the ball larger by the day. The training both increased the speed that my body accepted the mana needed for the spell and also increased the density of mana I could pull on, meaning that more power flowed through my body as I cast. I could easily visualize how to use both spells while riding Hestia, but I was still working on a way to utilize [Fire Elemental] without hurting her.

Continuing to cycle through my spells, I paused in shock, my mouth dropping open.

[Wind Burst]?

[Wind Boost]?

What the hells?

Chapter Five

It didn't make any sense. I was a fire mage, and yet here I was flicking through wind spells I'd never seen before. This wasn't supposed to happen. You were lucky to even receive access to one variety of magic. Most of the population had none. Having more than one type was unheard of. At least, to me.

I needed someone to talk to.

I leapt to my feet, grabbed my weapons, turned back toward the smithy, and sprinted out. Once again, I swerved past Froom as he pushed a barrow across the mud-slicked yard.

Skidding to a halt outside the doors to the smithy, I cast an eye over everyone waiting.

"Have you seen Brom?" I asked Helstrom. The dwarf sat waiting patiently, twin axes resting on his lap.

"Just left, Jadyn. Said something 'bout more packing," he replied, lifting his eyes to meet mine.

"Ah, thanks, man. Appreciate it!"

He grunted and smiled in response as I turned on the spot, got my bearings, and sprinted off again toward my next destination: our room.

I dodged through the crowd of students as I ran, skidding across the gravel courtyard. My path led straight and heading left for the boys' fourth-year dorm rooms. Crashing through the main door, I barely slowed in the hall before barging into our room.

Brom startled as I entered. A glass tankard slipped from his hands and shattered on the wooden boards, spreading a stain of a brown liquid that I suspected to be some spirit or other .

"What the hells, man!" he cried, shaking his head at the mess.

"Sorry, buddy. I'll help you clean it up in a minute. Just take a seat for a second. I've got something to share with you."

"Er, right... What's up, Jadyn?"

Having sprinted here from the stables, via Tad's smithy, I really should have been bent double, trying to catch my breath, but I felt fine. Weirdly fine.

"Have you ever heard of anyone having access to more than one branch of magic before?"

Confusion crossed Brom's face. He paused before answering. "What now?"

"More than one branch. Like wielding both wind and water? Fire and earth?" I explained, hoping from foot to foot in nervous energy.

"Hah. What's going on? Is this some kind of joke to get me back for the water thing?"

"No, buddy." I paused, thinking on the best way to explain. "Right, so... you know how I can do this?" I started, drawing on my mana and creating a whirling ball of fire in the palm of my hand.

"[Fireball]? Yeah, you've been able to do that for years, man." He shrugged, struggling to see where the joke was going as I withdrew my mana and the fire dissipated.

"Well, how long have I been able to do this?" I asked, calling on [Wind Burst] and shooting a forceful burst of wind straight across the room, knocking the mirror off the far wall above the wash basin and sending it crashing to the floor.

Brom jumped to his feet in shock, limbs flailing.

"Whoa!"

"Well?" I asked. "Any idea?"

"Nah, man. Not the faintest. If anyone is going to know it's going to be Sars, though. He's even in the library right now."

"Thanks, brother!" I called, spinning on the spot and heading back out into the hall, barely hearing Brom's curse as he realized he had double the extra clean-up to do now.

As I'd expected, I found Sars bent over a book on the third floor of the library. The library was located in a tower that was actually a former griffin roost, with huge ornate stained-glass windows on all four levels. It was annexed off the main academy hall, and it was where I'd spent a good chunk of my time in the first year, scrambling to catch up with others who'd known they had magic their whole lives.

Sars still frequented these halls, always looking to improve his knowledge and make himself a better mage. The recent deaths of his brothers had only served to harden that focus to the point where I doubted he'd even started packing yet.

I flopped into a chair beside him, and he looked up startled like he hadn't heard me charging between the bookstacks, bumping into a trolley full of books on my way in.

"Oh, hey, Jadyn."

"Hey, Sars." Despite my current 'situation', I still wanted to check on him first. "How are you holding up?"

A distant look crossed his face, and the sadness rolled in after. "I am okay, I guess. I just wish I had been there to help, you know?"

"I do," I admitted. "We all do."

"I do not know what I am going to do without their letters. And who will tell Mother?"

"I'm sure that will be all taken care of," I reassured him, "but I'll follow up with the dean to make sure for you."

He smiled softly and then shook his head as though attempting to banish the grief a little longer. I admired his grit. It took a lot to keep it together after what'd happened.

"So, what is up, anyway. Don't see you in here all that much anymore," he said.

"Got a question for you actually."

"Yeah?" he replied, perking up a bit.

"You ever heard of a mage with more than one branch of magic available to them?"

He laughed. "What... like wielding fire *and* wind?"

"Exactly!" I sighed in relief. It was so much easier than explaining things to Brom. Couldn't say I'd been looking forward to setting the bookstacks alight or blowing tomes across the room in another attempt at providing an example.

"That is not possible. Mages have been trying for centuries to open themselves up to the possibility of multi-wielding, but it has never happened. At least, it has not to the best of my knowledge."

I leaned over and whispered, "Until now."

"What? Are you serious?"

"On my life."

Sars scrambled to his feet, closing his book and shoving it under his arm. "You get the other guys, I will grab the girls, and meet in the arena in ten minutes."

He shot off through the doorway, leaving me more confused than ever.

By the time I reached the arena, Brom and Mallen in tow, Sars and the girls had already arrived. They sat on the first row of benches to our right as we entered. Sars spoke in an animated fashion, throwing his arms wide as he explained something as we made our way over.

"So," Sars started, looking up and meeting my gaze as we reached them, "I have not filled them in at all yet. Fancy going over it again?"

I shrugged. "Sure, why not? Be good to see if anyone has any answers."

I gestured for Brom and Mallen to take a seat with the others. Once they had, I drew a deep breath and proceeded to go over it all again for a third time.

"Okay… so, have any of you ever heard of a mage with access to more than one branch of magic…"

It turned out that it was indeed only Brom who needed a physical manifestation to get the gist of what I was trying to say. That didn't stop the incredulous looks across the board.

"Some kind a joke?" Fitmigar asked.

I sighed. "Look, how about I show you all?" I offered. It was surely safer to do so here in the arena, and thinking about it, that was probably why Sars suggested it. It would be a definite improvement on my dorm room mirror-smashing experiment anyway.

A few exited nods returned my way. I hopped down off the seats and headed a few steps out into the arena.

"Okay. You've all seen this little trick before," I started, pulling on my mana and casting [Fireball].

A ball around six inches in diameter grew on the palm of my hand, and I fired it across the arena floor. With a lack of any suitable target, it hit the ground around fifty feet away and merely blackened the dirt in a five-foot radius.

"Yeah, but you've clearly been practicing, Jadyn," Elandra said, "because it never used to be that big."

Ignoring Brom's waggling eyebrows, I replied, "I guess when I think about it does seem a bit bigger, but that's beside the point." I took a deep breath and smiled at my friends. "Now, check this out."

Drawing mana from within my body, I cycled through my available spells, this time mentally selecting [Wind Boost]. After a brief pause as I pulled mana from my core, the soles of my feet shot into the air, pushing me up and across the arena on a torrent of wind before easing off and landing me safely over eighty feet away.

"Huh," I mumbled to myself, "probably should have tried that out beforehand. Could have been headfirst in some seats there."

I jogged back over to the others and looked at them expectantly.

Six blank expressions stared back at me.

"Was that [Wind Boost]?" Sienna asked me.

I nodded. "Sure was."

"I have that one, too."

"Huh. What else do you have?" I asked.

She didn't need to look through her spells before she said, "[Wind Burst] and□—"

"—[Wind Wall]," we said together.

"How did you know that?" Sienna asked, mouth agape.

"That's the third one I have, too. And I think I might know what's going on here…"

"And that is?" Mallen asked, leaning forward.

"Well, at least as far as I can make out, whatever happened has taken place in the last twenty-four hours, and only one thing of note has occurred in that time related to wind magic…"

Knowing looks crossed the group's faces as they turned and stared at Sienna.

Brom stood, briefly glanced at her, then looked straight at me with a huge smile on his face. "Yeah… gonna need those fuckin' details now, man."

I chuckled and shook my head. No details, but I'm guessing you're all aware that Sienna and I got —"

"Freaky?" Brom interjected.

I rolled my eyes. "Not what I was going to say, but sure," I replied, causing Sienna to laugh out loud. "And it looks like I now have access to all of her wind-based spells—as well as my own, still."

I focused on Sienna. "Anything different with yours?"

She paused. "Hang on…"

Her eyes widened. "I've got a new spell. [Fireball]."

"Fuckin' hells!" Brom shouted.

"OK. So, I've got to admit, I'm more than a little confused by this all. No one has any ideas?" I asked. "No one has heard of anything like this happening before?"

They all shook their heads. Brom threw in an exaggerated shrug of his shoulders for good measure.

"How about I take Mallen to the library, and we will spend a few hours trying to see if there is anything that might help us out," Sars offered.

"OK," I agreed, "but don't forget we leave the morning after next, so don't let it take too much of your time as I'm sure you've still got plenty to do."

"Sure," Sars replied with a nod before Mallen joined him, and they took their leave.

"Elandra, can you take Fitmigar and Brom and see if you can discretely question a few of the instructors?" I asked.

"Of course," the beautiful dark-skinned girl replied, and I nodded my thanks and watched her take the other two and leave.

I then turned to Sienna. "Can we chat a moment?"

"Sure," she replied, coming over and pulling me into a kiss. As her soft lips met mine, I slid my tongue into her mouth, exploring. I nibbled her bottom lip as I released her, eliciting a gentle moan in response.

"What was that about?"

"Just needed that first," she told me, slowly stepping back, a huge smile crossing her perfect face.

"Well, I'm not complaining," I said, already missing the feel of her lips against mine. "We good?"

"I hope so," she told me. "What happened won't change things from my point of view. We've just done what I've wanted to do for years."

"Me, too," I said with a smile and pulled her in for another kiss. "Actually, I wanted to ask you something."

"Yeah?"

"Yeah. I know you said you have access to one of my spells, but is there anything else at all different? Anything that could help me?"

She lowered her eyes. A faint blush crept into her cheeks. "I'm feeling more powerful. Like my mana is denser, stronger. I'm also feeling closer to you."

I raised my eyebrows.

"Not in a crazy way," she continued. "I just feel like a small part of me is… linked to you now? I know this sounds stupid—"

"Not at all," I reassured her.

"—but ever since last night, I just feel a connection to you that I've never felt before. I'd wanted last night to happen from the day I met you, but it's like something's opened up, and now I could never see myself near anyone else."

I must have looked confused because she added, "It feels like a magical thing. A bond of some sorts."

"I feel it, too," I admitted. "I feel stronger. Better. Like I could do anything."

"I hope someone finds something out then, Jadyn, because we need answers." She slipped her hand into mine. "Where to?"

"I think the others have most everything else covered. Let's go see if the dean is around."

We left the arena and walked through the gardens in companionable silence. My thoughts raced a mile-a-minute, so it was all I could do to place one foot in front of the other.

The dean's office was located upstairs in the main hall, so we headed to the front, past the benches, and took a left toward the stairs.

Footsteps rushing down the staircase gave us pause. A moment later, Rivers appeared, looking flustered.

"Yes?" the small Beastkin asked, clearly expecting more issues on top of whatever he was currently dealing with.

"Ah, hi, Rivers. We just wanted to have a word with Dean Hallow if that's possible?"

"Not in! Village till tomorrow!" he shouted, racing away to his next pressing engagement.

I looked at Sienna, shrugging. "Guess that's not happening then."

"Doesn't seem like it. I've still got some packing to do anyway. You got anything to keep you occupied?"

"I might head over to see Hestia again. It got kind of cut short earlier, and I could really do with a chance to clear my head. Might take her out for a ride."

"Sounds good." She leaned over and kissed me on the lips before spinning away and heading for the dorms.

After watching her walk away, I jogged up to the main stables, finding it empty of staff. They'd probably already finished for the day.

I headed across the yard and entered Hestia's stable. She was up on her paws, pacing around and looking restless.

"You fancy taking a ride, girl?" I asked, stroking her neck.

She nuzzled me in return, and I took that for confirmation. We weren't supposed to take the griffins out at this hour, and certainly not alone, but I still had my weapons on me, and there was seldom anything remotely dangerous near the academy grounds. Couldn't imagine returning here having been mauled by a particularly angry fox or something.

A few minutes was all it took to get Hestia all strapped up. I led her out and around the side of the stables, thinking of taking her down the little-used track that ran towards a wooded area four miles away or so.

She paused, and I pulled myself onto her back, tucking my knees in. We set a slow pace at first, trying to be as quiet as possible. We might be leaving soon, but I didn't really want to get caught, especially as the dean mentioned we'd likely be back at the academy to continue our studies once we sorted out the situation at the border. If we survived.

Once I felt we were far enough clear, I leaned forward and forced my knees in harder. Hestia took the cue to pick up speed, her wings tucked in as she ran, releasing whatever tension she had been struggling to contain. The track blurred by as we raced on, the wind rushing through my hair.

The ground was hard from the recent lack of rain, letting us gallop at full speed. Before long we reached the woods, slowing down to walk as the path narrowed between the trees. Early evening birdsong greeted us as Hestia stepped over or around the odd fallen tree before heading across a clearing and through the other side.

There were more trees down this side—definitely more than the last time I rode through the path. I paused her stride and jumped down to inspect one.

"That's odd." I noted claw marks across the trunk of the tree. Judging by the size of the marks and the height they would have been at when the tree was standing, I was looking at one big fucking bear.

What the hells is that doing around here?

I turned Hestia around and walked alongside her as we started to head back. I didn't fancy running into trouble, not with the evening approaching. I wasn't supposed to be out as it was.

Turned out, trouble still found me.

Right as we walked back out into the clearing, a black bear ambled from the trees to our right, its eyes as black as its fur in the dwindling light.

Fantastic...

I'd hoped we could continue back into the woods on the other side without issue, but a deep huff caused us to pause. I looked over to see it had risen to its back legs, standing at maybe five feet and change.

OK. No reason to engage. Let's get out of here, I thought.

As I grabbed Hestia's straps and went to pull myself up, a second huff followed, this one deeper still. An even larger male black bear trundled out after the first, slapping the ground before rising to what must have been clear of seven feet.

Shit. Now, we're fucked.

Both bears immediately dropped back down to all fours and charged. Normally, bears bluffed their first charge, veering away—at least, that's what I'd been led to believe in class—but this didn't strike me as a normal situation. What was with those eyes? It was like staring into a void.

With no time to return to Hestia's back, I slid my scimitars from their sheaths and dropped into my stance, nodding to Hestia. "You take the smaller one, girl."

She chuffed in response and stretched her claws out.

Catching the eye of the larger bear, I stepped to the right, pulling its charge away from Hestia and giving her room to fight. I trusted her to handle herself. We'd never fought outside of training before, but I had absolute faith in her ability to handle herself.

The larger bear swerved across and threw out a huge right paw. I rolled, evading the claws, and they raked deep furrows through a tree trunk. Roaring in frustration, the bear reared up and approached upright, slower now, aiming to overwhelm me with its sheer size and weight. It had to be five hundred pounds of pure muscle facing me down.

I was shorter than the bear at six-two, but I fancied myself to be quicker. My blades flicked out, whirling before the bear. The couple of times it threw out a swipe, I caught it with my blade, slicing shallow cuts into the fur and skin beneath. Any normal animal should've ran by now, confirming my hunch that something nefarious was up.

Alongside me, Hestia had risen to her back legs, wings spread, claws flashing out and striking the smaller bear across the nose. Its pitiful whine encouraged Hestia to continue to push it back, giving it no chance to retaliate and buffering it away from me, allowing me to focus on my own fight.

With frustration quickly setting in, my assailant opened its huge jaws and threw itself forward in a desperate barrage of lunges. My heart raced as I ducked to evade its jaws, spinning right and arcing a swipe of my right hand upwards. I caught the bear across the side of its face, eliciting a pained roar. Blood flowed from its muzzle, the skin hanging down and revealing a sharp incisor beneath.

The bear shook its head, seemingly trying to dispel the pain before coming at me again. Both paws swung, six-inch-long claws whipping past my face. I leaned back, swaying left and right and backing up. One good hit from that paw would have me on my ass, and if it got its weight on me fully... well, I was fucked.

Assuming I was afraid and backing away in fear, it threw itself forward again, harder now, all four of its paws leaving the ground.

Exactly what I'd been waiting for.

Pulling on my mana, I selected [Wind Boost] and dropped to my knees. A surge of wind behind me shoved me forward, my knees sliding rapidly across the ground as I lifted both scimitars above my head. The blades slashed into the bear's chest as it dove over me, slicing through fur and skin alike and opening it from its chest to its groin.

Coming to rest twenty feet from the bear, I spun on the spot and pushed myself to my feet, ready to defend myself again.

However, the bear lay motionless on its front. Blood pooled around its corpse.

A grin spread across my face.

"Fuck yeah!"

Across the clearing, I watched Hestia dominate the smaller bear with her size, batting it from side to side with her paws. Her claws tore through its fur, her beak darting out and snapping at its muzzle with bone-shattering impacts.

Forcing it to back up against a tree at the edge of the clearing, Hestia threw both front paws forward, smashing the bear's head up and back. Driving her head forward, she jabbed the sharpened end of her beak into its jugular and ripped across, tearing its throat open.

With a whimper of defeat, the bear slid down the trunk, crashing to the ground as it died.

Hestia spread her wings and screeched defiantly, and I nodded in respect.

"No one fucks with us, girl," I agreed, fist-bumping the end of her wing.

Interlude 1

Geilazar tucked his huge red wings, lowered his head, and dived. Time was running out. His little remaining mana ebbed away. If he didn't make the entrance to the cave soon, he'd face an arduous climb up the mountain—one he wasn't certain he had the strength left to climb. Tucking his wings tighter still, he picked up speed. The wind behind him pushed him ever faster as he pushed on with every draconic bone in his body, every muscle tensed despite him knowing he needed to relax them to land.

There, an orc sentry…

He would make it. Just.

Landing at too high a speed, his red-scaled chest crushed the sentry on impact. Thick blood splattered the mountainside as he slid by, careening through the entranceway and deeper into the tunnel. His left wing came untucked and hit the solid stone passageway, sending him spinning out of control. He struggled to slow as another orc was crushed by falling debris.

His red wing, still tucked into his side, gradually shrunk until it disappeared into his back completely. The left soon followed. Still, he continued to tumble end over end as his claws retracted into his skin, the deep red of his arms lightening a touch. The scales blended into hardened skin, softening with each bounce, each crack.

His eyes, previously narrow slits, widened as he rolled, his pristine vision blurring as the worked walls of the cave span by.

His long tail, whipping from side to side in an effort to arrest his landing, retracted into him, first an inch, then a foot, until it disappeared completely as he came to rest. His back thumped hard against the rear wall of the cave, his head bouncing off the stone wall.

His snout was the final part of the transformation to vanish, gradually returning to a heavily bruised nose. He blinked away the pain.

Geilazar—dark mage... shapeshifter... human...—looked around, meeting the eyes of wyverns, basilisks, and drakes alike, naked as the day he was born.

It would be a while before he could take such a form again, but he had achieved what he had set out to do.

The griffin knights were no more.

Soon, the entirety of Atania would be in his grasp.

Chapter Six

The events in the woods had to be reported at once, so I hurried back to the academy grounds. With the dean away, the first authority I found was Galen. He was still in the combat halls, finishing up an after-hours top-up class with several second years. I waited at the side as they departed.

"Everything OK, Jadyn?" he asked, looking me up and down and noticing my disheveled appearance.

I let out a sigh and proceeded to fill the combat instructor in on what had transpired in the woods. He was far from impressed that I'd snuck away without alerting anyone, but I noticed a look of pride on his face when I talked of the fight. He fired a few questions at me, which I answered to the best of my ability, and then he nodded.

"You best get going, Jadyn. I'll get another couple of people together—Tad and Thom most likely—and we'll head down, burn the bodies, and see if there are any more in the area."

"Do I need to let the dean know tomorrow?"

"Leave it with me, Jadyn. No reason for you to get in trouble. Our little secret."

"Appreciate it, sir," I said, giving him a thankful smile.

We bid our goodbyes, and I headed for a quick shower before returning to my room.

Elandra and Fitmigar caught up with me as I crossed the courtyard, having had brief chats with Galen, Algernon, and Madame Summerstone earlier and now heading off to bed. They'd phrased their questions as hypothetical, but none of the instructors knew of any previous instances where multi-magic-wielding had been possible anyway.

When I finally reached my room, I just crashed on my bed, Brom already asleep across the room from me, snoring softly… for him. I could wait till morning to hear from Sars and Mallen. I doubted they'd found anything of note, so the chance for a few extra hours of sleep seemed worthwhile.

Rising early, I headed down to the showers again and took my time there, letting the hot water soak away my stress. I wanted answers to what was happening and why, but I couldn't afford to let it distract me from preparing for tomorrow and leaving the academy. We would be on the road and heading for war, after all.

Showered and half-respectable, I arrived at breakfast before anyone else, and I was sitting drinking my second coffee when the others started drifting in, Sars and Mallen looking like they'd barely slept.

Once everyone had grabbed something from the kitchen, they all took a seat. We leaned forward and spoke in excited, yet hushed tones.

"How'd it go in the library?" I asked immediately.

"No luck so far," Sars replied. "We have got a whole mountain more texts to wade through, though. Miss Benner has even agreed for us to be able to take a few books with us on the road, providing we have extra copies still here in the academy."

Miss Benner was the academy's librarian/administrator, and as one expected for such positions, she was sharp-eyed and organized. She was also a lovely lady and had helped me tremendously in my time at the academy with settling in, always happy to help answer any questions I had.

"And did you ask☐—"

Sars rolled his eyes and cut me off. "Yes, Jadyn, the first thing we did was ask her if she knew anything. No luck, though she did give us a few of the books on our list."

I nodded, deep in thought.

"How about the dean? Anything?" Mallen asked, and I shook my head.

"In the village overnight, apparently. At least, that's what Rivers told us yesterday. Not sure what's so important that he'd be away right before we leave, though."

"Instructors about as useful as a hipflask full a water, too," Fitmigar added, and even Mallen cracked a smile.

"So, we've got nothing," I surmised, looking around the table.

"Yet," Sienna added, resting a hand on my leg and giving it a squeeze. "We'll find out something. If we don't... well, we'll just learn as we go."

"You're right," I said. If the answers couldn't be found, we'd just have to come up with them ourselves. Everything happened for the first time sometime, right?

"How's everyone feeling about departing the academy?" Sienna asked, and more than a few spoons and forks paused. "I'm sure we'll do fine, but it's still a little scary, isn't it?"

"Yeah. I'm nervous as well," Brom admitted. "I'm mean we'll be seeing real combat."

"As a team," I reminded him. "I'll have your back, just as you'll have mine."

"If you're lucky, I'll guard your overly handsome face, too," he replied, laughing. "The girls of Atania will be mad if that gets ruined."

I groaned, rolling my eyes at him.

"We would be devastated!" Elandra said.

"See?" Brom pointed, as if her joke somehow validated his.

"Have any of you written letters?" Sars asked. "To your families?"

I fell to the background of the conversation for a bit. With Wendia long gone, I had no family to speak of.

"Wrote mine," Fitmigar confirmed.

"And I sent one yesterday," Mallen added. The elf never really spoke much about his family, but it was good to know he was thinking of the future.

"I'll be writing mine this evening," Sienna said, and Elandra nodded.

"We'll write them together."

We spent what remained of breakfast discussing our plans for the rest of the day. Elandra still had to visit Tad in the smithy, and Sars and Fitmigar were due to collect their lances and walk their griffins up. Mallen offered to get started in the library, and it turned out that Brom, Sienna, and I had some free time before the dean was likely to be back.

"Any ideas?" I asked the pair.

"Madame Summerstone was looking for volunteers to help load potions onto the various wagons we'll be taking with us. Apparently, her assistant, Elmar, needs a hand with his equipment, too," Sienna said.

With nothing better to do, we headed over to the potions workshop.

A series of carts had been set up outside the workshop, and already a short blond-haired man was loading them with jar upon jar of ingredients.

"Ho, Elmar, how goes it?" I asked, watching as he hoisted the jars onto a cart, the contents swirling within.

"Oh, hey, Jadyn. Sienna. Brom." He greeted us each with a gentle nod. "Got my hands full here. Don't suppose you can spare an hour or so?"

"That's exactly why we're here," I said, and he smiled gratefully. "But I thought you were going to be collecting ingredients as we traveled?"

"Some," he confirmed, "but others I just won't be able to source. Hence all these jars."

"Fair enough. So, where shall we start?"

Elmar pointed over his shoulder toward the workshop. "Everything's already been sorted, and it's all grouped together near the front. Just bring it out, and I'll work on stacking everything on. We'll only have to relocate it onto the main wagons down at stores anyway."

Nodding in understanding, we got to work. The next couple of hours were spent carrying everything out. Elmar was so glad for the help, he didn't even mind all that much when Brom took a tumble and smashed a jar, the mysterious-looking powder within causing everyone to sneeze non-stop for the five minutes that followed.

With the four carts all packed up, we took one each and headed toward the courtyard.

Stores was located across the other side of the central courtyard and down by the shower block. We slowed while rolling the carts across the gravel, careful not to damage the flat steel tires.

Despite all of us knowing the way easily enough, I offered to walk at the front of the group as we walked backwards. I told Sienna that it was so I could watch and offer assistance if she got into trouble. Truth be told, I was just keen to watch her ass strain against her tight-fitting pants as she pulled her cart, backing toward me as she went.

When we paused after crossing the courtyard, I noticed thin rivulets of sweat running down her chest, disappearing under her shirt and between her breasts, and almost lost it. It appeared she noticed me ogling because there was that smile again.

I smiled back. I'd been caught fair and square. Might as well own it.

We dropped the carts off with Tordlum, an aging, grey-haired, bearded dwarf who minded the stores. After bidding Elmar goodbye until the next morning, we headed to the stables.

We arrived to find several griffins were already out in the field. The team had forty to prepare today, and they hadn't gotten to Hestia or Sienna's partner, Dawnquill, yet.

Brom noticed his own griffin—named Shadowtail in typical shadow mage fashion—wasn't to be seen either, so he wandered off to find her.

After Sienna and I hopped the fence and sat down under an old oak tree in the far corner of the paddock, Hestia and Dawnquill approached and lay near to us in the shade of the warm autumnal afternoon. I still didn't feel tired, though the energy I had the previous day had ebbed somewhat. That didn't stop me from closing my eyes and relaxing.

Sienna's voice whispered in my ear, her breath warm across my face, "Not sure how to tell you this, it's pretty embarrassing, but my body is aching like mad for you since the other night."

I opened my eyes and stared at Sienna. She bit her lip and smiled, a faint blush reddening her cheeks.

"I was serious about that connection, Jadyn," she continued. "I can't get you out of my head... Thoughts of your cock between my thighs."

I grinned as I pulled her to me and kissed her, tenderly at first and then harder. My hand wandered around the back of her head and pulled her closer.

"How about I fuck you right now?" I growled, feeling her nipples harden against my chest.

"I'd let you," she replied, grabbing my stiffening cock through my pants and easing her hand up and down, "I want you. But we can't."

A cough jerked my attention away, and I saw Brom standing there, barely suppressing a smirk.

"Can't leave you alone for a minute, right? Beguiling the women of the nation with your good looks again."

Sienna reluctantly pulled her hand away, whispered, "Another time," in my ear, and then rolled away.

I pulled Sienna back for a final kiss before turning to Brom. "Guess not, buddy. Everything OK?"

"Yeah," he told me, tactfully avoiding the fact part of my body was still thinking of Sienna and the things I wanted to do to her. "Froom is in with Shadowtail now, so not much I can do."

"Join us then," Sienna said, budging across so Brom could take a seat against the trunk.

"Sure," he mumbled, careful not to sit between us.

With no chance now for any fun, I closed my eyes again. Without the need for talk, the three of us rested, all mulling over our own hopes and fears of what the coming days, weeks, and months would hold.

Dean Hallow called me to his office later that day, along with Lana, Enallo, a dark-skinned, short-haired water mage from the Darlish Coast, and Bernolir, a brown-haired dwarf.

"OK, listen up," he started, voice snapping and authoritative. "You four are the leading lights of the fourth year."

I could see Bernolir about to speak, but the dean waved a hand.

"You are. That's all there is to it."

We all nodded. I had a faint idea where this was going.

"So, with the forty of you out on the road, we need to maintain a rigid structure. Can't have you all not knowing where the orders are coming from." He paused a moment before continuing. "Algernon, Thom, Elmar, and Mirek will be joining you, but the leadership and orders will come from Galen. He is a well-respected combat instructor and spent many years in the elven army. You'll be sure to listen to every word he says."

We nodded in unison.

"Now, you four will be squad leaders. Next in line, so to speak. That doesn't mean you can ignore the other adults, but orders-wise, it goes from Galen to you."

"And the squads, sir?" I asked.

"Choose them now. You will know yourselves better than I do. This conversation is now over. I have full trust in all of you."

With that, we were excused and decided our squads outside his office.

I'd be joined by Brom, Sienna, Elandra, Sars, Mallen, Fitmigar, Helstrom, Syl – a tall, black-haired wind mage who specialized in the bow – and Rammy, my favorite man-mountain.

A brief chat with Dean Hallow after confirmed that he knew of no instance where a mage had collated multiple magics, though he wanted more information from me when we returned if I discovered more. Afterwards, we made sure everyone was set for the next morning's departure and then headed to the Molerat for one final drink.

With the seriousness of the situation, Joff, the innkeeper, had barred anyone but the fourth-year students from attending that evening. He'd likely pissed off more than one or two Persham locals in the process, but most would understand. Almost everyone had someone they had lost in the war, or someone they hoped to return. We arrived to find that he had even pushed tables together to create one long table large enough to seat all forty of us.

"Evening, Joff," I greeted after spotting him behind the bar, somewhat reluctantly polishing glasses.

"Jadyn." He nodded in greeting, placing the glass down and then scratching at his short beard. "Gonna give you all a proper send-off this evening, so I hope you've got your big-boy drinking pants on!"

"You know it," I told him, laughing.

"Hope that applies to you all," he continued, running his gaze across the entire group. He paused a moment before adding, "Especially you, Brom."

Brom feigned offense before laughing and heading over to get some drinks in. The rest of us took a seat at the top end of the table to wait for our fellow new recruits—as that's what we were, I supposed—to join us.

I glanced around the table as the other fourth years filed in. I noted Lana at the other end of the table, sat with the triplets, Orna, Orfan, and Oscar, their blond hair matching my own, and a couple of elven males, Rylunder and Aernon. Lana came from what Atania considered the nobility, and she tended to surround herself with others of that social standing. She'd even tried to bring Sars into her clique, without luck.

Farther up the right-hand side of the table sat a group from the nation's mountainous northwest regions. Helstrom and Rammy, our squad members, sat with Bernolir -- one of the other squad leaders. He was an earth mage dwarf with the most powerful single spell of anyone in the academy – [Rock Fall].

Down the left-hand side of the table sat a group from the eastern Darlish Coast. They all had darker skin, similar to Elandra's, and they spoke with a slight accent. I'd spent more than a few nights in their company as we'd celebrated their many festivals over the course of each year. The Darlish people loved their parties—and other people's parties.

A couple of their group, Enallo and Harlee, noticed me glancing over and raised their glasses. They were drinking that favorite blue concoction of theirs again. Blue Lightning they said it was called, though I had a feeling they were messing with me.

I raised my own glass in reply and smiled. We'd be heading off to war tomorrow. Tonight was a night for strengthening bonds. We had to be prepared to fight alongside our brothers and sisters against any enemy, to the death.

That thought should have scared me more than it did.

The scraping of chairs brought my attention back to Elandra and Fitmigar as they sat down with us.

"How about we get this party started!" Brom shouted as he arrived with our ales, clanking them down onto the table, ale sloshing over the sides.

The entire table cheered as one.

"Charn, how about a song?" someone shouted, and the sandy-haired boy sprang up from his seat a few down from us.

"You've got it! Any requests?"

"The venereal tales of the farmer's daughter!" shouted Brom.

Charn laughed and shook his head. "Maybe later, Brom. Best we start with something a little less bawdy, don't you think?"

The boy burst into a fine rendition of 'The Watcher in the Hills', ales were raised to lips, and our final evening as students of the academy commenced.

The conversation started off relatively serious when Mallen leaned in and asked, "What have you made of our four years so far?"

"Could be our *only* four years," Fitmigar said.

"I've enjoyed them," Sienna said, trying to raise spirits. "From the quiet farmer's daughter with no real magical know-how, I feel I've come on so much." She looked around at us all. "We all have."

"Sienna's right," I added. "Each one of us is so much stronger now than when we first met."

"Is it all going to be okay?" Brom asked.

"Of course, it is, man," I told him, a flutter of anxiety setting root in my stomach. If it took me pretending to be perfectly confident and unafraid to help the others through tonight, and all the nights that followed, then I'd fake it till my grave.

"Yeah, Brom," Elandra added. "Look around you. Everyone here is right by your side."

Brom smiled and took another chug of ale.

"Alright then. No more moping. Time for a few drinking games!" he shouted, and the table immediately cheered again.

"What are we playing?" Mallen asked.

"Con," Brom replied, and we all immediately dug into our pockets. We'd need coins for this.

The aim of the game was a little subterfuge, trying to disguise how many coins you held in an enclosed fist – zero, one, two, or three – placed out in front of you along with everyone else. We played in groups of eight, giving a maximum of twenty-four coins, a minimum of zero.

We went around the group guessing the total number, with no one repeating a guess that came before. Whoever got the correct total was out.

Seven then continued, and it went around again until only two remained. The loser paid for the next round of drinks for all eight.

The first loser was Brom, and he trudged off to the bar, immediately falling into conversation with Joff.

The beauty of the game was that it was quick, and it allowed us to talk while we played. The longer the night went on, the sillier the conversation got as we let loose. No one really knew what we'd find in less than a week's time, so if this was one last hurrah, we wanted to make sure we all enjoyed ourselves.

At some point, Elandra moved next me, clinging to my side.

"I'm worried about the war," she slurred, and I could tell she been drinking a lot. She was clearly anxious, but then we all were. Some just dealt with it differently.

"Me, too," I admitted quietly, putting an arm around her and giving her a squeeze. "It's normal to be, I think."

"What's our future going to hold for us? Will we all make it out the other side? Will you ever be with me?"

As I went to answer, her head dropped onto my shoulder, and she groaned.

"Uh… I think I'm gonna be sick."

I looked across at Sienna and gestured that we might need to help Elandra back.

She nodded, gave Sars and Mallen quick goodbyes, and came back around the table to join us.

"Brom, we're gonna head back," I told my friend as he approached the table again.

"I'm telling you, *Squad Leader, Sir*, there's no way she'll beat me this time," he slurred back as he placed down another ale. I counted six full ones in front of him. Beside him, Fitmigar had a matching number of drinks. I could already see where this was going.

Most of the table had already left for the evening. Het had been the first to go, taking her glasses off and rubbing her eyes as tiredness closed in. She was soon followed by others, some hand in hand, clearly off to fuck, until barely ten or so remained.

At some point, Helstrom had taken on five others in a drinking challenge—it really was a dwarf thing it seemed. He was now in the process of being carried out the door and homeward by a couple of friends—also very traditionally dwarvish. We were about to do the same with Elandra.

"Shall we get her back?" I asked, nudging Sienna gently.

"I think that's best," she agreed. "Maybe we can find somewhere to get cozy once we've done so…"

"Absolutely," I agreed, leaning over and kissing her.

After saying a quick goodbye to Joff, who was already in the process of pulling further ales for Fitmigar and Brom, we left the Wandering Molerat. The early hours of the morning were as chilly as I'd feared, but it provided a good excuse to keep Sienna close to my side as we took the track back towards the academy.

Once we reached the academy grounds, we walked Elandra back to her room, easing her into bed. Sienna tucked her in, and we left her to rest and sleep it off.

"You want to take a walk?" I asked Sienna.

"That would be nice," she replied, brushing her hair away from her eyes.

We left the girls' dormitories and strolled across the courtyard, towards the gardens illuminated by the soft moonlight. The wind picked up as we walked, rustling the shrubs and flowers.

As a tension hung in the silence between us, my mind ran rampant with all the things I wanted to do to this beautiful girl on my arm.

Then Sienna paused mid-step, pulling me to a halt.

"Did you hear that, Jadyn?" she asked, glancing around, her black hair swishing back across her face.

"Hear what?"

"It sounded like glass smashing, and it's coming from over by the stores."

"The wagons!"

I released Sienna's hand, all carnal thoughts forgotten, and together, we sprinted across the grounds towards the stores.

Chapter Seven

I reached the storages building a fraction before Sienna. The large wooden doors were open wide, swaying in the wind. Pausing, I signaled for her to slow as she approached.

The interior of the warehouse was dark. Lanterns that hung on the walls had been extinguished by someone. On closer inspection, I found the glass shattered on the ground.

"Whatever's going on, we need to be careful. If someone's up to no good inside, they could still be here," I warned, feeling a shiver go up my spine. This didn't feel right.

She nodded in understanding. Together, we stepped through the doorway and into the gloom beyond. The wagons were parked up to the left, tarps flapping in the wind that had now found its way inside. We headed over, steps light and our heads on a swivel, at least as well as one could after an evening of pretty heavy drinking.

Part of me wanted to be protective of Sienna and keep her behind me, but that would be doing her skills as a mage a huge disservice. I restrained my instincts but stayed close by her side. "Sienna, pull up your mana and get something ready to use to protect yourself. You circle around to the right of the wagons, and I'll head left. We'll meet up around the other side. OK?"

"Sure," she whispered. "I'll whistle if I see anything."

I nodded and then she snuck off to the right.

As I did likewise, slipping through the shadows around to the left-hand side, I heard the sound of running feet and then the banging of a far door way past where the wagons were parked up.

Shit.

I jogged around the wagons, jerking to a halt when I spotted a dark pool on the floor by the rear of the second wagon. Kneeling to inspect it, my eyes widened in shock.

The still form of Tordlum lay under the wagon, his head resting in the middle of the pool.

"What do we do?" Sienna asked, kneeling next to me, eyes scanning the area where we'd heard the door slam shut.

"Well, whoever that was is long gone," I said, shaking my head in frustration. As I spoke, I felt the store master's wrist for a pulse. "Plus, we need to get Tordlum to the infirmary."

"He's alive?" She sighed with relief. "Agreed. What's all this glass?" She poked the small shards in the pool of liquid.

"Best I can tell, whoever was in here was destroying potions. There's far too much liquid present for this all to be blood," I concluded, shuffling around to ease Tordlum's unconscious form from under the wagon.

As Sienna bent over to assist, the elderly dwarf started to come around, murmuring something unintelligible.

"What's that?" I asked, leaning closer.

"Damn… bastard… hit me… from behind…" he mumbled before passing out again.

Sienna and I lifted Tordlum and hurried him up to the courtyard, then through the main hall and up the stairs. The infirmary was located past Dean Hallow's office. Due to the late hour, we had to ring a bell and wait. We didn't have to wait too long before we heard the familiar shuffling feet of Beralda, the academy's resident nurse and the proud owner of roughly eighty-five years of hard-worn life.

After handing Tordlum off and being insured that there would hopefully be no lasting damage, we woke the dean to pass on the news of the attack. By the time we'd covered the events, it was almost dawn. Despite my insistence that we help investigate the stores to discover what had happened, we were told in no uncertain terms that it would be dealt with by the dean himself.

I looked at Sienna and shrugged. "Can I walk you back?"

"That would be nice." She rubbed her eyes and struggled to stifle a yawn.

Taking our leave, we headed back out to the courtyard and entered the girls' fourth-year dormitory building. Nearing Sienna's room, I slipped my hand into hers again and pulled her in for a deep kiss.

"Not the end to the night we planned, hey?" I asked, trying to hide my disappointment with a smile.

"There'll be other nights, Jadyn. Plenty of other—"

She stopped mid-sentence, her eyes widening as what could only be described as dwarven screams of ecstasy echoed from Fitmigar's room across the hall. The wooden door shook on its hinges.

What came next caused my mouth to drop open as we heard a slurring male voice come from behind the often-hot-tempered dwarf's door.

"Listen. We can't tell anyone about this…"

I looked at Sienna. "Was that Brom's voice?"

"Seemed like it to me," she replied, smiling. "And you know what that means…"

"Looks like my room's free."

I smiled and took her hand, and we slipped briefly back out into the night and into my dorm, making our way down the hall and inside my room.

As soon as the door closed, I pulled her to me, my lips meeting hers tenderly at first, then deeper as she sank into the kiss.

If everyone else was going to be hooking up this evening, I saw no reason why we couldn't do the same.

For the few hours of sleep that I managed to get, I felt amazing when I woke. That full of energy feeling from couple days ago was back in full. My eyes widened as I looked across the room to see Brom passed out in his bed. Guess he snuck back in after Sienna left.

It didn't take long to get ready as I'd left clothes out the previous day, everything else packed away for our journey north. I didn't purposely bang around as I got ready—OK, maybe I did a little—but soon Brom was up and staggering around the room.

"Still drunk?" I asked, suppressing a grin.

"Probably," he mumbled, plodding over and splashing cold water across his face.

"Good night?"

"Can't remember," he admitted, grabbing a towel. "Though, that damned ox has booted me in the head again it seems…"

"Can't remember anything or choosing not to?" I asked, lifting my eyebrows a couple of times.

"Last thing I remember I was trying to outdrink Fitmigar in the Molerat again."

"Right… Nothing after that?"

"No. Just a blank space. Can't even remember getting back. Why?"

Brom looked genuinely confused, so I left him to it. I was sure he'd find out soon enough.

Once Brom had finished getting ready, including falling over after failing to keep his balance while pulling his pants up, we grabbed our bags and weapons and headed out into the courtyard. A gentle rain greeted us as we stepped outside. Breakfast would be on the road today, so once the wagons pulled up front, we'd collect our griffins and be on the way.

The wagons!

"Back in a minute, buddy. Just got to run across to the infirmary." I dropped my bag at his feet and lay my weapons on top. "Keep an eye on that for me."

Brom mumbled something in response, placed his bags next to mine, and lay down against them, eyes closed. That would have to do, I supposed. Hungover Brom wasn't the most vigilant. I ran across the courtyard, dodging a couple of puddles on the way to the infirmary. Inside, I found Beralda still shuffling around.

"Morning, Beralda," I greeted. "How's Tordlum doing?"

"Go see for yourself, Jadyn. He's the only one in there," was her quick reply before she carried on her way.

"Thanks," I replied, but she was already out of earshot, which considering her age wasn't hard and only amounted to being about ten feet away.

I entered the small infirmary ward to see the elderly dwarven store master propped up on a couple of pillows. A few grey hairs sprouted through a thoroughly bandaged head. Enallo and Lana sat by the side of the bed keeping guard, the Darlish Coast native at least giving me a smile in greeting.

"Good to see you looking a bit better," I said to Tordlum as I pulled over a chair and sat down with the others.

"That was you that brought me here, Jadyn?"

"It was," I confirmed. "Sienna and me, actually. Found you unconscious under a wagon in stores, surrounded by broken potion bottles."

"I supposed you'd like to know what happened?" the elderly dwarf asked.

"Only if you feel up to it," I said, not wanting to make him feel any worse.

The academy was on full alert, so he'd surely been questioned already. Sabotage at the academy would be a serious business, and the dean had acted appropriately. Still, I wanted answers if I could get them.

"There isn't an awful lot to tell you, really," he admitted, rubbing his eyes and audibly exhaling.

I waited for him to speak in his own time. I didn't want to rush him in case he forgot anything that might help. He'd taken quite the bang to the head, after all.

"I'd locked up an hour or two earlier," he started after shifting in the bed to get comfy, "but I'd remembered something I needed to add to one of the wagons, so I went to head back inside."

Tordlum lived alone in a small cottage annexed to the back of the storeroom, close enough for it to have been no trouble at all, even at that late hour.

"I arrived to find the doors open and the lanterns smashed. I was about to alert the dean when I heard the sound of someone moving around inside." He paused for a second to take a sip of water before continuing.

"I grabbed a crowbar from inside the doorway and moved inside to check it out. We've had rats in there before, some real big, nasty buggers mind, but I could sense there was something else there. Something bigger still. Too much noise, you know? And no rat was going to force a door open or smash a lantern."

I nodded. We hadn't found the crowbar near him when we discovered him, so his attacker must have left with it as they made their escape.

"Well, I heard glass smashing, and immediately, I knew what was going on. We'd spread the potions across all four wagons, and someone had located the bottles on one of them and was destroying them."

I leaned forward, hoping for any clues that might help discover the motive behind the attack.

"I walked as quickly as I could around the back of the wagons and knelt down by a puddle on the floor," he continued after another sip, "and some bugger must have snuck up on me and clocked me good an' proper."

"So, you didn't see them at all?" I asked, frowning.

"Nothing. Next thing I knew I woke up here to the sound of Beralda's shuffling feet."

I thought about pressing Tordlum some more, seeing if I could jog free any details. The idea was interrupted by a familiar shuffle of feet. I turned to see Beralda gesturing for me to leave him be. I'd already outstayed my welcome.

Nodding to acknowledge I got the hint, I turned back to the elderly dwarf.

"You take care of yourself, sir," I said. I then bid Lana and Enallo goodbyes and headed out of the door.

Beralda gave me a gentle smile of appreciation in passing for not hassling her patient too much.

I took the stairs to the main hall, my mind still on the night's mystery assailant. I was no closer to finding anything out, and we were leaving soon. Could it be an infiltrator from north of the border, a shapeshifting monster, a sneaky goblin?

My stomach churned as I considered the possibility that it was someone inside the academy. Surely not? I'd spent nearly four years with these people. No one would sabotage their brothers and sisters in arms. Not the ones I knew anyway. I didn't know the younger years anywhere near as well, but still I doubted anyone at the Griffin Academy would do it. I did resolve to keep an eye out for trouble, though, and I'd need to let the others know there might be some creatures stalking us in the night.

The looming reality that we would be fighting for our lives and our kingdom before too long was all the stress most of them needed. I didn't like the idea of adding more to their plate, but they had to be made aware.

The rain had picked up a little during my infirmary visit, yet Brom was still lying on the packs, presumably fast asleep despite the water running down his face. Fitmigar was standing near him, not-so-gently kicking his side while the others stood around waiting.

The last of the students appeared as the first of the wagons made their way into the courtyard from stores. Galen pulled the first on a large black horse, followed by Algernon, Thom, and Mirek on the three others, each astride a similarly large pack horse. Elmar trotted alongside on a smaller horse, mumbling to himself, presumably about the destroyed potions. I'd have to have a word with him later to see if he knew why anyone would set out to destroy them.

Once all the wagons had pulled up in front of the dormitories, we tossed our bags into the last one. We then took the path around the back to retrieve our griffins, carrying our weapons, for the initial departure at least.

Brushing wet blond hair from my forehead, I noticed Sars and jogged over. Hopefully, he had discovered something about these new spells of mine.

"Anything?" I asked, unable to hide the anticipation in my voice.

"Nah, man. Nothing," he replied, shrugging his shoulders. "I have been through maybe two-thirds of the books that might have something, and the third that remain I have loaded onto one of the wagons."

"There's still hope then," I accepted. "It would be good to know what's happening to me."

"Agreed," he said, a small smile appearing before he added, "what is up with Brom and Fitmigar this morning?"

"What do you mean?" I asked, playing dumb.

"I am not sure. She just seems different around him. I swear she punched him in the shoulder before and it was not even hard."

"Maybe she's gone soft on him," I said, trying to keep a straight face.

"Ha. Doubt it. Must be something else." With that, Sars shrugged and went over to join Mallen, the elf retying his ponytail before we left.

As I walked on, a hand touched my back, and I turned to see Sienna alongside me.

"How's Tordlum?"

"Yeah, he's doing a bit better..." I filled her in on my recent conversation with the convalescing dwarf.

It turned out that Sienna had already spoken with Dean Hallow in passing that morning. Apparently, the stores had been thoroughly searched, but nothing of note had been discovered. However, she had been assured that the academy would continue a diligent hunt for the attackers after our departure.

Reaching the stables, I was delighted to see Froom had all forty griffins lined up and looking fierce, straps all fitted, lances attached to each. Walking down the line, I smiled as I saw Hestia study me from the corner of her eye.

"Very discrete, girl." I reached her and ran a hand down her brown, feathered neck. She lifted a wing and wrapped it around me in greeting. After she released me, I stepped around the side to pull myself up as she lowered her head, chirping softly.

Once all forty of us were on our griffins, we marched in a line back down the courtyard, shouting our thanks to Froom and his team as we passed. They'd done a great job in getting the griffins ready for departure—and I'd expected no less.

I glanced over my shoulder and noticed Sars struggling a little at the back of the line. I guided Hestia to step aside and fall back.

"Everything OK?" I asked as he pulled up alongside me.

"Not sure," he admitted. "Ralartis is just a little slow and favoring her left-hand side somewhat."

"What did Froom say about it?"

"Just said maybe she turned it over on her way up from the jousting stalls," he said, running a hand down her light-brown-feathered neck and giving a gentle pat.

"Damn. Not an ideal time for that, but let me know if the pace we set gets too much. The first two or three days at least should be fairly slow before we reach the wider, flatter tracks north of Riverhaven. If you need to put your lance onto one of the wagons, too, just do so. The added weight can't be all that helpful right now."

Sars gave me his thanks, and then I guided Hestia back into the back of the line, watching Ralartis's movement as we splashed through the rapidly forming puddles to join the wagons. We'd spent some time with Galen learning about formations for safe travel, back before the more physical combat classes, so we only needed a quick refresher before the march.

"Listen up, everyone," he started, and the gentle sound of conversation died down. "The tracks for the first couple of days are going to be pretty narrow and riddled with ruts."

A griffin screeched from the rear of the group.

Ignoring the brief interruption, Galen continued, "So, you'll be riding two abreast to begin, with the wagons spaced between you. The land is pretty open and flat, for the most part, so there'll be a few times where we need to scout to the left and right. We'll run groups of four a couple hundred yards ahead of the main party, and then we'll do the same at the rear, watching our tail."

We nodded acknowledgments. The plan was simple enough. Later, as the path winded and the surroundings closed in, we'd revert to brief aerial scouting trips and several of the party traveling to the sides of the main column, but that was some distance off.

"Now, it has also come to my attention that one of the griffins is walking a little lame, so we'll be setting a slightly slower pace to begin, but that should pick up soon enough."

I looked across at Sars, and he mouthed a silent thanks at me. I'd spoken to Galen and explained the situation, so it wouldn't become a problem on the road.

"Any volunteers for taking point?" Galen asked.

I kept my hand down. I wanted to be at the rear of the column for the first day, at least. That way I could keep an eye on how Ralartis coped from behind.

With four students chosen and moved into position, Galen continued, "And for the rear?"

I immediately lifted my hand and noticed Sienna, Fitmigar, and Brom do likewise.

Galen agreed, and the rest of the students moved into position. As Elandra passed, she whispered, "Don't leave it too long before we get to ride together, Jadyn," and threw in the least subtle wink I'd ever seen.

She was throwing more than a few hints my way, and after her wandering foot at breakfast the other morning, I knew she wasn't just playing around anymore. What's more, Sienna had pretty much already hinted that she didn't require being the sole object of my affections. I had a feeling Elandra was exactly who she was referring to when she mentioned another woman wanting a piece of me.

A rational part of me urged that a relationship before war, let alone a more complex arrangement, was a bad idea. However, that perfectly rational Jadyn was in the losing minority. If worst came to worst and some of us didn't make it back, I wouldn't want to live with regrets over not pursuing what we wanted.

With the column all set, a shout from the side set the wagon wheels to creaking motion. The griffins chuffed in eagerness, and we set a gentle pace across the courtyard toward the academy gates that led north.

All the younger students and most of the staff had come out to see us off. Passing by, I noticed the dean and Rivers deep in conversation. They both paused to catch my eye and nod. Was there something they hadn't told me?

I looked across at my friends around me, caught their eyes in turn, and said, "Off we go then. Whether we're ready or not, we'll soon be knee-deep in orc blood. Whatever happens, just know I've always got your back."

They each passed on similar promises as we exited the academy grounds, perhaps for the final ever time, and moved north. To war.

Chapter Eight

Our first half-day on the road passed by quickly. Conversation flowed effortlessly, and even Fitmigar seemed chattier than I'd ever known her. She was insistent on riding alongside Brom for the entirety of the day, much to his confusion. I was more than happy to be near Sienna, so that worked out well for me.

The land in the southernmost half of Atania was open and flat. Other than small infrequent groves in the near distance, the horizon stretched on with field after field. The various crops had been mostly harvested in the late summer months, and farmers now plowed the land, laying fertilizer, and in some instances, sowed winter crops such as carrots, cabbages, and kale.

The rain eased off mid-morning, and, by the time we stopped in the afternoon, the ground was dry enough to pause briefly and eat. We circled the wagons to an empty field, set the griffins to roaming and hunting small game, and set up a fire. The academy kitchen couldn't spare anyone to join us on our journey, so it fell upon Thom to prepare the food. Tamar and Syl, who'd grown up around kitchens, assisted him.

As we sat and ate, Brom sidled over to me. He attempted to be discrete, but as with most things about my stocky friend, it fell some way short of what he wanted, several faces turning our way as he got my attention.

"Hey, man. Can I ask you something?"

"Sure." I wiped my mouth with the back of my hand and placed my now-empty bowl down on the grass.

He looked a bit embarrassed, which was unusual. Brom had a seemingly effortless ability to own all his various fuck-ups. Eventually, he started, "Don't suppose you know if something's up with Fitmigar, do you?"

I suppressed a grin. "What do you mean?"

"Ah, it's probably nothing, but she keeps staring at me. If I didn't know any better, I'd call it almost affectionately."

"Really?" *Keep it together, Jadyn*, I thought, having to bite my lip to prevent myself from laughing out loud.

He shook his head in confusion. "Yeah. And it's freaking me out."

"And you have no idea why?" I said, thinking that maybe talking about it would bring back some of my friend's memory.

"Nothing," he admitted. "It's starting to get weird." He picked up a piece of meat from his bowl and popped it into his mouth.

I jumped to my feet, picked up my bowl, and started walking over to wash it clean. "Not surprised, buddy, after what you got up to in her room in the early hours…"

Brom's eyes widened, and he coughed mid-chew, spluttering food from his mouth. "WHAT?!"

I continued walking away, my shoulders bouncing with laughter.

A warm breeze blew across our temporary rest stop as I strolled over to the wagon where we'd set up a cleaning station. My chuckles were only now dying down. It was strange to be marching towards the unknown, knowing our lives would be on the line, and still finding humor in everyday situations. I was lucky to be surrounded by such close friends.

I dropped the bowl into some tepid water for a quick scrub, then passed it off to Syl with a thanks. I returned to Brom and found him deep in conversation with our young dwarven friend. I guessed she was filling him in on the gaps in his night that I couldn't—and wouldn't want to even if I could.

Walking around the pair, I noticed Sienna and Elandra sitting together. Approaching, I dropped down, leaned over, and kissed Sienna on the lips, pulling her close and feeling her breasts against me before leaning away and smiling.

"And where's mine?"

I turned to Elandra expecting a teasing grin, but instead, I met eyes burning with desire. I paused, but only long enough for Sienna to giggle softly behind me and then speak.

"Yeah, Jadyn. It isn't nice not to share."

Okay? So this was happening. Well, what the heck. I'd already resolved not to leave regrets, and if the girls were fine exploring this then so was I.

I laughed, shrugged, and pulled Elandra close, meeting her full, perfect lips with my own. She tasted fruity, reminding me of recent summer days.

"My apologies," I said trying to keep my cool as I leaned back, the bulge below my waist already pushing hard against my pants.

"Sienna tells me you've got some unfinished business from yesterday in the paddock," Elandra said, her eyes avoiding mine, "but once you've got that out of your system, you'd better believe I'm going to get me some of that."

It was happening. I laughed in disbelief, taken aback a little at where this was all coming from. I put it down to knowing that our lives were changing faster than we could process. That and I knew Sienna and Elandra talked together all the time. Maybe she'd passed on *everything* about what happened the other evening.

Her eyes lifted up, meeting mine. Elandra ran her tongue across her lips and blew me a kiss.

I felt a warm breath at my ear. Sienna's voice added, "You'd better give her as much as you gave me. Neither of us wants to be missing out on that perfect cock of yours."

"Right. Uh, wow. Don't worry, girls." I coughed. *Keep it cool, Jadyn. Keep it cool.* "There's plenty of me to go around," I said, hoping it didn't sound too corny.

Evidently not, because Elandra leaned over and grabbed my cock firmly in hand. She squeezed, purring with anticipation.

Before the temptation could grow too intense, a call came out over the camp. We gathered ourselves, packed up, and were back on the road again within minutes.

Our caravan wound northward. The gentle warmth of the day dropped away, and a soft chill flowed in as we followed the track between the fields, fording a couple of small streams along the way. Thanks to sparse rainfall before today, they were still far lower than one would expect at this time of the year.

Twice, a small pack of wolves was spotted at the far edge of our vision. They rarely wandered this far from the more northern forested areas. The packs kept their distance and disappeared pretty quickly both times, their appearance shrugged off without much thought.

Due to the condition of Sar's griffin, Ralartis, the first day's pace was rather more sedate than we'd hoped for. The plan had been to reach the village of Millford before nightfall, but we'd fallen short. Not the most auspicious start to our journey.

As dusk approached, we pulled off the side of the track into an unplowed field and set up camp. Once the wagons were arranged, Mirek and several students set about setting up a temporary griffin enclosure.

The rest of us threw up tents that were spread across the wagons. I'd hoped for a bit of privacy, maybe a room at an inn or something similar, at least this first night, but the cold, hard ground beckoned instead.

Food ran the same as earlier in the day. Once we had taken our fill of meat and vegetable stew, we sat in groups around the large fire and discussed the day. Sars was nose-deep in a book, so we left him to it.

"How are you both doing?" I asked Elandra and Mallen.

Brom had spent the majority of the day deep in hushed conversation with Fitmigar, but when he wasn't, he'd done little else but complain. First, it was the rain, and then it was the uneven track beneath Shadowtail's feet. It was relatively lighthearted, but I could tell my friend was on unfamiliar ground.

Mallen looked to Elandra and gestured for her to speak first.

She smiled at me, brushed a strand of hair from her face, and spoke. "Better than I expected," she admitted. "Once Veo found his feet, I got balanced pretty quickly. Company was pleasant"—she looked at Mallen and nodded—"and the time passed quickly."

"Yes," Mallen agreed. "For the first day of our travels, and the slow nature, it went well."

"Did you notice the wolves?" Elandra added, and I nodded.

"Twice. They followed us from a distance. Likely they're just inquisitive, but it might pay to keep an eye on them."

"You think they'll come closer?"

"Not sure." I thought on it for a moment. "They don't normally approach large groups, especially griffins, but if they're hungry or lost who's to say how they'll react? Didn't even expect to see any this far south, to be honest."

"It's unusual to see them here for sure," Fitmigar said. Wolves were a near-constant in the low, mountainous region in the northern part of Atania where she hailed from, so she probably knew more than most of us. "Other than the mountains, they tend to stay near forests and the like."

"We'll see how tomorrow—"

A howl echoed from somewhere out in the darkening night, followed swiftly by another.

Our steeds responded, and for a moment, all else fell silent as forty griffins responded to the challenge with a bone-chilling cry.

The wolves did not reply.

"We'll see if the watch reports anything tonight, and then keep a look out tomorrow, too."

"Speaking of the watch," Sienna said, "who's pulled duty on the first night?"

"I've got next watch actually," Brom said, "with Fitmigar and Mallen."

"And I've somehow managed to end up being roped into helping document any information Sars thinks might be relevant," Elandra said, rising to her feet.

A short while later, a whistle sounded, and Brom, Mallen, and Fitmigar jumped up and headed off. Fitmigar usually carried her lance, but she'd persuaded Brom to pass her a couple of his daggers. Mallen had his war hammer leaning on his shoulder.

"So… I think we might have some time," I said to Sienna, turning to her as she reclined next to me. Her face was gorgeous in the flickering of the firelight.

"Where are you taking me then, Jadyn?" she asked in perhaps the sultriest tone I'd ever heard from her.

"My tent. Now." I pulled her to her feet, keeping her close behind me. "So forceful," she said. "I like it."

"You'll like what comes next more." I shoved the flaps of the tent aside, pulling her inside.

"Oh, I'm sure. I do love this. It's amazing and helps take the mind off everything. Hard to think of much else when I'm with you."

"You know you don't have to try make me fall for you all over again anymore?" I asked, teasing. Sienna smiled as I pulled her in and pressed my lips against hers, arching her back. My tongue parted her soft lips and slipped between them. Easing my hand around her back, I pulled her closer, kissing her deeper, and she let out a soft moan as she responded.

I brought my hands around her sides and caressed them through her curves. Sliding my hands over her chest, I felt her hardening nipples through her shirt and her pulse quickening.

I brought our kiss to an end. Our eyes met, both burning with want. Slipping her top buttons out, I dropped my hands, took the hem of her shirt, and lifted it over her head, eliciting a gasp of delight.

I smiled as I leaned forward and took her right breast in my mouth. I ran my tongue around her areola and flicked it over her nipple before sucking gently, then harder as my left hand found her other breast and squeezed. Little moans of pleasure escaped her lips under my tease.

I let her catch her breath and left a trail of kisses above her chest and across her collarbone, before dropping again and seizing her left breast in my mouth this time. Every part of her needed my attention, and as my mouth was busy, my hands moved to the waistband of her pants.

Slipping a couple of fingers under the waist, I lowered myself to my knees, slowly kissing every part of her skin as I eased her pants down and off, my face level with her waist.

"Jadyn..." she breathed. Her fingers dug into my shoulders as my kisses wandered lower, meeting the thin section of soft, curly hair that led me lower still.

I ran my hands up the back of her thighs, reached her perfect ass and grabbed. I pulled her down, easing her on her back before me.

A growl left with my exhale as I took in the sight of her naked body in the dimming light. Her pert tits heaved with excitement, her dark hair fell loosely around her face, and her thighs rubbed in anticipation of my cock.

I pulled my shirt over my head and tossed it into the corner, then placed a hand on the inside of each of her knees to ease her legs apart.

"Jadyn…" she whimpered as I trailed kisses up the inside of her thigh, her sweet tangy scent intensifying as I moved up, pulling me in, threatening to make me lose all control.

Pushing her legs wider still, I ran my tongue across her folds. The finger I'd inserted helped part them. She was burning hot and wet. Juices soaked my fingers and met my lips as I continued to explore her sex, licking it with increasing speed as my finger moved in and out.

She grabbed my hair, moaning as I pulled my finger out and found her nub. Her lower body tensed, abs and ass tightening. Teasing my finger around her sweet spot, my tongue continued to push her onwards until her legs seized and jerked, and she arched her back, her tits rising as she reached release.

I smiled and flicked my tongue across her again, tasting the sweet tang of her orgasm before I pulled slowly away.

Rising to her knees to join me, her chest pinkening, she fumbled at the waist of my pants before shoving me backward and yanking them free.

She looked from my hard cock to my eyes, a smile spreading across her face.

"Get over here," I growled, leaning up and pulling her legs forward until she sat before me. Her hands flew to my waist, and she let out little sounds of excitement as she started to pump me up and down, using both hands as she worked me into a frenzy.

I needed to fuck her senseless and tried to pull her forward, but she refused. Sienna gave me a 'be patient' look, while guiding my tip past her lips and setting her tongue to flick up and down me. Her hands snaked beneath my length, slipping to cup and caress my balls.

Moments of pleasure stretched, and the urge to fuck her grew impossible. "Sienna... stop."

"Hmm?" She rose briefly, meeting my eyes as she licked her lips. "Did I do it wrong?"

"You did it too good." I lifted her up and onto my cock in one smooth motion, shuddering with delight as I glided effortlessly inside her, stretching her wide. Sienna clasped a hand to her lips to stifle her moan. Her eyes closed. Fingers dug into my shoulders.

We started moving our hips almost simultaneously. I gyrated mine, while she pushed me back again and then rocked back and forth, my length fully inside her. The muscles in her hips tensed, tightening the grip of the strokes to the point I was fast approaching release.

"You're so tight," I murmured.

"Pretty sure it's you who is big," she groaned, slowing her movements to prolong our ecstasy. We continued the steady strokes, relishing the pleasure of just fucking each other until I couldn't take it any longer. I grabbed her thighs and started lifting her up, increasing the speed. I pushed deep into her, faster and faster, then had to let go. Hot spurts of cum shot into her as her own juices ran out and onto my thighs.

Arching her back, she screamed, "Jadyn!" before collapsing on top of me, sweaty and perfect.

"That... was... so... nggh," she huffed between breaths.

I smiled at her as I lay back, eyes closed, savoring the feeling of still being inside her, not wanting this to end.

We cuddled for a while before, Sienna spoke again, "What are you thinking?"

"About us?"

"About us, about the war, about the future."

"Us feels right," I told her, and she leaned into me. "The war is coming, and there's nothing we can do about it. I'm not scared, but I am concerned. About how if we don't do this right, there won't be a future for us to worry about."

"And if we do secure a future?" she whispered.

"Wherever I am, I see you there, too," I told her, kissing her softly on the forehead.

"Me, too," she whispered back, and I felt a warm glow inside my chest.

A short while later, Sienna slipped away into the night to make it back before the shift change and the return of my tent mates.

A content smile still lingered on my face as I lay back and closed my eyes for the night. We'd be heading out as soon as dawn broke, so without being down for watch tonight, I took the opportunity to rest. I'd just earned it after all.

Chapter Nine

Howling woke me constantly during the night. Each time, the griffins screeched back defiantly. I also stirred when Brom and Mallen returned from watch duty. Sars, however, obeyed proper watch etiquette and snuck in at some point during the night without making a sound.

Still a little sleepy, I tried to put on a sharp face when our combat teacher and commanding officer, Galen, pulled me to one side just as I was heading for breakfast.

"I've got a favor to ask of you today, Jadyn."

"OK," I replied. "How can I help, sir?"

Not one to preamble, the elf dove straight in. "The wolves were around again in the night. I'm sure you heard?"

I nodded.

"Well, we need a plan of action in case that continues today. The watch reported numbers far higher than anything we saw in the daylight. What's more worrying are the eyes. They're black, the same as those bears you reported at the academy."

"That's worrying," I agreed. "What can I do to help?"

"From the little practice you've all had, Algernon reports that Hestia and you are our best option if we need to scout aerially."

That made sense. We'd been able to stay up longer and with greater success in the one and only lesson we'd had so far.

"I can do that. Just me or others, too?"

"We've had a brief think about it," the elf explained, "and we've decided that too much activity might cause them to try and attack, so we thought you could go up alone and check the situation out from the air, and then we'll send Brom, our shadow mage, to get close from the ground."

"Is all this really necessary for wolves?" I asked.

"According to Mallen's report, noises were coming from multiple points during the night. They could be numbering in the hundreds."

"Understood."

"So, do me a favor and ride at the rear again today, Jadyn. Sars mentioned he'd like to ride back there with you today for some reason, so add another couple, and if we need you, I'll send someone back to alert you."

"I'll get right on it, sir," I confirmed, then I turned and headed over to grab a bit of food.

As I walked across the camp, I felt invigorated and fully awake. The earlier sleepiness had faded strangely quickly considering how badly I'd slept. I was positively overflowing with... *power?* Was that what it was?

I paused and cycled through my spells again.

[Fireball]

[Fire Burst]

[Fire Elemental]

[Wind Burst]

[Wind Boost]

[Wind Wall]

Nothing had changed since I received the new wind spells a few days ago. I didn't know what to think, so I didn't bother thinking and instead grabbed some food and ate it quickly before helping the others to take down the camp.

With the tents all away, the paddock broken down, and our preparations complete, we returned to the track heading north. Despite tensions rising with the wolf situation, Charn, Lana, Enallo, and Bernolir thought that it would be good to have a sing-along as we marched to help diffuse some of the tension. Charn, using a low-mana casting of [Ballad Boost], projected his voice across the caravan, singing songs that the others could join in with. Some were not even aware that the magic behind them boosted their own mana levels as they sang.

The chill of the morning soon dissipated, and I reminded myself to enjoy the last moments of warmth before winter closed in. A couple of grey clouds floated in an otherwise mostly blue sky. We'd likely be lucky enough to miss the rain.

Sars joined me at the rear, and Ralartis's leg seemed to have improved somewhat from the previous day. Mallen and Elandra rode with us. Since Sienna was elsewhere, I made sure to ride behind the dark-skinned beauty to watch her ass sway with the griffin's steps. I would've stared at her butt all day if Sars hadn't sought me out.

"Jadyn," he began excitedly, "I think I have found something."

"What kind of something?" I asked.

"The multi-wielding."

"OK. So, what have you discovered?"

"It is not much," he admitted, trying to temper my expectations, "but it is something, at least."

"OK… go on," I encouraged.

"I found it in a really old text. I do not even think it is Atanian in nature. Possibly something from north of the border. Maybe from somewhere else entirely."

"There is nowhere else, Sars," Mallen interjected from in front, looking over his shoulder. "There's just us and Urg-frei, north of the border. You'll be talking of across the seas soon!"

Mallen and Elandra laughed, but Sars still had his serious face on, so I nodded at him to continue.

"So… this text mentions, hypothetically it seems, the possibility of certain people potentially having the ability to wield two, sometimes three, branches of magic."

"OK. So that's good," I hedged, raising an eyebrow.

"Seems so," Sars agreed. "Apparently"—a blush rose in his cheeks—"they could be passed on through… um… *carnal activities* between magic wielders."

"That would make sense after what happened," I told him, feeling no shame in talking about it.

He nodded. "But then it gets a bit weird."

"Yeah? Weird how?"

"It talks of the possibility of mana surges happening at the same time. Both ways."

My eyes widened. "That's it!"

"Er, what is, Jadyn?" Sars asked, confused.

"That's what I've been feeling." I smiled, barely able to withhold my relief. "Does it say how it works? How long it lasts?"

"It was not very clear, to be honest. The new spells would be permanent, at least to my understanding. The mana surge, perhaps two or three days? I struggled to translate those bits."

"It wasn't written in Atanian?" Elandra asked.

"I thought I explained that already?" Sars shook his head. "Anyway, that is all I have got so far."

"That's great, man. Thank you," I said, and he smiled back at me. "So, we know how I've got the new spells, and Sienna has got hers, and we know what this extra energy might be that we both have. This power. I also think three days might be about right, too, because I felt a little drained yesterday, and then after Sienna and I partook in"—I winked at Sars—"*carnal activities* again last night, it feels like I'm better than ever again today."

"Hah!" came from in front of me, and Elandra spun around on Veo's back to stare at me. "That means it's my turn next!"

"You got it," I replied, already undressing her with my eyes.

"I'd better have, Jadyn," she finished. "Can't let Sienna have all the fun."

With that, she spun back around. I continued my conversation with Sars, discussing the text again, but he didn't have much else to share. Sars promised to look into the book more that evening, and then we fell into more general chatter as we continued on our way.

A few hours in we skirted the village of Millford, which should have been the sight of the previous night's camp. A few villagers came out of their small stone and wood dwellings and waved as we passed, the children gawping on in awe as our majestic griffins marched past.

A little before lunch time, a shout came from the front and was passed down the line. We all looked to the east, where several lines amounting to what must have been over a hundred wolves appeared a few fields over.

"OK, that's way more than a few small packs," I mumbled.

"They normally travel in sixes and sevens," Sars explained, "so you're right. The numbers are huge."

We continued on, our shadow remaining with us for a good half-hour before they peeled away and out of sight.

An hour passed by before the next sighting. This time to the west. The pack seemed to be of a similar size.

"Do you think that's the same group?" I asked the others.

"Hard to be sure," Sars said. "They have so many more with them now."

"Yeah," Mallen agreed. "They're fast enough to have gone ahead or behind us and traveled across there. But why they'd do that is a mystery."

"It's creeping me out now," Elandra said, making a point of shivering in her seat.

"Well, if gets much more than this, we'll need to be ready. Everyone, keep your weapons to hand," I warned them.

"Agreed," Mallen responded.

They all placed a hand on their weapons, another on their lances. Sars rested his lance on his shoulder in preparation for action.

The third sighting was after we'd stopped for lunch. This time, even more wolves appeared in one long line that ran parallel to our caravan, now only two fields away. As we pressed on, they dipped in and out of view as the land gently undulated.

"That is odd," Sars noted at my side. "Downright unnatural."

"What is?"

"You never really get packs of more than thirty wolves. Ever. And now there is a pack more than three times that size now that all those lines have merged."

"Are you sure?" Elandra asked, a hint of worry in her tone.

"Absolutely. I remember Fitmigar talking about it when she spoke of home. She said one of the main similarities between the mountain wolves and the forest ones was that they ran with similarly sized packs."

"So, you think this is definitely more than one pack?" I asked, running a hand through my hair.

"Lots of packs, all converging, becoming one."

"Maybe they're doing some wolf Autumn mating gathering?" Elandra suggested. "Lots of that going on these days."

Sars scoffed, shaking his head. "No. I am sure. This is not normal."

Hmm. "It feels off somehow," I agreed. "And those black eyes. Just like the bears."

"Agreed," Mallen added.

Helstrom rode up on his griffin from the middle of the column, one of his twin axes spinning in the palm of his left hand.

"Galen says to go aerial, Jadyn. Says you'll know what he means."

"Understood," I said, moving back and out of the line and allowing the dwarf to take my place. "I'll pause and give myself some space to get off the ground. Brom?"

"Already moving across as we speak," he confirmed.

I nodded and let them go on ahead. Leaning forward on Hestia's back, I whispered, "We're going up, girl. Nothing crazy. Let's just take a look at what's going on, and then we'll head back down."

Hestia chirped in response, then she lowered her head and ran forwards, quickly picking up speed before jumping with wings extended. A couple of powerful wing-strikes kept us afloat and pulled us up. I exhaled as we rose, my heart rate picking up as the cold air streamed past my face. I'd only had that one previous day practicing with her in the air, and now we were using it for real. The feeling was still as magical as ever, the view of a patchwork of groves and fields breathtaking.

Running my hand down Hestia's neck, I nudged her gently with my right knee, and she instinctively knew what I needed. We swooped down and glided left, heading east toward the line of wolves.

They soon appeared directly below us. A dozen or so raised their heads, briefly, to check us out. The rest remained transfixed on stalking along the route of the wagons. Since I'd taken to the air, they had moved a little farther away, and now the rest of the caravan would be unable to spot them from the ground.

"A bit lower," I encouraged Hestia. She lowered her head as we descended. More wolves took note of us, but they continued to track the column while remaining out of its view.

I wonder how Brom's getting on, I thought, just as a dozen wolves at the rear of the line broke away and moved towards our line.

"Ah, that's strange," I said.

The wolves that had left the pack picked up speed, suddenly running as though in pursuit, uncontrolled, crazy with rage. The others remained committed to their tracking, so I left them momentarily to keep an eye on the wolves that I assumed were following Brom.

It was a hunch that was soon confirmed by metal glinting in the sun. A dagger flew out of nowhere, burrowing itself deep in the flank of the lead wolf.

Rather than dropping the pursuing wolf, it growled and picked up speed. Heedless of the bleeding or the obsidian knife buried in its side, the wolf chased down the elusive shadow mage. It moved its head from side to side, seemingly losing the scent multiple times, only to find it again as Brom led them back and away from the main caravan.

"Jadyn, I can't lose them!" came from below, a touch of panic in the tone.

"Hold on!" I shouted and encouraged Hestia to dive down with a gentle pat.

I leaned forward against her neck and cycled through my casting options as we descended, coming to rest on [Fireball]. Mentally selecting the spell, I pulled on my core, twisted my fingers around, and a ball of flame appeared on the palm of my hand, growing as I poured mana into it. My eyes widened as the ball bloomed far faster and larger than anything I'd created before.

A nudge of my knees was all it took for Hestia to take us down over our first target. Mentally calculating speeds and distances as we flew, I released my hold on the spell. The fireball flew forward, erupted around the wolf, and consumed it in an explosive inferno. A whoop of delight from below reached my ears, and I realized Brom was nearby. I might have only just acted in time.

The other wolves continued to hound him, charging past the fallen leader and after Brom as he evaded their pursuit. It was time to show them the power of a magic-wielder and a griffin working together.

I flew lower still, firing off [Fireball] after [Fireball]. The smell of burning wolf fur soon filled the air. A couple evaded my spells, but with a nudge of my feet,

I guided Hestia to swoop low. She plucked both from the ground in her claws, eviscerating muscle and crushing bone before dropping their limp corpses to the ground with a screech that seemed to shake the very skies.

One wolf remained, still determined to catch Brom despite the destruction I had wrought against its kin. However, as it leaped over one of its fallen packmates, a dagger flew from its left-hand side, embedding itself in its brain and sending it crashing to the ground, dead.

I twisted on Hestia's back, peering over my shoulder to check out how the larger line of wolves had reacted. They hadn't. The pack continued to follow the line of the main column, a few more fields to the east now, still out of sight of the main caravan.

As I guided Hestia back toward the wagons, Brom appeared below me on Shadowtail, his [Shadow Cloak] either dismissed or expired, I couldn't tell which. He had retrieved his daggers and slid them into the bandolier across his back.

"Did you see that?" he shouted up. "I took it out with one shot!"

"I saw, buddy! Great job!" I shouted back, before being unable to resist adding, "shame you couldn't do that with the first one or any of the others, hey!"

Brom had a great big grin plastered across his face, but I couldn't match it. Something about this didn't feel right. *Why were the wolves tracking us? And why did a dozen leave the line but the others keep on, transfixed on the actions of our main column?*

As we landed behind the column and ran to catch up to the rear, my friend chattered away in delight at his first real action. Mine, too, I supposed.

Once Brom joined the middle, I relieved Helstrom from my place and filled the others in on the wolves' movements.

"That first one you released must have been the biggest fireball I think I've ever seen," Mallen said as I settled back into the pace of the column.

"Yeah." I realized they would have still seen me in the air, even if they couldn't make out my targets. "Think it might be that mana surge at work."

"You think?" Sars said excitedly, scrambling for a small notebook he kept in his pocket.

"That's my best guess."

"Any idea why some attacked?" Elandra asked.

"Not really. I think somehow Brom managed to spook them, but the way they attacked felt wrong somehow."

"Wrong how?" Sars asked, leaning closer and writing the conversation down as we discussed events.

"I don't know," I admitted, unsure whether I should voice my true concerns.

I'd seen the way they acted. With no concern for the other wolves, they left the line and headed out, eyes as black as the night. The main group just carried on without them, and even when we took them down, the others didn't flinch.

It was like they weren't even controlling their own minds…

It was like the bears all over again.

"I think someone might be controlling them."

Interlude 2

For as long as Ugrea had been alive, the Kre'Hrez clan had been at war with the Kre'Speiw clan, battling in the northernmost mountains of Urg-frei. The two clans slaughtered each other indiscriminately, brutally removing any who stood against their dominance of the region.

When Ugrea murdered his predecessor and became Warchief Ugrea of the Kre'Hrez clan, that pattern continued. The slaughter a way of life. Brutal. Unforgiving.

Then one day, two full cycles ago, all of that changed.

Dreiz, warchief of the Kre'Speiw clan, left behind his elderly and his young, and he took his males and his females south to fight against the humans and the elves in an effort to conquer the land where everything was so very soft. So very pitifully soft and weak.

No matter how hard Warchief Ugrea strained his mind in the intervening seasons, he couldn't work out why anyone would choose to leave the harsh mountainous region that had been their home for centuries. The harshness made them strong. Made them powerful. How could an orc clan succeed if they surrounded themselves with the squishy and the soft?

Not one to let such an opportunity slide, Ugrea had rounded up his best warriors, and he had ransacked the weak and the young that Dreiz had left behind.

The elderly were killed on sight, dispatched and left to rot, food for the vultures. The young were kept alive. Not through any sense of compassion.

No, they lived only because they would grow to become useful fighters. Fighters for the Kre'Hrez clan that now ruled the entirety of the Grikk mountain range of Urg-frei.

Now, as Warchief Ugrea sat surrounded by his wives, batting them away as they tried to tend to his needs, the situation changed again. He closed his eyes as a vision assailed him.

Ugrea walked across a bloody battlefield, three thick stripes of blue warpaint across his grizzled face, the corpses of griffins and griffin knights strewn across the ground. None remained to stop him. He snarled as he lifted the blond-haired head of a young griffin knight into the air. The orcs around him roared in approval.

The war was over. Now, Warchief Ugrea could march south and take anything he desired from the soft, weak animals of this pitiful land.

Warchief Ugrea called a meeting of his council. When he explained what they were going to do, voices and grunts were raised in dissent, only calming to a low mutter when the head of the warchief's main advisor rolled across the floor.

As Ugrea wiped the blood from his greatsword, he told his clan of their mission. They would round them up in their entirety and leave the young and the elderly behind. They would then march south, and together with the remaining Kre'Hrez clan members, they would fight for complete control of the land south of the border.

The land of Atania.

Chapter Ten

After our earlier skirmish, Algernon and Galen wanted to excuse me from watch duty that evening. Brom was off anyway after being on the night before, but I refused. I was still bursting with energy and fine to take my watch. We'd only be on around every third night anyway, with groups of three running three-hour shifts, so it wasn't such a big deal.

I agreed to take the second watch, running from after dinner until the turn of the next day.

Eating as quickly as I could, and with barely a word to spare for the others, I headed over to the third wagon to meet the pair who would be sharing the shift with me. A couple of minutes later, Helstrom and Het arrived, the girl pushing her spectacles down and peering at me over the top.

"Helstrom, Het," I greeted.

"Squad leader," Helstrom said, coming up and clasping arms. The dwarf was a touch taller than Fitmigar at around four-foot-three.

"Nice work earlier, Jadyn," Het added, and I struggled to hide my shock. That was surely the first time she'd been openly nice to me.

"What?" she asked, face scrunching up in annoyance.

"Nothing." I shook my head. "Thanks, guys. Any preference for which point you'd like to take?" We'd set it up, as out in the open as we were, to take triangular watchpoints.

"Happy for you to choose, Jadyn," said Helstrom.

I nodded, turning to Het.

"I don't mind either way." She shrugged. "You seem to have a handle on things." Was that two compliments in a row? This was a day for the history books.

"OK. So, the last time we saw the huge line of wolves, they were settling down in the east still. So, if you both are OK with it, I'll take the easternmost point."

Both nodded in agreement, so I continued.

"Helstrom, you take the north-northwest point, and Het, you take the south-southwest point. Does that work?"

"Fine with me," Het said, turning and immediately heading straight across camp to relieve whoever preceded her.

"Aye, sir," Helstrom added, "that's fine with me, too. Whistle if you need me, or I'll see you in three hours."

With that sorted, I headed over to my watchpoint. I switched with Rammy, the huge red-haired fire mage of few words who looked like he was made of pure lava. And a member of my squad.

"All clear?" I checked before he left.

"Yep, all good, Jadyn. Keep us safe." He nodded and headed back into camp, likely hoping that Tamar and Syl had put some food aside for him. And by some, I assumed a lot. You didn't get that big living off scraps.

After erecting the camp, Enallo had taken his squad and set up perimeter traps. Harlee had created pits with her earth magic, which they then filled with sharpened wooden spikes. One of their group, Glymavor, an elf, was an excellent logger, despite being a lightning mage. He'd also chopped down and provided wood for a crude palisade, leaving easily defensible points between it.

It paid to prepare. Hundreds of magically enraged wolves could pose a problem... if they took us unawares. But so long as we kept a tight watch during the day and set up a properly defended camp and faced them on our terms, we didn't have much to worry about. My attention was drawn from the defenses to the night by a howl in the darkness. One followed by another, then another, each answered by the loud shrieking of the griffins in a challenge.

Are they closer than before?

I couldn't make out any skulking figures in the gloom, so I put it down to a trick of the dark night and relaxed. They'd be daft to try and attack an entire caravan of magic-wielders and forty griffins.

With my mana levels still high, I had no issues keeping awake and alert on watch. With all that energy to spare, I figured I'd practice some spells.

This would continue to strengthen pathways and increase the density of my mana, allowing me to cast faster and with more power.

I was tempted at first to call upon [Fire Elemental]. What better way to locate any potential wolves than by walking an elemental eastward until I heard a howl or it was snuffed out by force? Then again, the wolves were acting really strange, and an attack might trigger them into attacking us. Even if they didn't pose a threat in a fight, I didn't want to ruin our rest.

I brought up my list of spells and scanned through it. I'd worked with all of them with the exception of [Wind Wall]. In fact, I hadn't even thought to ask Sienna more about it. It still felt weird how the spells had just appeared. My own spells I was perfectly confident in. I'd spent three years learning them, growing them, improving them. Them I had earned through hard work.

With these new ones, I honestly had no idea how they worked. Using them was going to be trial and error. Well, it was when you didn't think to ask simple questions. Although, to be fair to myself, being too busy getting naked with Sienna was a valid excuse for not thinking about magic questions.

Right, let's give [Wind Wall] a go.

I let out a long breath, relaxed my body, and cycled through my spells, pausing on [Wind Wall]. Then, I pulled mana from my core. First, a trickle, then a little more, until I could feel I had enough suffused through my body to give it a go. Careful to aim away from my campmates, I mentally released the spell.

A solid wall of wind, perhaps twenty feet wide and six feet high, moved away from me, pushing back the evening breeze until all was still around me.

I wonder if that pushes people back, too? It seemed pretty strong. I shrugged the thought away. I couldn't practice that right now, and I wasn't sure anyone would really volunteer to be my assistant, so I settled on just waiting to ask Sienna in the morning. At least, I'd started practicing it. Next, I wanted to see if I had any control over the wall...

A sudden yelp caught my attention, and I grimaced. The wall had traveled a little farther than I'd expected it to.

Immediately, I begin to mentally calculate the speed the wall had been traveling at and the time that elapsed before the wolf yelped. Providing the wall had traveled at a constant speed into the darkness, that would put the wolf at roughly four hundred feet away. A little closer than earlier. Were they spying on us?

I waited a few minutes, ear out towards the woods.

When no howls followed and no wolves came running out, I settled back down and resumed my watch. I decided against flinging more magic out into the dark beyond camp, no matter how much I was itching to test the magic out.

I spent the rest of my watch trying to remain alert, while thoughts of Sienna and her magic kept trying to worm into my mind. That first night in the showers with Sienna wasn't my first time, though I still suspected it was hers. However, it *was* my first time with another magic wielder, and something about it had created a connection between us. Sienna had spoken of feeling closer to me, and I had to admit, even if just to myself, that I felt it, too. A magical connection of sorts.

But, we weren't the first magic users to ever fuck. So, what was different here? Sienna was the daughter of a rural farmer, and from what I knew, that was all pretty regular. The missing piece here were my origins.

Wendia had found me on the streets of Farrenport as a five-year-old—at least she assumed that to be my age—and had taken me into her home. I had lighter skin and blonder hair than the locals, but I carried no accent in the few words I'd spoken, so it was difficult to pinpoint where I'd come from.

Unfortunately, I remembered nothing from before that, so pondering where I came from would be nothing but dead ends.

I focused on something I could try and work out.

What was it that had established that connection between us? Was it her orgasm? Was it mine? If I'd pulled out like I'd thought she'd have wanted, spurting thick ribbons over her chest, would it still have happened? It felt weird to think about how I'd manage to test any of these theories. Perhaps, I'd just hope that Sars found out a little more.

And then there was this increase in mana. Fucking Sienna again the previous evening had seemed to replenish it, after I'd felt it gradually draining again.

Was there a ceiling on the amount of mana I could receive from Sienna? And was the surge she received as large as mine? I assumed I'd always top up to the same point, but I'd need to find out.

Then what if I fucked someone else?

My mind sprinted off on its own, painting a vivid image of Elandra, bent over on all fours, her perfect dark ass on full display while she looked back over her shoulder at me as I thrust deeper and deeper.

I shook my head. *Concentrate!*

Would giving Elandra what she wanted gift me even more spells? What was I thinking—it was something I wanted, too. I could see myself with Elandra almost as easily as I did with Sienna. Would I receive water-based spells, and would Elandra receive one of mine as Sienna did? And then would that also give me another mana surge, and her the same?

Would it top me up to the levels I got from Sienna, or if I fucked them both together, would it boost me higher still?

Despite the uncertainties ahead, I smiled.

I would enjoy finding out, that much was certain.

My shift ended when Tamar came to relieve me. It turned out that helping with dinner duties each evening didn't excuse you from your spot on the watch.

We clasped hands, and I mentioned both the howling and my [Wind Wall] experimentation. After giving him the wolves' approximate distance, I returned to the center of camp.

Brom's snoring led me back to my tent. I snuck inside, got my head down, and was asleep within moments.

The noise around our makeshift camp by morning was louder than normal. Galen was running a combat class for anyone who had the energy to join in, which was almost everyone. Practice and preparation helped give us some confidence for the war ahead.

I spent a while running through some familiar drills with Brom, Mallen, and Elandra. We sparred using some wooden swords that Galen had bought along.

The weighting was different from my regular practice scimitars, so some of my techniques were off, but sparring helped loosen my muscles and experiment with some new scenarios.

We had limited time before we reached the border, so it made sense to keep learning and practicing as we traveled. Any increase in our mana capabilities could be priceless.

After packing everything away and waiting for us to set off, I headed over to Hestia and spent a while gently grooming her. There was little we could do without being in a town or village with suitable facilities, but I did my best to make her presentable. She appreciated the attention, chuffing gently as she nuzzled at my ear.

Heading to the rear of the column again, I was surprised to discover four other griffin riders already present. Brom, Fitmigar, Het, and Rammy were mounted and ready to go.

No Sienna, I noted, feeling a pang of disappointment. *No Elandra, either.*

As I moved into position, Elmar -- Madame Summerstone's short, blond-haired assistant -- rode up on his horse and pulled in alongside me.

"Elmar," I greeted, wondering why he was joining us.

"Morning, Jadyn," he said, then added, "Brom, Fitmigar, Het, Rammy," nodding to each in turn. "I suppose you're wondering why I'm here?"

"Ya got that right," Fitmigar said.

Brom groaned.

Elmar ignored him and continued, "Algernon told me to join you this morning so we can run through the various ingredients that grow along our route. Every now and again, I'll also need to wander off the track slightly to make collections, so Jadyn will join me."

I groaned internally. *Weed collection duty. Fantastic...*

It turned out to be not as bad as I feared. Despite being a little flighty, Elmar talked us through various herbs and plants required for potions with teacherly patience. He was also happy to ride along in silence once the questions we raised were exhausted.

As he'd forewarned, a couple of times we headed a short distance from the track, and the sack full of jars that clinked at his side began to fill up with various ingredients. He told us he would start replacing the potions that had been destroyed the night before we left the academy -- a situation I still wished we'd had the chance to investigate properly.

The third time we traveled off-route, the wolves were back. My eyes widened as I counted up the numbers.

There's got to be well over a hundred and fifty now.

"Make it quick, Elmar," I warned. "It looks like we might have trouble soon."

The man glanced up nervously. "You think they'll attack?" he asked, forcing yellow flowers into a jar quicker than I thought possible.

"No telling," I replied, "but it's certainly escalating. Just finish up and head back to the column. It's easier for us to keep you safe there."

Nodding, he screwed the lid onto his latest jar, dropped it into the sack at his side, and hurried to mount his horse.

"Let's get back then," he said, flicking his gaze rapidly between the main column and the wolves.

"Keep calm," I said. "It won't do for you to show any weakness. Let's just ride back now and join the others."

"Right…" he mumbled, fumbling at his horse's reins and trotting back to join the others. I moved Hestia and myself to block him from the wolves, guarding his back. Joining the rear of the column again, I passed my observations on to the other four. I then escorted Elmar back to the center of the column, hoping he'd feel safer there.

Galen sought my attention as we approached.

"A word, Jadyn?"

"Sure," I said, keeping pace alongside his wagon.

The track had widened a little over the course of the morning as we traveled farther north. It hadn't done much about the deep ruts I noted as the wagon bumped and jumped, Galen momentarily pausing to make sure all was well behind him.

"We might have a situation shortly," he started, and I cleared my mind of other thoughts.

"How so?"

"First, the good news. We'll be reaching Riverhaven before nightfall today, so we'll have a better place to rest up."

"OK… and the bad news?"

"There's a spot an hour or two before we get there that can be difficult to defend, where a shallow river runs alongside the track. It's one of the few areas where the land rises, creating a low valley, with hills on either side."

"Right. Understood. So, what's the plan?"

I need you to organize a few others and take them ahead. Get set up on the hills to either side and ensure we can take the route between without any extra attention from those wolves."

"Consider it done. How many, sir?"

"The ten of you should do. Five of you on each side, patrolling the hills. Replace anyone you need to at the rear."

"Absolutely, sir," I confirmed.

"That's great, Jadyn. We've got a few hours yet, but do make your squad aware during lunch."

"Will do, sir."

I eased Hestia out of line, allowing the rest of the column to pass me by, waving and nodding to instructors and students alike as they passed before I joined the rear of the column again.

When we stopped for lunch, I pulled the others aside and explained the plan. We took our leave once we'd eaten and grouped up to head out, leaving the other students to pack the kitchen utensils.

"You really think the wolves will attack?" Brom asked, riding at my side. Hestia and Shadowtail chirped at each other as though lost in a conversation of their own.

"Feels that way. The numbers have been building, and they've been getting closer each day."

"They're not here now, though," he replied, making a show of looking around.

"Yeah," I admitted, "not sure if that's a good thing or not."

"You getting the same feeling with the wolves as those bears?" he asked.

"Pretty much," I said, running a hand through my hair. "There's just something off about it all. Like, why are they following us if not to attack? And why are they traveling in a pack way larger than anything anyone's seen before?"

"We'll be ready," he said, sounding confident.

"That we will, buddy." I smiled and let the conversation fall away as I ran through all the various permutations that could greet us when we reached the valley.

A couple hours later after we'd moved on ahead of the rest of the column to scout ahead, we took a turn in the track, and our destination came into view.

The place was quiet aside from birdsong, with no wolves in sight. "Set up on the hills, everyone, and we'll see what's around."

As I waited, I cycled through my spells. I'd been mulling over something since I'd received the new spells. Now was a good opportunity to see if my intuition was right.

I mentally selected [Fireball], but rather than start to pull mana from my core, I reached out and tried to select [Wind Wall], too. At first, I couldn't get the mana to move, but then it clicked, and I pulled it to [Fireball], locking it into place. My eyes widened as the letters blurred, shuffled, and reformed.

[Fire Wall*].

Holy fuck. I've merged them into a new spell...

"Sir!" Syl shouted, and I looked across at the ranged attacker as he waved at me.

"Yes, Syl. What is it?" I asked, choosing to ignore being called sir. I'd told him enough times that it wasn't necessary, but he wouldn't have it.

"I can see smoke, rising from farther down the trail toward Riverhaven."

I pulled myself up onto Hestia's back. "Understood. I'm going up to check it out. Wait here with the others."

Syl nodded.

I nudged Hestia's flank, and she responded immediately, powering forward and taking us airborne with rapid beating of her wings. Cold breeze rushed through my hair as we ascended above the canopy and into the skies.

It didn't take me long to make out what was happening up ahead. The townspeople had left Riverhaven to face off against the pack of wolves. There had to be three or four hundred wolves, crazed, erratic, and seemingly focused on death and destruction.

They were never after us at all, I realized.

The townspeople were armed with flaming torches and tools, and they weren't faring well. The able-bodied had already joined the army under Commander Flint's command. Those left behind were the weak, old, disabled, and children. They had no chance against the wolves. I couldn't allow this slaughter to take place.

Wolves were no trouble to powerful griffins and mages, but regular people wouldn't fair nearly as well against a horde of magically dominated beasts.

A soft nudge was all it took for Hestia to return and drop low and join my squad. The griffins must have sensed the battle because they stood alert, mane feathers standing up, knife-long claws pawing at the ground.

We had trained these past four years to trust our griffins, and as one, my squad mates joined me in the air. They hovered beside me as I addressed them all.

"Magic control or not, they are just wolves!" I shouted. "And we are Griffin Knights!"

They all nodded in understanding.

"We are going to save these people now. We fly by, and we blast the wolves apart with spells and ranged attacks. Standard fly-by tactics. Understand?"

"Absolutely," Brom confirmed.

The others gave me nods and affirmatives. "Then follow me."

I turned Hestia in the air and led my squad towards the bloodthirsty wolves.

I pondered as we flew. The townspeople were using fire to keep the wolves at bay, and even when under a spell, there was still some hesitancy there. Whatever magic controlled these beasts, it didn't quite override their base fears.

So, fire it was. I cycled through my spells, and my eyes widened. That would do it.

I mentally selected [Fire Wall*] and pulled mana from my core. More and more suffused my body, growing denser. Approaching the closest wolves, I released the spell.

A wall of blazing inferno, thirty foot wide and ten feet high, streamed forward and decimated the beasts below, sliding rapidly across the ground and incinerating everything on its path. Dozens, perhaps scores had died, and I was just the first attack.

Brom came in next, covering the wolfpack in shadow to blind them, making it impossible for them to evade our attacks. Then came the salvos of death. Griffin knight after griffin knight hurled spells, blasting apart wolves with elemental explosions.

With our initial barrage complete, we flew low. Griffin claws ripped wolves from the ground and pulled them apart in the air before tossing away their broken remains until none remained.

We landed just after to the relieved cheers and thanks of the villagers. They had come out today fearing the worst, prepared to die to give the children a chance to escape the town. And then we had swooped in and mowed through their opponents like they were nothing.

It felt strange to realize how powerful we were. Strange and exhilarating. This was what I'd strived for, to become someone who could save others, to give hope.

But seeing the teary faced relief, the sobbing, the hugs of disbelief between the townspeople... It was more humbling than I'd expected, and more than a little intimidating, knowing for real that the fates of so many relied on us.

"Helstrom, Rammy, fly back to the main column and let them know what transpired here. We'll await their arrival."

Both nodded in acknowledgment and took to the skies.

Chapter Eleven

With the main caravan still a good hour or so out, we sat and waited outside of the town, allowing the residents to head back home while we talked over what had taken place.

Brom cleared his throat, and I turned to face him. "So… you want to tell everyone what that was back there?"

I considered for a moment how to play it, but I didn't see any point in hiding the truth.

I took a deep breath and addressed the group.

"That, I think you might all have guessed, was a new spell that I created."

"So, how did you do that?" Sars asked, that notebook of his ready, his writing implement poised. He'd mentioned before our journey started that he'd likely be documenting our discoveries, and I found I didn't mind. As long as it didn't turn into some weird biography.

"I saw the people needed assistance," I explained, "and I recognized that fire was likely the best approach, being something the wolves still hesitated near. I knew that merging two of your spells together doesn't work —"

"I think Therbel's told us that once or twice!" Sienna interjected, laughing.

I chuckled. "Yeah, only every other lesson. Anyway, I assumed that would be the case still, even with my new wind-based spells, meaning I could merge two spells from two different branches of magic."

"But?" Sars pressed.

"But, it wasn't. I managed to select both [Fireball] and [Wind Wall], creating this new spell: [Fire Wall*]."

"What happens when you cycle through your spells now?" Sars asked, scribbling away.

"Huh. I haven't checked them all that closely yet."

The others looked on in interest as I pulled up my spells.

[Fireball]

[Fire Burst]

[Fire Elemental]

[Wind Burst]

[Wind Boost]

[Wind Wall]

[Fire Wall*]

"Well?" Brom asked, leaning closer as if they would appear written out before him.

"It's still there. I've got seven spells now." I let out a shuddering exhale and repeated in disbelief, "I've got seven spells now."

Brom whistled.

"So, you have still got access to this new one you have created then?" Sars asked.

"Seems to be the case. I can now call upon [Fire Wall*], though there is an asterisk next to it."

"Think you could repeat it now if we pointed you away a safe distance?" Mallen asked, while peering over Sars' shoulder to read the notes he was making.

"Let's find out." I hopped to my feet and walked a short distance away from the track that led towards the village.

"OK. Here goes."

I mentally selected [Fire Wall*] and pulled on my mana. Nothing happened.

I tried again but couldn't pull it off.

"It's not working, guys," I said, turning back to face them. "Not sure why."

"If I had to guess, I would say you need more mana than normal to work the casting, due to the fact it is an amalgamation of two branches," Sars said, tapping his chin in thought. "When you did it before, you would have used up a huge amount."

"That wall of flames was pretty immense," Brom agreed.

"That actually sounds right," I admitted. "I am feeling pretty empty, mana-wise."

"I know just the way to get your levels back up," Sienna said, smiling and winking suggestively.

"Hey," Elandra butted in, "he's all mine next!" She pouted and crossed her arms in mock annoyance, and I laughed at the pair of them.

"Don't worry, girls. There's plenty of me to go around."

"There is. I can confirm," Sienna said, staring at my crotch.

Sars coughed into his hand, pretending to be really busy with the notebook.

Brom sighed and rolled his eyes. "Get a room, guys."

"That's the plan," I told him, smiling at the thought of what I'd be getting up to soon.

We continued to chat as we waited for the others. A couple of times I noticed Brom and Fitmigar whispering to each other. I caught my friend's eye and smiled. Whatever was happening there, I was glad to see them both happy. Well, as happy as Fitmigar could be I supposed.

I was sitting with Sars, answering his questions, when Mallen alerted us to the appearance of the lead griffins of the main column.

Jumping to my feet, I whistled to call Hestia. We all hopped on our mounts and got ready to join the caravan. People waved and hollered greetings when they appeared over a hill on the road. I allowed the first half of the column to pass me by and dropped in next to Galen.

"Looks like it was a success," he noted, "though not in the location I expected."

"It was," I confirmed. "We had to change plans a little, but luckily it all worked out to our advantage."

"I'm sure luck had nothing to do with it," he said, offering a rare smile. "Helstrom and Rammy passed on the basic details, but do you want to run me through it from the start, and we'll see if there's anything you could have done differently."

I took a deep breath and proceeded to fill our combat instructor in on our actions.

Galen nodded as I talked, stopping me a few times for me to repeat a line or go over something again in more detail. By the time I finished up, he seemed happy enough.

"Nice work, lad," he said. "There are a couple of small bits you could have done differently, but considering the scene that greeted you when you arrived, the townspeople in immediate peril, you did well to get out without any bad injuries or losses."

"Just have a really good team around me," I said. "Everyone played their part, reacting to all"—*hmm... orders sounds too harsh*—"requests without question. To be honest, sir, those wolves didn't stand a chance."

The elf laughed and nodded. "I'd say you're right about that."

"What's next?" I asked.

"Well, we head into Riverhaven. It marks the approximate halfway point of our journey north."

"Accommodations?" I asked.

"Plenty," Galen confirmed. "We sent a messenger bird ahead from the academy, so they'll be expecting us all. And they'll know we're here now anyway after that brutal show you put on for them. There are stables sufficient for the griffins, and we'll all be staying at the Flying Chub."

"Can't say I'll mind a proper bed again," I admitted.

"I'm sure an ale or two wouldn't go amiss either," Galen suggested. "But keep it sensible because we'll be away early tomorrow. Every minute we delay, more of our army suffers."

"Understood, sir," I acknowledged. We'd been slowed by the initial injury to Ralartis, and the precautions against the wolves had added to the delay. A couple of drinks sounded great, but I'd need to make sure that Brom, in particular, knew we had a new responsibility now. We needed clear heads tomorrow.

The conversation over, I excused myself and dropped back in next to Sienna, Elandra, and Sars. Hestia chuffed a greeting to their griffins, nudging Dawnquill with her beak affectionately.

My aim had been to flirt with the girls a little more, but I didn't want to make Sars feel uncomfortable or unwanted, especially while he was still sorting through his grief. So, I searched for a topic to discuss as we rode.

Elandra saved me from thinking by asking about the upcoming town of Riverhaven.

Sars' eyes lit up. He'd done some reading on our journey before we left, and now was his chance to shine.

"It's the first town on our route, though I'm sure you've noticed that," he started, watching us nod in confirmation. There had been a few very small villages off the main track at points on our journey, but we hadn't passed through any as we had no need to do so, especially after not reaching Millford that first night.

"It's situated at the point where the stream we're currently following converges with the River Tyrell. From there, it continues southwesterly to the sea."

"Don't we follow the river upstream for a while after we leave?" I asked, and Sars nodded.

"We do indeed."

Sars gestured for Charn to join us then as this was his hometown. The bard proceeded to fill us in on some of the local information while we traveled.

As hard as I tried, I still couldn't help checking out both girls—something they reciprocated.

Before too long, the first buildings came into view. They appeared to be almost wooden lean-tos, barely held together by rust and hope. The place also had a stench of feces and garbage, making us wish we were back in the farmlands. Locals came out of the homes. Some I recognized from before, and they thanked us again for saving them from the wolves.

Gradually, the shacks disappeared behind us, the smells replaced by cleaner air as we entered the more affluent part of Riverhaven. Two-story buildings stood in stark contrast to the earlier shacks. Their lower floors were stone brickwork with no natural light going in, giving the impression of above-ground cellars, while the upper floors were wooden and allowed plenty of light in. Solid beams ran perpendicular to each other, smaller beams crisscrossing between them against a whitewashed outer wall. Some buildings had wooden roofs, while others were an older thatched style.

As we traveled, the stream beside us widened, until it joined with the Tyrell in the center of town. Here we also found a central square full of stalls offering all sorts of products and baked goods. The aromas in the air made my mouth water.

The locals stared as we passed. Griffins were far from a common sight, and forty traveling through the town, two abreast, brought on murmurs of conversation.

"They're barely children," one particularly ruddy-faced man said, shaking his head.

"How are they supposed to help the real men and women holding the line?" his friend replied.

I looked over, caught their gazes, and formed a rotating ball of fire in the palm of my hand as Hestia looked at the pair and screeched defiantly.

"We're far from children," I replied, most of us nineteen, with a few eighteen years olds amongst us. "We're about to risk our lives for you, so have some faith. It's the least you can do."

The doubtful looks turned away in shame. I faced them and the adoring stares with a serious expression on my face. It wouldn't do to appear too happy and juvenile. I was no child but a knight.

As we passed the food stalls, I noticed Brom briefly disappear from Shadowtail's back. He must have activated [Shadow Cloak] as he dropped, because after a minute, he was back astride his griffin with a steaming pastry in each hand.

I caught his eye, and he winked back.

The bridges here in the center of town were narrow walkways, too small for the griffins and wagons. We headed right and followed the river, passing out of the square and past a few storefronts before our destination came into sight: The Flying Chub.

As the lead riders pulled up outside, a couple of young-looking boys ran out, followed swiftly by another pair. They took each griffin in turn, passing them fresh cuts of meat and leading them down the side of the inn, presumably to the stables. The storage for the wagons must have also been around the rear as Algernon, Galen, Thom, and Mirek pulled them straight around the side, barely slowing.

When our turn arrived, I patted Hestia's neck and whispered, "See you soon, girl," before sliding down, weapon sheaths in hand, lance still on her side. We'd need to grab our bags for the night, but for now, we all headed inside with Elmar, keen to find a table and get a drink inside us.

The inn was quieter than I expected, though the sounds of our peers were quickly bringing it to life. As we got our keys, the jovial man behind the bar explained that they'd closed to the town while we were passing through. They'd served groups heading off to join the regular army at the border, and the nights had seldom ended well when soldiers mixed with the locals.

There was a lot of pent-up frustration going on, even if we were fighting for them. Too many had lost someone in the war, and some of them blamed the army for stealing their loved ones away.

That was fine by me. I'd much rather spend my evening surrounded by friends when we had to be out at first light. Normally, I didn't mind mingling, but I didn't think I was in the headspace to be hanging out with locals right now.

The ten of us were still sweaty from our slaughter of the wolves, so before we joined the others we were spirited off to the two shower rooms out the back of the inn. As Elandra and Sienna were led away by Fitmigar to the female showers, I looked on wistfully. Could have had some fun right there.

After a quick clean-up and change, we returned to the bar to find the ales already flowing freely. The students sat together on tables of ten, while the instructors and assistants were seated in the far corner and deep in conversation.

The inn was brighter lit than the Molerat we were used to, with windows bathing the oak tables in cool daylight, dusk soon approaching.

As we squeezed through, dodging elbows and knees, I tapped Bernolir on the shoulder. "You guys are next for the showers."

He sighed in relief. "Not a moment too soon, Jadyn. Some of these be stinking like those shanties back there."

The others at the table roared in disapproval, flinging insults the dwarf's way. Then they all headed off to get clean while we continued to our table by the solitary fireplace.

A couple of logs burned away, chasing away the slight chill seeping from the doorway. The soft crackling soon relaxed everyone, and we all watched it for a bit until a young girl appeared with an armful of ales.

"Food's coming soon, mister," she said when I looked up and caught her eye as she deposited the drinks.

"Sounds good," I replied, smiling.

She blushed, ran a hand through her hair, and then hurried back towards the bar.

"Seriously, you handsome devil. How do you have that effect on every female?" Brom asked.

"Not every female!" Fitmigar interjected, and I noticed a broad grin appear on Brom's face.

So that's still going on then... I noted.

Elandra sat down next to me, snuggling close again like she had the night before we left. Although, I presumed she wouldn't get so drunk to become sick tonight.

I'd noticed she'd become less in my face with her comments lately. Maybe she realized I wasn't sure how to take them. Her hand brushed mine under the table, and I smiled and leaned my head against hers.

"Hey, you," I whispered.

"Hey, Jadyn," she murmured. "That wall of fire today was super impressive, you know."

"Thanks," I replied, nudging her gently. "You weren't so bad yourself. What was that spell you used that left the wolf corpses looking all dried-up?"

She smiled. "Awesome, right? That was [Dehydrate]. I've been practicing it a lot, trying to raise its density to make it work faster."

"It certainly did that."

The firepit crackled.

"Well?" she asked, while the others began admonishing Brom for snatching baked goods.

"Hm?"

"All this talk about sharing makes a girl expect some contact," she said.

She shifted a little closer, eyes staring at me expectantly. Carefully, I slipped my arm around her and pulled her closer. "Better?"

She was close enough now that I could smell the floral scent of whatever she'd used in the showers, and it woke part of me up. She smiled at me, clearly having noticed the movement below, and I shrugged.

"This feels nice," I said.

"It does, Jadyn. I hope we get to do this some more."

"I'd like that," I admitted, glancing at Sienna.

She gave us a sly, almost Elandra-like, smile. Her cheeks had a light flush that couldn't be explained with the drink alone as she mouthed, 'go on' and winked at us. Go on we did. Hands began wandering beneath the table, Elandra's groping my hips and groin so hungrily I feared the others might notice. They didn't though, and the night went on.

After the day we'd had, conversation at the table remained light. More than once Mallen had to nudge Sars awake after we ate, the waiting staff still topping up our drinks.

Gradually, the room cleared, the students disappearing to their allotted rooms. I'd managed to secure one with Brom on the upper floor, while

Fitmigar had picked one up with Sienna and Elandra just across the hall.

We headed up together, leaving Mallen and Syl the task of getting Sars to their room. I noted Syl already seemed to be at home with the group. Fighting together really brought you closer.

As we reached the top floor, I smiled as Fitmigar grabbed Brom by the hand.

"Yer coming with me," she growled and pulled him into her room, leaving me standing in the hallway with my two favorite girls.

I opened the door to my room, looked them both in the eye, and said, "Shall we?"

Both girls put out a hand, and I took them in mine and pulled them into the room, their giggles already stirring my cock to life.

Chapter Twelve

As Elandra pushed the door closed behind us, Sienna pulled me in tight, brushing her lips against mine. She ran her fingers through my hair. I slipped my hand down and grabbed her ass, but she dropped her hand and pushed mine away.

"Nuh-uh," she said, shaking her head.

"What?"

"I'm only here to watch, Jadyn. It's Elandra's turn. We promised."

She stepped back, and I felt a soft hand run down my back. I turned to see Elandra, eyes wide. A grin lifted the corners of her mouth, forming a small dimple on her beautiful dark-skinned face.

"My turn to have Jadyn."

Her voice carried to me in sultry tones, and a grin split my face. I slid an arm around her narrow waist and pulled her body against mine, her back arching as her lips parted.

I moved in hungrily, my lips meeting hers as she rose onto her toes, her nipples stiffening against my chest. I drove my tongue in, and she moaned, closing her eyes, her fingers tugging at my shirt.

I took the bottom of my shirt and lifted it over my head, stepping away from her. She took in the sight, panting, breathless, her gaze roaming over my body.

I lifted my hands to her top, slowly unbuttoning, easing it aside. Her perfect breasts fell free, standing perky. I'd been yearning to see these for so long. I cupped them both, kneading the sensitive flesh gently as I flicked my tongue across each, first the right, then the left, drawing involuntary gasps of delight from her.

My breath caught in my throat as I gazed over her body. A moment passed as I drank in the sight, then I lowered myself, running a trail of soft kisses down her stomach. Kissing, I eased her pants down past her thighs, tugging them to the floor.

A small, trimmed patch of dark hair crowned her sex. My cock stiffened at the sight, straining against my pants as I thought of fucking her senseless.

I lifted my gaze to see her staring back at me, no hint of shyness on her face. As I rose back to my feet, she placed her hands on my chest and pushed me backward, her eyes locked on me as I obliged and sat on the bed. She dropped to her knees, tugging my pants off, my cock bouncing to attention as it came free.

"Whoa..."

Her eyes widened as she took in my size. She licked her lips seductively as she brought her head down and flicked her tongue across the tip.

"It's so fucking big, Jadyn," she murmured.

I smiled. "And it's all for you."

I lifted my waist up from the bed and pushed my length in past her lips. She immediately sucked, gently at first, then harder as she bobbed up and down, pumping me with her mouth, making soft moans of pleasure as she flicked her tongue down my shaft.

She added one hand, then another, stroking the base of my cock, while her lips remained gripped on the tip. I groaned in ecstasy, leaning back, moving in rhythm as she plunged deeper.

"Is this okay?" she asked, coming away, hesitant for a moment.

"Don't stop," I panted.

She returned to sucking, and I lay back in total bliss.

A noise from the chair in the corner of the room caught my attention. I looked across to see Sienna naked, her legs raised and knees spread, her fingers teasing around her folds, rubbing, her breath hitching as she slipped first one finger inside, then a second.

I propped myself up on my elbows and looked back down at Elandra. Her eyes bore through me as I lost myself in their dizzying depths.

"I need you to fuck me, Jadyn," she growled, her hands still gripping me, pumping me closer and closer…

I took her hands and pulled her up onto the bed. "Oh, you're gonna get fucked alright…"

"Where do you want me?" she asked, running her tongue across her lips, swallowing the precum she had licked from my cock.

I bent her around and over so her rump was in the air. "Get on your knees," I told her, slapping her across the ass.

She let out a moan and obeyed, lifting herself up to all fours. She looked back over her shoulder, wiggling her hips and making tiny sounds of whiny arousal. I nearly lost it right there, imagining my cum spurting across her ass, stark white against her dark skin.

Maybe I could get Sienna to come over and lick it off?

Grinning at the thought, I slid a hand down past Elandra's ass cheeks, running it under and feeling her soaking pussy. Juices dripped over my fingers. She was ready. I didn't want to hurt her in case she was as virginal as Sienna had been, so I took the tip of my cock and gently pushed it around her entrance, teasing.

"More…" she moaned.

I eased inside her, shuddering at the tightness gripping me. I entered slowly at first, bringing myself back out with each probing thrust. First, a couple of inches in, then a couple more, then more.

"So… fucking… big," she panted.

"Give her all of it, Jadyn," Sienna moaned from the chair, her face flushing. She continued to finger herself furiously, driving in and out, letting out soft moans of ecstasy. "Fuck her silly!"

"Yes, Jadyn!" Elandra cried, backing onto me, trying to force all of me inside her.

So, I gave it to her. Every fucking inch.

I grabbed her hips and slammed into her, making her cry out, but I didn't stop.

I gripped her tighter and pounded her harder, deeper, again and again. She soon spasmed on my cock, crying out as she came. But I wasn't done.

I held her tightly and kept her pinned into the bed, continuing to thrust into her. Sienna's screams from nearby joined Elandra's as she brought herself to the edge and past it, gushing over the seat. I realized I was so… fucking… close.

I hammered into her until furniture creaked. As Elandra cried out in ecstasy for a second time, I joined her. My pleasure peaked. Hot spurts of cum filled her slit and gushed out as I leaned back and cried out, draining me completely as every drop filled her tight hole.

She collapsed forward onto the bed in a shivering mess. I slipped out and fell beside her, both of us wide-eyed and gasping.

"Holy shit…" she murmured, "is it always like that?"

"Gets better every time," I replied.

"Fuck… that was amazing," Sienna added, dropping down naked next to me on the bed and draping her arm across me, running her fingers across my mouth. I tasted her sweet, tangy juices.

I closed my eyes and smiled as I slipped an arm around each girl and pulled them close.

"Next time, I'm fucking you both," I decided.

"Yes, please," Sienna replied, and Elandra smiled in agreement. Her heartbeat still raced in her chest as I dropped kisses across her breasts, gently sucking at her nipples as she came back down from the best high of her life.

Morning arrived far too quickly. I opened my eyes to find the girls both still there, curled into me, naked as the moment we closed our eyes.

A quick glance across the room confirmed Brom never returned in the night—or he had, received quite the eyeful, and then made a quiet exit. I doubted Fitmigar would have let him go, though, judging by the way she'd dragged him into her room.

I spent a couple of minutes simply appreciating the gorgeous nakedness before me. Then I realized if I didn't stop now, we'd never get up in time.

I could feel extra mana running through my body—more than ever before—and could think of several things I'd like to do to burn off some of that extra energy.

"Hey," I whispered, nudging both.

"No…" Sienna moaned, "it's too early."

"We've got to be up," I said apologetically and stirred the girls awake.

I stayed lying down as I watched them rise, those perfect tits, those curvy asses... I was going to have to close my eyes, or I'd definitely be trying to drag them back into the bed.

I kept my composure while they dressed, though it was a close thing. Soon we were downstairs with our bags and weapons, joining the other students and instructors. A couple of the party looked like they'd been up far later than us. Or at least, drinking later. We'd been busy late enough.

The jovial innkeeper appeared a few minutes later. We followed him out the back door and into the stables, Brom and Fitmigar coming down just in time to catch us. The dwarf's normally braided hair flowed loose around her shoulders.

I winked at Brom and smiled. He returned the wink. A soft chirp reached my ear as we entered the cool morning air. I jogged across to Hestia's side, running my hand over her dark-brown feathers.

"Morning, girl," I greeted. "I hope they've been looking after you?"

She tilted her head and bounced slightly, chuffing. I took that to be confirmation she was well and set about preparing her for our departure, retrieving her straps from where they hung in her stall.

As I worked on Hestia, Algernon appeared beside me, tapping me on the shoulder to get my attention. "A word please, young man."

My eyes widened. What had I done?

I asked Mirek to keep an eye on Hestia and followed the elderly instructor past the stables. We left the hearing distance of the others and joined Lana, Enallo, and Bernolir.

"What's up?" I asked, exchanging greetings with my fellow squad leaders.

Algernon must have sensed our unease. "Nothing any of you've done, so relax. We just received some news this morning, and we thought it would be good to talk it over with you before we head out."

"Okay…" I said hesitantly.

"So, it turns out that the elves of Birchvale are sending reinforcements to the border, coinciding with our arrival."

"How does that affect us now?" I asked. Birchvale was the largest elven settlement, located in the Lower Helerean Forest, so this was good news. I expected their reinforcements to be big.

"Well, Lord E'lyn has requested several of our party take a detour to meet them as they leave the forest. They are worried about traveling without air support toward the border with rumors rife of multiple wyverns present in the area."

"And you'd like one of us to go?" Lana asked, stepping forward.

"Jadyn and his squad, yes," Algernon confirmed, and Lana's face fell.

I paused to consider my response, then said, "Leaving thirty to defend the wagons? You think that's enough?"

"Thirty, plus myself, Galen, Thom, Elmar…"

"And Mirek?"

"He'll be coming with you on Elmar's horse. He might not have magic, but he has jousting experience."

"OK. Sounds like everything's decided," I said, rubbing my eyes. "I'll take my squad," I confirmed. "How many elven warriors will there be?"

"A couple of hundred I would imagine."

Algernon then gave me a small nod. Truth be told, I was proud that he'd come to me over choosing any of the other squad leaders. Lana, in particular, looked pissed to miss out.

"Gather the others and pass on the news," he said. "We'll chat more on the road as you won't need to split from us for a couple of hours or so."

Dismissed, we rejoined our squads to bring them up to speed.

"Why us?" Rammy asked, a look of confusion crossing the red-haired giant's face when I pulled him aside.

"They must have thought we were best equipped to follow it through," I replied, shrugging.

"Well, I appreciate it, Jadyn. Been looking for some more excitement."

"Hah. We certainly have a way of finding that."

"Too right we have. Massacred those wolves we did." He laughed and went back to preparing his griffin for travel.

I continued on, passing the message along to everyone else who needed to know. Mallen was less than keen about the change in plans, but I didn't press him on it.

As the wagons rolled out, I noticed Elmar still astride his horse, grumbling. He likely wasn't excited about having to pull one of the wagons. I also knew that he'd still been working away late last night replacing the missing potions, so tiredness was surely a factor, too.

Mirek appeared chipper in contrast. The young man looked happy with the change in plans and gave me an energetic salute in passing. It didn't seem like he would be put off by anything as insignificant as a complete lack of magic.

I smiled and pulled myself up onto Hestia's back, patting her neck and running my hand through her feathers. She cooed gently and swished her head. The rest had done her good and rejuvenated her naturally cheery mood.

After everyone mounted, we eventually moved to depart. The young boys from the inn waved us off, and I noticed the female server from the previous night watching me from inside, a faint blush on her cheeks once again.

Brom leaned over. " She seems sad to see you go. Young strapping man that you are. Does your handsomeness know no bounds?"

"Idiot."

I ignored his laughter as he moved on ahead.

Hardly my fault if I had that effect on the opposite sex. Anyway, I already had my hands full with my two magic-wielding girls. I didn't have time, nor want, for more. At least, not currently.

I lost myself again in thoughts of the previous night, imagining Elandra's lips around my cock again as Sienna watched on. Clearing my head, I encouraged Hestia forward.

Yeah, I wasn't going to be waiting too long before I got some quality alone time with my girls again.

Chapter Thirteen

We exited the town of Riverhaven and followed the river. On the way, I noticed a few fishermen out early, seated on the bank and looking for a catch or two before most of the population was awake. It was still early, but plenty of market traders passed us by to set up for the day, not paying us any real attention.

There was no sign of the shanty-type housing on this side of the town. We passed several other drinking establishments, the shutters closed on all but one that was doing a slow breakfast trade.

The town then abruptly transformed back into endless farmlands. The track here was far wider and even—a vast improvement on the previous day's route.

With a good road beneath our wagons, we picked up the pace. The conversation continued to revolve around the wolf situation, and I heard various versions of how we'd dispatched them. I felt a little embarrassment from all the praise being heaped on us, but I smiled and answered the curious questions all the same.

The general mood of the group seemed good. Clearly, I wasn't the only one happy to have spent the night in a proper bed, even if I hadn't spent all that much of it sleeping.

It came as somewhat as a shock twenty minutes or so out of town when Thom's wagon hit a small rut in the track and the rear axle snapped. The back of the wagon crashed to the ground and our convoy drew to a halt.

Thom dismounted and ran back to inspect the damage. I pulled up alongside on Hestia to see if I could be of assistance.

"Need a hand?" I asked.

Galen's red-haired assistant looked up at me and shook his head, before sliding closer for a better look. "This shouldn't break like that. Not from a small bump."

I dropped down off Hestia's back and bent down to join him. "Seems quite a clean break," I noted.

This was far from my area of expertise, but it seemed a little odd. We'd traveled along tracks much rougher than this over the previous days, and there'd been no hint of damage yesterday when we'd arrived at the Chub.

"A bit too clean if you ask me. See there?" He pointed to the broken section.

I nodded. "Looks like someone's sawn part of the way through."

"That's what I was thinking, too." He shook his head in disbelief. "But who?"

"And why?" I added, deep in thought.

There were plenty of people around us when we arrived last night, but I suspected the saboteur from the academy had followed us. Anyone determined enough could've had access to the wagons overnight. They had been secure, but we hadn't exactly set up a strict perimeter. Or perhaps it was a foreign agent from the village? Surely, it couldn't be one of the party.

"All it does is delay us reaching the border," he said.

"That makes no sense, though, right?" I mused. Everyone in Atania would surely want us to reach the front sooner rather than later. As we spoke, Algernon joined our side.

"This won't do at all," he stressed, rubbing at his temple.

"We've no spares," Thom informed him. "Who scored the highest in pioneering among your year?"

"Glymavor, sir," I replied.

Algernon nodded. "OK. Someone go and grab Glymavor, and he can get to work fashioning a replacement for us." He paused then for a moment, scratching the back of his head and meeting my eyes. "Jadyn, it makes no sense for you all to be delayed, too. Round the others up and go on ahead."

"Are you sure?" I asked. "I don't mind helping out if needed."

"Yes, lad. Lord E'Lyn won't be best impressed if you're not there to meet the elven reinforcements on time."

"Understood, sir." I turned and headed back through the line, gesturing for the others to join me up front ahead of the main column.

Galen joined us as we prepared to depart, leaving Thom and Algernon to organize the wagon repairs.

"You've got everything?" he asked me.

I nodded. "Best I can tell. We've all got our weapons, and then Mirek here's loaded his saddle bags with food, potions, and more."

He looked across at our magicless companion, and the young man nodded in confirmation. "OK. So, you'll need to take the right-hand fork just as the next village comes into sight," Galen explained.

Sars scribbled it all down rapidly, while he explained. "You'll cross some pretty barren land, but continue until you meet the southernmost section of the Lower Helerean Forest. Then head north, following the tree line, and you should be with them by early tomorrow evening. Before you reach the River Yorn."

"And they'll be waiting?"

"As far as I know, yes. They should be camped at the forest's edge by then."

"OK," I said. "And after that?"

"It's a day's march to the border from there, and you'll need to cross the river first. We'll meet up with you along the way after you cross."

I nodded. "We'll see you in a couple of days then, sir."

"That you will, Jadyn. Be sure to rotate air patrols as you go, too. You'll need to be perfect in your execution by the time you reach Lord E'Lyn."

"Consider it done."

We bid our goodbyes for now and he rejoined with the caravan.

I nudged Hestia to a march, and we began our way north. Sars joined my side as we traveled northward, two abreast, towards our elven allies.

The track grew busy with a steady trickle of people, wagons, and beasts of burden the farther we traveled from Riverhaven. Almost all of them headed in the opposite direction as us, presumably to barter with the market traders we'd seen earlier in the day. The fields we passed were near indistinguishable from any other fields of Atania. Farmers were out plowing and sowing seeds for the winter crops, huge horses pulling the metal contraptions through the hardening ground.

Here and there we witnessed the late harvesting of apples and pears. We paused to purchase a few to help make up for the fact we'd skipped breakfast.

Together with Sars, I organized a schedule of sorts for air patrols. We'd barely begun flying with our griffins, so we were going to need to get up to speed quickly to not let down our allies' expectations.

Everyone here could stay airborne for at least five minutes at a time, so we decided on a system of pairs going up, then resting for twenty minutes before going again. Five up, twenty down. Simple.

While we called it patrol, the main point really was to practice how to fly and work together with our griffins. Even without the added pressure of needing to appear strong before the elves, we needed to get better. Building that confidence was paramount to our success at the border, so every minute counted.

I considered suggesting using magic to test our spells from griffinback, but the chance of finding danger, especially after the situation with the wolves, seemed high. It was a gut feel, but after the black eyes of the magically possessed bears and wolves, trouble felt like only a matter of time.

I thought it might be best we all saved our mana. It replenished far slower than we could use it up, so it made sense to be careful.

Hang on... spells?

Fuck.

We'd been up for hours, and I hadn't even thought to check my spells after last night with Elandra.

Signaling to Rammy and Helstrom to take the first watch from the air, I then gestured for Elandra to join me at my side.

"How are you feeling?" I asked her as she pulled up next to me, her smile beguiling.

"Really good," she replied. "Thanks to you."

"Good how?"

"Um..." she struggled to find the words before adding, "this is going to sound ridiculous, but I feel better connected to you."

"That actually makes sense," I admitted. "Sienna said something similar."

"And you?" she asked, that almost shy look returning to her face, only making her more perfect.

"I feel better than ever. I have more energy, more... power, I guess, than I've ever felt in my life."

"And the spells?"

I'd forgotten again. Those damn lips...

[Fireball]

[Fire Burst]

[Fire Elemental]

[Wind Burst]

[Wind Boost]

[Wind Wall]

[Water Burst]

[Ice Blast]

[Dehydrate]

[Fire Wall*]

"Holy shit!"

"Jadyn?"

"Elandra, these are fucking awesome. [Water Burst] is similar to others I have, but [Ice Blast] will confuse enemies, and as for [Dehydrate]…" Possibilities raced through my mind. It hadn't escaped my attention that [Fire Wall*] had remained at the bottom, still accompanied by an asterisk.

I'd need to think on these for a while. I could likely merge some of these spells, but I had no idea where to start. This sounded like a job for Sars. He was the smartest of us all, and he'd surely be more than happy to discover something no one else had ever done before—at least, to our knowledge.

I was pulled from my thoughts by Mallen as he landed beside me, the elf's ponytail flicking out as he turned to address me.

"Your turn, Jadyn."

"Right…" I muttered, finding it hard to keep myself in the here and now. I turned to Elandra and said, "It's our time to scout."

"Up we go!" She pulled back on Veo's straps, pressing with her knees to nudge him into a run. As she did so, I pulled Hestia out to the left of the column and joined her in pushing Hestia forward, her dark-brown wings spreading in preparation.

Tucking her shoulders and forcing up with her back legs, her wings forcing down, Hestia took off and rose into the late-morning sky.

The next five minutes were spent swirling through the skies. The view from above took my breath away. From here to seemingly the end of the world stretched gently sloped land, fertile and lush with vegetation. Smatterings of trees hugged the meandering river below. Distant homesteads, dirt roads, and crumbling stone fences only added to the cozy charm.

We would soon be leaving the River Tyrell behind, as we continued eastward. Peering ahead, I could just make out the start of the barren plains that our elven combat instructor had warned us about.

The afternoon arrived and continued in much the same vein. The trips into the air let us enjoy the grand view of the surrounding land. For the most part, we simply enjoyed the scenery. That was until I spotted a herd of bison turning to note our presence.

From our studies, I'd understood them to be predominantly wallowing animals, more prone to rolling in the dusty plains than threatening travelers, but again it seemed that we'd enraged the local wildlife.

"This doesn't make any sense." I took Hestia lower, trying to better judge if they intended to intercept us.

Hestia chirped, and I stroked her neck.

"I agree. They're closing in. Better warn the others."

Swooping down, we landed behind the rest of the group. Elandra and Veo set down behind us, having followed our rapid descent.

"Bison incoming!" I shouted.

The group immediately tensed up.

"How are we playing this?" Mallen returned, and I thought through our options.

"Everyone halt!" I cried, and we came to a standstill. "Let's face them down. Bison don't normally act this way, so let's see if we can avoid another bloodbath and scare them off."

The cloud kicked up by the bison slowly approached. Again, I considered how bizarre they behaved. First, the bears, then the wolves. It didn't make sense. Yes, individuals caught in bad situations sometimes lost their lives to attacks, but never like this. Looking into their eyes was like taking on the void, and that didn't seem right.

Was it a disease? Some orcish curse perhaps? We'd never been taught anything about magic like that.

"What the fuck be going on?" Fitmigar shouted, echoing my sentiments.

Everyone could sense it. Something wasn't right. These animals shouldn't be behaving like this. Something—or someone—was controlling them.

"If we can do this without magic then do so," I called, wary of the fact we'd need every edge in the coming days, "but if it's a matter of life or death, do what you need to."

"Damn right!" Brom shouted.

"They don't deserve what's happening to them. But if it's them or us, we take them down," I replied.

He pursed his lips together, giving me a resolute nod. The dirt of the plain rose into the air as the animals closed in, charging across the grassland.

"Not yet!" I called.

Griffins strained. Their riders waited, some hesitant, some keen to battle. I watched over it all, keeping an eye for how my friends handled the pressure.

I'd sensed times in the past when Elandra looked nervous, but that was all gone now. She sat there on the back of Veo, resolute, her sword resting on her shoulder, her hand other twitching by her lance. She was also likely cycling through her spells just in case.

Sienna had already nocked an arrow, her gaze concentrated. Whatever connection I now had with both girls, they seemed stronger, more confident.

Sars and Mallen conversed, no doubt deep in thought about the best approach for taking down rampaging four-legged mammals.

Brom and Fitmigar likewise chatted away, gesticulating wildly. I couldn't tell if that related to the approaching threat or whatever it was they got up to after the door closed at night.

Syl, Helstrom, and Rammy, waited with us. The wind-mage archer sighted his bow as the axe-wielding dwarf took a glug from a flask he'd pulled from his person. Rammy remained the big red-haired force of nature.

The first bison to reach us was also the largest. Likely the pack's dominant bull, the one they expected to drive through us, opening us up to attack from those that followed.

Instead, I met it head-on, both scimitars sheathed, my lance in my hand. As we clashed, I drove the lance into the beast's neck, driving it deep with the weight of Hestia's charge.

It bellowed in rage, skidding to a stop, turning, and pawing the ground. We circled to face it again. Stubborn beast. My lance poked out of its neck, but I'd only managed to make it angry.

I drew my scimitars. Hestia let out a challenging cry. Lowering its head, the bull rushed at me, horns leading. We waited and let it pick up speed.

Then, as the beast was seconds from clashing, I called upon [Wind Boost] and kicked off. Hestia dodged left, while I flew over the seven-foot-tall bison. Throwing in a somersault to gain momentum, I landed on its back, plunging my scimitars straight through the ribcage and into its heart.

It took a couple of seconds for its brain to register it was dead. The bull bellowed and continued onwards. Then its legs gave way, and it crashed to the ground, plowing through the grass. When it skidded to a stop, I smiled, pleased with my attack, and hopped off.

As I'd come to expect, there was no hesitation from the bison herd after witnessing the death of their lead. The herd charged us as one, their eyes black and glazed over. We formed up. Lances plunged into chests, arrows protruded from eyes, swords cut through muscle, fat, and bone, and a war hammer crushed skulls as if they were melons. In all fairness, they never stood a chance.

Their charge broke upon us like water on a cliff.

But they came around again.

And broke again.

Each charge whittled the herd, until the last calf charged me and died on my lance. I rubbed my eyes and stared at the others. No one looked happy. This had been senseless slaughter. Simple beasts were never going to take us down. They barely even delayed us. It was the act of a desperate person—someone who'd use anything at their disposal to prevent us from reaching the border on time.

I hadn't wanted to kill these animals, but whoever was controlling their simple minds had left us no choice.

As I scanned the blood-soaked ground, I mulled over whether or not we should dispose of the corpses. In the end, the bodies might attract wolves and harass the farmers, so we decided to do it even if it added a bit of a delay. We set the griffins to work together to stack the bodies, and I tossed on a couple of [Fireball]s, burning the beasts as we got back on our way.

"That smell…" Brom muttered from beside me.

"Ha. Hungry, buddy?" I asked.

"Don't you know it."

"It'll be all that extra exercise you're getting," I replied, waggling my eyebrows.

"You're a fine one to talk," he shot back.

I laughed. "Yeah, good point. Only difference is I get up the next day feeling better than I ever have before. You on the other hand…"

"What can I say," Brom said, shaking his head. "Fitmigar takes a whole lot of loving."

"I'm just glad to see you happy, brother," I told him.

"Likewise," he replied, tilting his head as Sienna approached on Dawnquill.

"Hey," I said, smiling broadly.

"Hey, you," she replied. "Brom," she added as he smiled and moved back to join Fitmigar.

"What do you think's going on?" she asked me, and I shrugged.

"To be honest, I'm not sure. It seems pretty obvious that the animals are being controlled."

"Those eyes…"

"Right. There's nothing natural about that," I said, shaking my head.

"You think they are trying to stop us reaching the border?"

"Seems the most likely option," I said. A moment of pause passed. "Enough about that. How are you doing today?"

"Good." She smiled and brushed her hair back from her face in that way that made my chest feel funny.

"I miss you when you're not next to me," I said.

She grinned. "Elandra and I were just saying the same thing."

"It's more than that though. I feel more powerful, like I can do anything when I have you both near me."

"And that's what you'll have, Jadyn. We aren't going anywhere."

We chatted amongst ourselves as we traveled. Flight and scouting practice continued throughout the day.

A few times, we noticed distant animals grazing, but each time we passed without incident. They were either too far from our route, or whoever was controlling them had moved on from that approach.

We stopped briefly for lunch in the early afternoon, much to everyone's appreciation. The twenty-minute breaks between aerial duties were fine at first, but the griffins had been tiring a little this past hour. Also, we started to really feel the effects of that skipped breakfast. Sensing the opportunity, Sars shuffled over, notebook in hand. He cleared his throat to get my attention.

"Ah, hey, man." I noticed the book and added, "Got a few questions for me?"

"If that is OK?" he asked, shrugging.

"Sure. Might be good to talk it over."

"So, from what Elandra has told me, I assume you have some new spells available?"

"Yeah. I assume you don't need the details about how I got them?"

"I think we're fine there," the water mage said, a faint blush appearing on his cheeks.

I shrugged. "So, I guess you'd like to know the spells?"

"Please." He got ready to note it all down.

I put my food down and took a deep breath. "OK, so prior to Riverhaven, I had access to my three Fire spells, the three wind spells I got from Sienna, and then the merged [Fire Wall*] that I created."

"Any idea how to utilize it again?" he asked.

I cycled through my options as I sat there, mentally selecting the spell, and then pulled on my deep mana reserves. My eyes widened. "Yeah, I think we were right in our assumption before. My mana is far higher now than it was after the wolf attack, and I feel like I could quite easily call it forth again."

"Hmm… makes sense." Sars made a few more notes and then looked back up. "And the new spells?"

"I spoke with Elandra before, and they are the same three that she has access to."

Sars lifted his eyebrows and leaned toward me, his right hand open and palm up. "And they are?"

"Oh, sorry, man. I thought you knew." I pulled them up again, reminding myself. "They are [Water Burst], [Ice Blast], and [Dehydrate]."

"Nice," he replied, nodding his head. "I've got the first two, also. My third is [Frostbite]. It works better when applied to my lance."

I'd caught a glimpse of it in action, though my focus had been on fighting. Sars had impaled a smaller bison with a huge, pointed ice shard that had coated his lance.

"You did well with it. It's a powerful spell."

"You think you could merge any of these spells into anything new?" he continued.

I shrugged. "I guess I probably can, but I'll need to think carefully on it first. [Fire Wall*] came about through after I spent some time considering which options would work well together, but there could be limits to how many I can combine. What if the limit is one between each branch, and then I ruin it by creating something useless?"

"Good point. We really should go through potential options and work out what would be the most useful to our quest."

"We should. If we had time for it," I said. "Sadly, we're on a mission and need to be on our way."

"Later then. This is the sort of discovery that requires proper study."

"Later," I promised.

Sars nodded once, put his notebook away, and turned to leave. Pausing for a moment, he then turned back. "Then there's the chance you could merge three branches together, of course."

Fuck... Now, my head was starting to hurt with the possibilities.

Interlude 3

Thrargud Ironmantle growled, crumpled the message in his hand, and tossed it into the smoldering fire. Sighing, he took a long swig of ale from his tankard and scanned the dark stone walls of his home before slamming it back down on the table.

Who did Lord E'Lyn think he was? Blasted elf.

Four hundred reinforcements he was sending to the front line. That pompous elf was showing off again. Nobody—elf or not—made the dwarves of Krag Ferris look bad.

Thrargud couldn't let it stand. Fitmigar would be traveling north now with those griffin riders he'd allowed her to join. He'd be damned if he wasn't going to support her. The dwarves had stayed out of this conflict for far too long.

He whistled loudly, and Vel appeared, slowly shuffling into the room. He squinted in the low light, but he'd never ask for more candles to be lit. It didn't do to show weakness in your later years. Vel had been the main advisor to the Ironmantles for longer than Thrargud knew, and he would know if this was his heart or his head talking.

"E'Lyn's sending four hundred," he told the dwarven elder, shaking his head, his red hair swishing free as he pushed himself up from his seat.

"Ye wish to send five?" Vel returned, holding his stooped position, eyes shrouded beneath bushy brows and curling grey hairs.

"I do," Thrargud admitted. "Fitmigar rides north."

"Then five we send. Doesn't do to be outshone by elves."

"Glad we be in agreeance," Thrargud replied. "See that it is done."

"Right away," Vel confirmed. "I'll be sending a tunnel hawk ahead to alert those at Fort Brickblade that we be sending them through the gap."

"Good," Thrargud said before taking another swig from his tankard. "No Ironmantle be leaving his daughter without aid."

Chapter Fourteen

Having finished lunch, we continued the road northeast. The ground dried up farther from the river, making griffin paws kick up the dust as we walked. We'd be traveling until we reached the tree line of the southern end of the Lower Helerean Forest.

Feeling well-rested, I'd volunteered to take the first watch. Mallen offered to join me, eager to see if he could push Svendale's abilities to remain airborne for longer spells.

We would be meeting with the elven reinforcements late tomorrow afternoon. After that, we had only a day's travel to reach the frontline. That is, unless we hit further delays. I doubted it, though. The wilder plains were behind us, replaced by plowed fields and small fruit orchards, and the animals we did spy from griffinback were now peaceful and oblivious to our presence. Only the odd farmer, guiding his plow horse across a field, gave us notice.

I'd wanted to run through what Sars had said before about triple-merging my spells, but the land here looked a bit dry, and I didn't particularly want to start any orchard fires. Instead, I continued my scouting, spotting a few meandering streams but nothing of real note. We wouldn't see a larger body of water until we'd joined up with Lord E'Lyn's men traveling north and had to cross the River Yorn.

With our time in the air soon up, I nudged Hestia into a dive. We landed at the back of our group, dust kicking up off the track as Hestia's claws found purchase.

Sienna and Elandra rode before me on Dawnquill and Veo, chatting away. I dropped into conversation with Mirek for a minute, noticing that he wasn't his usual smiling self.

"How are you finding traveling with us, Mirek?" I asked. Lance wasn't my primary focus in weapons training, and Galen took care of the early lance lessons, so I hadn't spent as much time with him.

"It's OK, I guess," he replied, eyes meeting mine. I noticed the dark bags under his eyes.

He'd seemed keen enough to come with us before, but now he seemed pretty down. "Missing riding with the wagons?"

"A bit," he admitted. "I can't help feeling that coming with you guys has just brought the trouble a bit closer to me, is all." He fidgeted with the chain around his neck, perhaps thinking about his family back home.

"That's fair enough," I replied. "We do seem to have a habit of finding ourselves in these situations. That said, we don't know how the others are faring. They could be having an even more difficult time than us."

"That's true."

I smiled and moved forward in the line. I couldn't say that I'd cheered Mirek up at all, but I'd definitely given him something to think on.

Yeah, nice one, Jadyn. Bad situations could always be worse. Bet he'll be smiling for the rest of the day.

I moved on in private contemplation for a short while. I'd fallen into the position of squad leader easily, happy to lead a group of my peers into battle. I had always wanted to be the best that I could be, and I was one of the strongest knights of our year. But that didn't really make the best leader. I found myself doubting my ability to keep everyone content and in good spirits, picking away at my earlier comments and trying to find flaws.

Maybe I was being too hard on myself. We'd gone from fourth-year students in a military academy to marching to war in a few short days. All of us had cracks left in our training, big and small. I didn't have family outside of the academy, not since Wendia passed, so other than the battle, I was still surrounded by my most treasured people. My only fear was losing them. The others had families and friends to worry about. I spent a moment trying to imagine what each was leaving behind.

Sienna's entire family farmed the land, and she spoke of them often. Sars' parents would be going through the same grief that my friend was. Brom's family were bakers in Erbury, a large settlement on the western coast, he their only child.

Mallen didn't really talk about his family much at all, but I knew his mother was around. Fitmigar's large extended family came from Krag Ferris in the mountains in the northwest of Atania. I recalled one of her drunken boasts, with her going on and on about how her father trained tunnel hawks. If drunk Fitmigar was to be believed, they were not only the best messenger birds in the world but nearly sacred to the dwarves. You had to take drunk Fitmigar with a pinch of salt, however.

Elandra's parents had both passed away, but I knew she had an older sister that —

"Jadyn!"

I shook my head to clear my thoughts. Our axe-wielding dwarf waved at me.

"Hey, Helstrom. What's up?" I asked.

"Just wondering how much farther we got to go today."

"Honestly, I'm not sure," I admitted, giving what I hoped was an understanding smile. "I only know that we follow the track to the edge of the forest, and we should be there before dark, giving us time to get set up for the night."

"Huh. Guess nothing to do but wait then," he said, looking a little downcast.

"I'm sure there's more we could be doing, but without instructors with us, it's going to be hard to study on the road."

"Meh. True I suppose. Shame we don't have Charn with us. A song would've been fun right about now."

"I could tell a few stories to help pass the time?" Sars offered from behind.

We all urged him to do so, happy to have a distraction. The villages were few and far between along our route, and there were only so many fields and orchards I could look at before they all blended into one.

The mood picked up as Sars told tales that some of us hadn't heard for a good while, and others we'd never heard at all. We were laughing at one particular tale about a mage who cursed himself into a mouse, when Syl shouted from above.

"Tree line ahead, sir!"

I waved at him to come back and join us, and Rammy also brought his griffin down as we circled up.

"So, what have you seen?" I asked.

"It appears to be the edge of the forest, sir. I could just make it out over some hilly ground ahead."

"And how close is the tree line to the hills?"

"Hard to judge at the moment, sir," he said, "but I'd guess around a couple of miles. It's pretty flat between the two."

"OK. So, with dusk approaching in a couple of hours, let's get to the hills and then camp on the top of the tallest one. That way we can easily keep an eye on every direction, and we won't be too close to the tree line to be caught unawares by anything coming from the forest beyond."

"Sounds good," Fitmigar said, nodding, deep in thought.

"Anything to add?" I asked, glancing around.

"Not from me," Sars said.

The others nodded in agreement.

"OK, so, Brom and Mallen, you're up next. Continue to watch our route carefully. See if you can get a better idea of the distance between the hills and the trees, and we'll head for those hills in the meantime."

"Right on it, Jadyn," Mallen said.

The two turned on their griffins, and with a couple of powerful beats, they were aloft again, circling the blue skies.

"OK," I started, looking around my squad. My friends. "Let's get going."

The land started to gradually rise as we traveled, the orchards becoming more prevalent than the recently plowed and seeded fields. Elandra pulled up alongside, and I was happy to chat. The lingering nerves from the attack faded over the hours.

"I can't remember feeling this full of energy before," she started, and I smiled.

"It's a side effect of the spells crossing between us," I said. "At least, as best I can tell. It seems to increase the size of our cores, albeit temporarily."

"Whatever it is, it feels good."

"It does," I agreed. "Have you had the chance to try out [Fire Elemental] yet?"

"I haven't," she admitted. "Haven't had the right opportunity. Figured I'd take a look when we stop in a while."

"I can help you," I offered. "It's no trouble at all."

"I'd like that," she said. "And it goes both ways, of course. We're going to need all our strength when we reach the battle lines."

"That we are. Great idea, Elandra. I'd love to have you explain the various spells for me."

"No time like the present," she said, grinning. "I could think of things I'd rather be doing"—she pointedly looked at my crotch—"but that will have to wait."

"Sure," I said, nodding, briefly distracted by her comment and the way her skintight shirt clung to her chest.

She coughed, and I smiled. Caught again. "OK, so [Water Burst] is pretty similar to Sienna's [Wind Burst] in that it's powerful but short range. A decent area of effect spell, affecting a specific range that I've manage to practice up to quite a substantial distance compared to what I started with."

"Yeah, I'm not sure where I'll be starting from, so it'll be interesting to compare."

"Mm-hm. [Ice Blast] is similar, in that I can cast it over a specific area, and it can do a great job of reducing visibility like a snowstorm."

"Makes sense."

"I would have used it against the wolves if Brom hadn't cast them all in shadow first."

"It's still a great option, though," I said. "Great for making arrows fly off course."

"Uh-huh, and just let me know if you get cold using it. I have ways of warming you up." She winked at me, repeatedly.

I laughed. She was darn adorable. "I bet you do."

"Now, [Dehydrate] is something a little different."

"OK, how?" I asked.

"It can make you really thirsty. Very dangerous if a girl hasn't had release in a while."

I snorted.

"Really, though, it involves a lot more feel. It's a single target spell, and I can use it over a decent distance now, but I have to be careful on how much mana I push into it."

"To make sure you don't waste mana?" I asked, leaning toward her, intrigued.

"And to make sure I use enough to debilitate whatever I'm casting at. Too little and it will carry on, potentially killing me or someone else. Too much and I'm just wasting precious mana."

"So, you saying it's going to take much longer to master?"

"I am," she said. "But if anyone can get to grips with it quickly, Jadyn, it's you."

"Let's hope so," I said.

"Speaking of getting to grips with…"

I winked. "I might be sharing my attention, but I won't forget about you, Elandra."

"I'd hope not. Pretty memorable, right?"

"Very memorable," I said, the image of the previous night seared into my memory.

She smiled and then nudged Veo onwards, joining Sienna. I watched her go, noticing not for the first time the way those tight shorts of her really accentuated the perfect shape of her ass.

She turned and caught my eye, giving an extra little shake of her ass before she continued away.

Another hour later, we crested the tallest hill, leaving the agricultural land behind. A few solitary trees dotted the grassy hillside on the way up, thickening to a small copse of trees at the top. From here to the forest there were no more fields. Syl had been pretty accurate in his initial estimation of the distance between these hills and the tree line. Two maybe two and half miles separated us now.

I walked back over to the others. The day was just starting to dim, so it was important we set up a camp before darkness fell.

Rammy and Fitmigar immediately set to work, knocking down a couple of trees to fashion rudimentary posts for a pen for the griffins. We then debated setting a perimeter. We had the high ground, and we could see in all directions, but once night fell, our vision would be limited, so it was important to be secure. In the end, Helstrom, Brom, and I decided to set about setting some traps.

As we dug holes, Syl started preparing our food. Mirek helped, giving him a hand, though from the comments I overheard he was more of a hindrance. I liked to think we were all pretty capable, but Mirek had received a pretty sheltered upbringing. He clearly still lacked some of the skills we'd all picked up along the way.

Sienna and Elandra prepared food for our griffins off to the side, while Sars and Mallen set up tents around the center.

"We're working well as a team, aren't we," Brom noted.

"That we are, fella," Helstrom agreed as he placed another spiked stick into the pit we'd dug out.

"I knew we would," I said. "There was never doubt in my mind about selecting you all for my squad."

"Means a lot," Helstrom replied solemnly, banging his fist against his chest.

"Agreed," Brom said. "We are fortunate that the most handsome man in all of Atania managed to fend off all the girls long enough to make the right decisions."

"Shut up," I chuckled, tossing a stick at him.

He fell back, laughing.

"He's not wrong," Helstrom added, face tight as he held back a smile.

"Don't you start, too," I warned, finger raised.

Not that I truly minded. Some goofy comradery was what we needed to distract us from the war we were walking towards. And as we finished up setting the traps, I was pleased to hear laughter coming from across our makeshift camp. It seemed like we weren't the only ones loosening up.

We decided to go with pairs on watch duty, each taking a couple of hours before waking the next. Maybe everyone was tired, or maybe worried they might not get to sleep much on the frontlines, but we were all keen to catch all the shuteye we could.

As people were settling down for the night, a few small fires sprang up in the tree line. My first guess was elven scouts, but I made sure to reiterate the importance of keeping an eye on them through the night. It wouldn't do to get ambushed here.

Once I was sure everything was under control, I lay back and closed my eyes.

"Jadyn?"

I woke with a start, an arm nudging my side. "Yeah," I answered groggily, rubbing the sleep from my eyes.

An elven man's silhouette stood outside. "You're up next."

"Thanks, Mallen," I mumbled, pushing myself up onto my elbows.

My turn meant dawn was only a couple of hours away. I hadn't personally requested the last shift, but I couldn't say I minded when it fell that way.

"Anything to report?" I asked.

"All quiet," the elf replied. "The fires are still out there, but there's been nothing else of note."

I sat up, pulled an extra overshirt from my bag, and rose to my feet. "OK, get your head down, and I'll see you in a couple of hours."

Mallen was down, eyes closed, before I even left the tent.

I pulled the flaps back and headed out into the early chill. Stars were still out. The approaching dawn was just a faint suggestion of bluish light on the far horizon, but it was still bright enough I saw my breath frost. It was the coldest I'd known it since fall arrived, but that's what you got when traveling north.

I shivered, rubbing my hands together and thought back to the hot summer days of my youth. I doubted I'd ever grow to tolerate the cold. Numb fingers and toes just felt fundamentally wrong, and the bone-penetrating chill was just unbearable. I genuinely could not understand why people would choose to live up north. There was still plenty of good farmland left down south.

I did a quick perimeter check, noticed Syl heading over, and then went and warmed my hands by the fire.

"Morning, sir," he greeted.

"Just Jadyn is fine, Syl," I repeated again.

"Not going to happen, sir."

I smiled and gestured to the log next to me. "Take a seat."

He nodded and sat next to me, warming his hands.

I'd spent far less time with Syl these past three years than my closer friends, so this felt like a good time to try and gauge how he was dealing with everything.

"So, how are things with you?" I asked.

"All good, sir."

Not the most talkative of starts.

"I'm sorry for not already being aware, but do you have family back home?"

"Just my father, sir," he started, slowly, perhaps not used to talking about personal matters.

I paused to let him continue.

"Mother died giving me life," he explained.

"I'm sorry to hear that," I said. I knew what it felt like to grow up with a parent, or two, missing. "How was your father about you joining the academy?"

"He understood." He paused, then added, "Eventually."

"Not keen?" I asked.

"Not at first. Father and I are close, sir. As you'd expect, I suppose."

"No brothers and sisters?"

"No." He rubbed the back of his neck. "Father never remarried, so it was just the two of us."

"I heard somewhere that he's a cook, is that right?"

"That's correct, sir. Works for one of the richest families in Atania, sir. Located in Olnfast."

I made a sound of understanding. Olnfast was the capital city of Atania, situated a few days' travel to the west from where we were.

"Well, Syl. I don't want you to worry. We'll have you popping by to see your father again before you know it."

"Thank you, sir."

I nodded and rose to my feet. "Time to check our surroundings again. You head left, I'll head right, and we'll cross around the back of camp and meet back here."

"Understood, sir." With that, I headed off, trusting Syl to do the same.

Being called sir still felt a bit awkward. I'd have preferred to be friends, but hopefully, I'd at least taken a step towards becoming a better leader if nothing else.

I reached the midpoint of my walk without incident, but there was no sign of Syl, so I pulled my additional overshirt tighter around myself and carried on. He was probably just walking slowly.

As I continued around the edge of camp, a dark shape on the ground alerted me. My senses screamed danger, so I ran over, scanning left and right.

It was Syl, lying dazed on the ground, holding the back of his head and groaning.

"You OK?" I whispered, continuing to glance around.

"Yeah, just... I'm not sure what happened, sir."

I knelt next to him and eased him into a sitting position. "Looks like you took a blow to the back of the head, Syl. Let's get the rest of camp up and see if we can't find out what the hells is going on."

Refusing to leave his side, I placed two fingers in my mouth and whistled loudly. The camp quickly sprang into life, tent flaps flying out as my squad mates emerged.

Chapter Fifteen

In less than a minute, I had nine people lined up in front of me. Syl had tried to rise to his feet, but I'd insisted he sit back down. It wouldn't do to have him passing out again.

"What's happening?" Brom asked, rubbing the sleep from his eyes.

"Someone attacked Syl," I said. "Given him a fair old whack on the back of the head."

"And no one saw anything?" Mallen asked, scanning the camp and its surroundings warily.

"Nothing," I confirmed. "He left to do a perimeter check, and I headed the other way. Found him on the ground."

"Fuck…" Brom muttered, shaking his head.

"Strange that the griffins remained quiet," Sienna mused, and I had to agree. They weren't shy about screeching at encroaching beasts.

"Maybe the attacker is still here," Sars said slowly, looking between the squad. "One of us could have—"

I coughed, cutting him off. "I sincerely hope not. But let's not rule anything out. Dawn is approaching, and we're all up now. So, let's take a seat, and as soon as it's light enough to do so, we'll spread out and see what we can discover."

"You want me to use [Night Vision] to check out the area?" Brom asked.

"I'd rather no one go off alone just yet," I told him. "Let's just wait a short while, and then we'll all look together in the light of day."

We each pulled up a log and took a seat around the fire. We were strong together, at least I considered us to be so, but now gazes flicked around, sizing others up in the firelight.

This wouldn't do. Not now. We had to fight together in a couple of days, trusting each other with our lives. Maybe that was the plan of the saboteur all along. To sow doubt. To create fractures between us.

I'd known everyone here for almost four years. Some I knew better than others, but it didn't make any sense for any of them to act like this. I paused as I thought about the bears, the wolves, the bison.

Unless they were under someone else's control.

If that was the case it must be fleeting. Coming and going. I'd certainly notice someone riding with us with permanent pitch-black eyes.

"What are you thinking?" Sienna asked from beside me, resting a hand on my leg.

"Just if it was someone here, they'd have to be controlled, surely?" I replied, deep in thought.

"I was thinking the same. Do you think they'd know about it when they weren't directly affected?"

"I'd have to say no. Otherwise, they'd surely do something. Tell someone. It would have to be against their will."

"Or…" she began.

"Yeah, I'm not willing to consider the possibility that someone's actively fucking with us yet," I said, shaking my head.

"We'll be checking the area soon enough anyway," she said, nodding toward the lightening sky.

"That's true." I pushed myself up and paced back and forth. We needed to be careful when we looked for signs. Could I trust everyone to look properly, or was there someone here who would actively destroy evidence?

As soon as it was light enough, I headed directly over to where Syl fell. My worst fears were confirmed.

The brief rain shower we'd gone through at the start of our journey hadn't made it this far north. The ground was hard and grass-covered, and there was absolutely nothing to be seen.

I cursed under my breath and waved the others over to spread out and check more extensively, though I already suspected that we'd find nothing. We'd come slightly off the dirt track to head up the grass-covered hills last evening, and already the griffins' pawprints had disappeared, the grass springing back into place during the night.

I kicked a stone away in frustration. This hadn't really slowed us down, and Syl was already recovering.

Other than sowing seeds of doubt, I couldn't see the point.

"Nothing," Brom confirmed a short while later, coming back to join me as I remained closely inspecting the ground where Syl fell.

"OK. Then let's have a quick breakfast, pack up, and get on our way. The track takes us within a couple of hundred yards of the tree line, and then it's north all the way."

With Syl still recovering, Brom rustled up a quick meal before we left. The fire had already been covered, so it was just cured meats and hard cheese, but no one really minded, their thoughts elsewhere.

"OK, let's head out," I announced, gesturing for Rammy and Helstrom to lead us down the hill and back to the track.

Helstrom nodded and nudged Mossrik forward, his griffin's grey feathers rippling in the early morning breeze. I allowed Sienna and Elandra to pass next and pulled into the line alongside Sars.

The situation was serious, and I fully intended on racking Sars' brains on it, but that didn't mean I wasn't going to appreciate the two fine asses bouncing before me at the same time. I didn't want to think that anyone here could betray us, purposefully or not, but my girls were without suspicion. I'd trust them with my life.

I looked around and realized I could say that for almost everyone here.

As we rejoined the main track, paws kicking up dust on the dry road, I turned to Sars.

"Any ideas now we've had a chance to think on things?"

He looked deep in contemplation. "I am reluctant to start pointing fingers."

"Me, too," I agreed. "Every one of us here has known the others for years."

"We could be being trailed by something or someone?"

"Like who?" I asked. If anyone was going to know it would be Sars with all that extra-curricular learning in the library.

The water mage thought for a moment. "There are a few possibilities. It could be a shapeshifting mage. They are not common, but they could be following us as a small bird perhaps or another animal?"

I couldn't help myself and scanned the trees ahead, squinting suspicious glares at every chirp.

"Or perhaps a rare, stealthy creature like a doppelganger or something?" he continued.

That had potential. I'd have to speak to Brom, our resident master of stealth.

"Then, there are those fabled orc special forces, famed for their fearsomeness and ability to stalk unseen in human lands."

OK. That got my attention. I hadn't heard anything recently pertaining to orcs spotted within Atania, especially this far south of the border, but we couldn't rule it out.

"Then there are shadow drake and other large creatures that can stealth through innate ability and magic…"

Bloody hells, the list was endless.

"Could be gnomes," came from behind, and I turned to look at Fitmigar as Sars and Brom laughed.

"Gnomes? Really?" I asked, shaking my head.

"Aye. Nasty little buggers."

"If you're not going to take it seriously," Mallen voiced from behind them, "is there any point?"

"Conversation isn't going anywhere anyway," Fitmigar groaned.

I had to agree. We could spitball ideas and possibilities for hours. But, without any evidence, we'd only ever be guessing at who or what was responsible.

"Whatever the case, we need to keep moving and stay vigilant," I said.

The others agreed, and I turned back to Sars as he spoke.

"Why start now, though? What has changed?"

"You mean other than us heading off to war?" I lifted my eyebrows.

"Good point. It does seem that events are conspiring against us. It is just all done on such a small scale. The few potions, the wagon axle, now Syl. Why not something bigger? More drastic?"

"Perhaps they'd planned on destroying all the potions. Maybe the wagons, too. But then Tordlum first, and then Sienna and I disturbed them."

"Could be." He paused, eyebrows furrowing in thought. "And then Ralartis was kind of lame as we left."

"That's a good point," I said. "Froom said he'd likely done it on the way up to the main stables, but what if it was deliberate?"

I dropped into silent contemplation for a while as I ran through events in my head. None of these events were derailing us, but just knowing someone or something was acting against us was a huge concern.

I was pulled from my thoughts soon after when Rammy shouted from up ahead, "Elves!"

"Halt!" I pulled out of the line and nudged Hestia forward, joining Rammy and Helstrom at the front.

We'd closed to within around four hundred yards of the tree line, and now a group of six elves on horseback were riding toward us. They had bows out, arrows nocked, and were dressed in dark green clothing with no real armor of note. Rangers, I surmised.

"OK. Wait here, everyone. I'm going to approach and let them know why we're here."

"Alone?" Sienna asked from behind me, her voice worried.

"I think that's the best option," I said. "I don't want us to threaten them."

"Be careful."

I smiled. "Always am."

I nudged Hestia again, and we made our way toward the newcomers.

As we drew closer, I gently patted Hestia's neck to settle her down. Horses could be skittish with unfamiliar predators, and the last thing we wanted was to cause an incident by spooking the elves' mounts with my huge griffin.

The bows remained trained on me as we pulled up before them. Six elven rangers by the look of them, five male and one female, all with serious expressions on their faces.

One, a tall, thin blond-haired male encouraged his horse forward a step. OK, so he was in charge here.

"Name your purpose here, Griffin Rider."

Not one for warm welcomes then…

I smiled, affecting a calm diplomatic tone. "I'm Jadyn of Atania, a knight of the Griffin Academy and squad leader in what is now the main griffin army of Atania. We've been tasked with meeting up with Lord E'Lyn north of here to help transport elven troops to the border."

"And who travels with you?"

"That would be my squad," I replied, suppressing a wince of exasperation. He had eyes, didn't he? "Well, Griffin Knight Jadyn, I am Nerimyn, senior ranger in these parts, and we have been tasked with meeting you here and escorting you north. Fall in behind us, and do keep up."

He turned his horse and prepared to head north.

Great, so it's going to be like that.

I motioned the others forward as the elves lowered their bows. Their glares remained stern, though the female elf offered a glimmer of a smile, or did I imagine that?

Dressed all in green, she wore skintight leggings and a tight shirt with straps crisscrossing the front, pushing up what I'd consider ample breasts for an elf. Her eyes sparkled lightly on her flawless face.

I shook off the thoughts, and noticed her briefly scan me up and down before returning to ride beside Nerimyn. Did I imagine that, too?

My squad joined us, and we were soon following the elves on a track that ran parallel to the trees. I'd assumed they'd have questions, or at least make conversation, but the six rode out ahead of us, barely even glancing back as they led us north.

"What's up with them?" Elandra asked from my side.

"Just doing their jobs, I guess," I replied, shrugging.

"Well, they do their jobs weird," she complained. "This isn't how you treat guests or allies."

"It's just how they are. At least we know they're alert and focused," Sienna added, pulling up on my other side.

Elandra went quiet for a minute, a thoughtful look on her face.

"She's very pretty," Sienna added, nodding her head toward the back of the female elf.

"That she is," I agreed. "They're all so serious, though."

"Not everyone can immediately fall to your charms, you know?" Elandra teased. "We're just the lucky ones."

"Ha. I wouldn't expect them to," I said, shaking my head. "Just be good if we can get along without issue. War is hard enough, without friction."

"There's a certain type of friction I'd like with you," Elandra said, loud enough for most of the column to hear. I glanced across as she blew me a kiss, leaning forward and dragging my gaze down to her pronounced chest.

"Now, some friction with Jadyn here does sound good," Sienna admitted, tucking a loose strand of hair behind her ear, and Elandra laughed, nodding.

I smiled, wishing I could drag the pair into the trees to release some tension.

It was almost like Elandra could read my mind as she wiggled both eyebrows, giving me a whole collection of suggestive looks and winks.

I chuckled at her silly antics. Despite having company and flirting occasionally, we maintained our aerial surveillance, rotating through the squad a pair at a time. Galen had stressed it's importance for when we met up with Lord E'Lyn, and I agreed. Not only were we close enough to the battle that we might run into some enemy deep raids, but we had to maintain the powerful impression of Griffin Knights. The elves needed to know we could be relied on.

There was nothing much to be seen through the dense canopy, even from above, but we still had a good view of the grasslands and small tributaries in the west. The River Yorn flowed into Atania from the mountainous regions of Urg-frei, north of the border, heading south for a period before curving east. It flowed between the upper and lower Helerean Forests and met the Eilerin Sea. At the point where it turned eastward, the Tyrell broke away, flowing south all the way to the western coast, south of Erbury, where it entered the Atanian Sea.

It would be the Yorn we crossed, but only after joining up with the elven reinforcements later today.

My latest sojourn through the skies coming to an end, I nudged Hestia to descend, and we joined up with the back of the column. Brom landed beside me.

"So, Elandra tells me you've got your eye on our new travelling companion?" he said.

I looked across at Brom, shocked. "What?"

"Ha. I'm just messing," he teased. "Elandra was just telling me how seriously hot she is is all."

"I'm heading to war, Brom, and trying to figure out two relationships as I go. Just because someone has a hot ass, it doesn't mean that I'm interested. Not when I have two hot asses already."

Brom chuckled again. "I know you, Jadyn, and I know the ladies can't resist your pretty face. She'll soften to your charms."

I rolled my eyes at him and pushed Hestia up in the line to escape. Noticing Syl, I pulled up alongside him and Rammy. "How's the head?" I asked.

Rammy dropped back a little to make room.

"Improving, sir," Syl replied, his hand subconsciously moving to the bump on the back of his head.

"Nothing come back that could help us?" I asked.

"Nothing, sir. One moment I was walking around the edge of camp, and the next I was coming around on the grass, pain coursing through my head."

"I'm sorry it happened."

"Not your fault, sir. I should have been more vigilant." He looked down, disappointed in himself. I needed to lift his spirits somehow.

"Not your fault, Syl. Something strange is going on here. I'm glad you're around to help us get to the bottom of it."

"Appreciate that, sir."

Our conversation was cut short by a whistle from the head of the column. I raised my eyes to see Nerimyn and the other elves had pulled up.

"Looks like lunch," I said to Syl and headed up to speak with the elves.

It turned out I was correct. We paused to take in some refreshments, the elves sitting separate from ourselves, consuming supplies that they carried on their mounts.

Syl insisted he was fine and prepared us a bite to eat. The rest of us gathered to sit down, relax, and massage our saddle-weary asses for a bit. I headed over to sit down with the others, fully intending on relaxing for a brief moment. Only Mallen didn't join us, since he had pulled griffin feeding duty. I noticed a couple elves head over his way as I sat and kept an eye on them. Their conversation soon turned odd. The two elves laughed, while Mallen looked downcast and refused to meet their gaze.

I quietly got to my feet and made my way over. As I approached, one of the elves turned and met my eye. He nudged his friend, and they turned to leave.

"See you later, *Naeryn*," the taller of the two said. They walked away, chuckling darkly.

"You OK?" I asked Mallen once they were out of earshot.

He raised his eyes to meet my gaze, offering a weak smile. "Fine."

"What did they want?" I asked.

"They know me. From before the academy."

"Didn't seem overly friendly," I noted.

"That would be accurate," the elf replied, shaking his head, "Aelen, in particular."

"And what does *Naeryn* mean? I assume it's elvish."

He looked away, declining to answer.

"Mallen?" I asked again. "What does it mean?"

He turned back around. Was that shame in his expression?

"It's a derogatory term."

I waited.

"Roughly translates to 'pitiful half-elf'."

I must have looked confused because my friend continued without prompting. "My mother is human. My father was an elf."

"And that makes you lesser somehow?" I asked, already dreading the answer.

"In his eyes, yes…"

"Right. Just a moment."

I turned on the spot and strode across to where the elves stood, talking amongst themselves.

The taller of the pair, Aelen, was around my own height, a touch taller than the others in the group, and he remained oblivious to my approach as I neared.

Nerimyn didn't, however, and met my eyes. "Yes?"

I stopped, hands clasped behind my back, my jaw tense as I held in the firestorm. My glare nailed Aelen down where he stood.

"We are allies heading to the same war," I said evenly.

Nerimyn raised a brow. "Yes?"

"Some of us are likely to die in the coming days."

His expression grew grimmer, more confused. "Speak clearly. We'll soon be back on the road."

"Then this is the perfect timing." My eyes stayed fixed on two elves in particular. "Griffin Knights treat their allies with respect, and I'd been taught the elven rangers shared our sense of honor. Imagine my disappointment when two such rangers decided to spend their last days before battle harassing one of *my* Knights. For all our sakes, I do hope that's not the standard of ranger behavior."

"Pssht. We were just joking around with the Naery--"

Aelen's words were cut off by a snap-fast fist from Nerimyn, sending him crumpling to the ground.

Nerimyn met my eyes, giving me the faintest nod of respect. "Thank you for bringing this to my attention. Rest assured, it will be properly addressed."

I returned the nod.

"To your feet, Aelen!" he roared, pulling the downed elf up by his collar.

Aelen struggled shakily to his feet, refusing to meet his eye.

"This true?" Nerimyn asked, glaring at his subordinate.

Aelen nodded meekly.

"You'll be heading over to that young elf to apologize then," Nerimyn told him, and the reprimanded elf slunk off, back toward my friend.

"My apologies, Griffin Knight," Nerimyn said, a stern look still present on his face. "That is not how we do things here. It will not happen again."

"Thank you for handling it," I said, before turning and heading back over to the others.

Without comment, I sat back with my squad and picked up my food from where I'd placed it.

"What was that about?" Sienna asked, concern on her face.

"Just needed to remind them to be polite to others is all," I replied. It wasn't my place to fill the others in on Mallen's secret. There was obviously more to it. He talked of his mother in present tense and his father in the past tense. And then there was the way he tended to avoid elven norms.

The others sensed they wouldn't get more details for the moment, but I noticed Sars give me a small nod of appreciation. Maybe Mallen had already confided in his roommate.

He'd tell me if and when he needed to. That much I was sure.

Chapter Sixteen

When Mallen came back to join us, he was quiet, but he whispered a soft, "Thank you," as he passed me. We then got back on track, ready to join up with the elven reinforcements, hopefully just a couple of hours ahead.

My confrontation seemed to have broken the ice with our traveling companions. Nerimyn dropped back to trot alongside me for a while as we traveled, his horse soon calming after initial shyness about traveling next to a huge, imposing griffin.

"I apologize again for Aelen's behavior before," he started.

I nodded. "It's been dealt with as far as I'm concerned. If it stops, then the matter is behind us."

"I appreciate your understanding. He's had something like that coming his way for a while, so it might not have been too bad a thing."

"It did feel pretty good to see you punch him," I replied, and the ghost of a smile appeared on the stern ranger's face.

"We should arrive with the others in the next hour or so," he said.

Pretty much what I'd calculated after my chat with Galen before leaving the main column. "How many will we be joining up with?" I asked.

"Around four hundred, from what I understand," Nerimyn said, and I had to keep my surprise in check.

That was quite the force and sorely needed. All we had to do now was support their journey to the war, keeping them safe along the way. Not much to worry about at all…

"Horses? I asked, wondering what kind of pace we'd be setting.

"Around one hundred I would suspect. Most will be on foot."

OK, so that would slow us, but I figured that would have been factored in with what I'd been told previously. "Will we cross the Yorn today?"

"Either later today or early tomorrow morning. It depends on how quickly we can mobilize the others, and if they have even arrived at the cross point prior to us."

"Appreciate the update," I said.

He nodded and headed back to the front.

I noticed Dawnquill approach from the side and smiled at Sienna.

"All going to plan?" she asked.

"So far, so good. The numbers are a little higher than I was expecting, though."

"How many?"

"Four hundred or so."

Sienna gasped.

I grinned. "It just means we have more allies at our side now. Less likely that anything will bother us."

"You think pairs patrolling the skies is still going to be enough to cover them?" she asked.

"Honestly, I'm not sure yet. We're going to be moving slowly northward. I guess it'll depend on how close to the Upper Helerean Forest we are, what kind of cover, that sort of thing."

"I trust your judgment, so just let us know what we need to do."

"Thanks. Will do," I said, smiling. "Seems like we haven't had the chance to spend much time together these past couple of days."

"I know. *We* know, I suppose. I've been talking with Elandra, and we know how busy, how stressful it is right now."

"Hopefully, we can get some time together this evening?"

"We'd like that," she replied with a smile.

I appreciated how understanding they were being. It felt like we were moving from one bump in the track to the next, issues cropping up and attempts to slow us down around every corner. I was focused on what awaited us at the border, but I was also enjoying what Sienna, Elandra, and I had together. I wanted it to grow and blossom not slow down.

I huffed in frustration.

The next hour passed quickly, my two trips into the air being relatively serene. The only thing of note I spied from above was that the point where the elven reinforcements were due to meet us was rather emptier than I'd hoped.

It remained that way as we came to a stop, a few hundred yards from the tree line. The elves would be taking that right-hand track from Birchvale to here, so it seemed we had little to do but wait.

There was no point setting up a camp, we would be continuing north as soon as they appeared, hopefully reaching the River Yorn before it was too dark to cross. For now, we dismounted and relaxed a little. We'd camp at the river. From there, it would be just one more day of travel to reach the camps close to the border.

I dropped off Hestia, patting her neck. She nuzzled against me, chirping softly.

"Won't be too long, and then we'll be off again, girl," I told her.

She tilted her head in understanding, then lowered herself to the ground, content to sit and recuperate while we waited. Our constant aerial scouting sessions were still spread out, but there was no denying that the griffins grew more tired as each day progressed.

Glad to recuperate myself, I lay down and rested my head against her, closing my eyes. A breeze tousled my hair, but Hestia's warmth warded off its chill. I didn't sleep, but I still felt a little groggy when a feminine voice spoke from right beside me.

"Jadyn?"

I eased my eyes open to see the beautiful blonde-haired elf crouching before me. "Hi, ...?"

"Ella," she answered, realizing she'd never been introduced properly.

"Hi, Ella," I rose to sit. "What's up?"

"Nerimyn said to come and let you know that Lord E'Lyn and the reinforcements are five minutes out. Thought you might want to be up and ready."

"I appreciate that, Ella," I said. Blue eyes, I noted. *Cute.* "Please pass on my thanks."

She nodded and rose back up, disappearing over to the senior ranger's side.

I climbed to my feet. Hestia did likewise, my mighty griffin shaking her wings out and stretching her back legs as she lifted her head into the air.

I did my leaderly duties and went around rousing anyone that had chosen to take a short nap while waiting. Brom lay, eyes closed, on Fitmigar's lap as she ran a hand through his hair.

I enjoyed waking him the most.

Judging by the sun's position, it had only been a half-hour or so since we'd arrived. Hopefully, that meant we could reach the river crossing this evening. Either way, we'd be camping close to the river, whether on this bank or the opposite.

With everyone up and about, now seated on their griffins' backs, we lined up facing the forest, ready to welcome the new arrivals. Nerimyn moved next to me, ready to point out anyone I needed to know.

The first to appear were armored elves on horseback, the silver of their chest plates, pauldrons, vambraces, and gauntlets reflecting the late afternoon light. I scanned down and noticed the poleyns and greaves. Relatively basic armor, but then they needed to be mobile. It was all finished off with green-painted leaves on the side of a silver, open-faced helmet.

As the horses filed around the clearing, the foot soldiers came next, four abreast, all bedecked in similar armor, swords at their hips, bows on their backs. Impressive.

On and on they came, an apparently endless line of elven warriors, all seemingly molded from the same cast—tall, thin, predominantly blond-haired, and cheek bones I figured I could slice cheese on.

Suddenly, a gap in the line appeared. Eight riders emerged, surrounding a central elf on the largest war horse I'd ever seen. His armor was golden, and his poise made the simple act of scanning our line seem like the most regal act I'd ever witnessed.

"Almost as handsome as you that one," Brom whispered from my right. I rolled my eyes.

"That's Lord E'Lyn," Nerimyn confirmed from my left, and I nodded.

I paused a moment to recall all I'd been taught on etiquette in these matters. "I let him come to me, correct?" I asked.

The senior ranger nodded in confirmation. "That would be wise."

Lord E'Lyn left the main line and rode towards us, surrounded by the eight who I assumed to be his guards. The leaves on their helmets glimmered with gold.

The footsoldiers and regular horseman continued to fill the area, when Lord E'Lyn paused before us. He removed his helmet and placed it under his right arm.

"Which one of you is in charge here?" he asked, every syllable carefully pronounced, almost like poetry.

"That would be me, my lord," I replied, speaking but staying in line. Hestia fidgeted under me, seemingly fed up with all the standing around.

"Then follow me." With a dismissive air, he turned and rode off without a glance back.

I looked at Nerimyn and whispered, "Just me?"

The senior ranger nodded again.

I nudged Hestia forward, following the lord across to where a makeshift tent had been erected. A young-looking elf came out, took the lord's reins, and he gracefully dismounted, striding into the tent.

Right, so this is going to be fun…

I ran my hand through the feathers of Hestia's neck, gave her a pat and gently nudged her right flank. At once, she lowered herself to the floor. I swung a leg over and slid off.

"Thanks, girl," I whispered. "Back shortly."

With that, I headed into the tent to find the lord already seated, a drink in his hand. He met my eyes, nodded once, and gestured to a seat opposite.

"Drink, …?"

"Jadyn, my lord."

"A drink, Jadyn?"

Was this a test? He had already begun drinking a cup of something, so I hedged my bets.

"Just a small one, please, my lord."

He gestured to another young elf in the corner, who walked across, a generously poured drink already prepared.

"Let's get down to business then shall we, Jadyn?"

"Certainly, my lord."

He sighed. "It's all pomp and ceremony, Jadyn. Just E'Lyn is fine here."

"Understood, E'Lyn," I replied, and he smiled.

"Good. Good. Now, how are you going to get my warriors to the border safely?"

Straight to it. Despite my first impressions, I found that I liked him.

"I assume that you are familiar with the way that we travel. We'll rotate watches between the ten of us, two up at a time."

"And two griffin riders are enough to spot anything untoward in protection of four hundred elven warriors?"

"From what I am led to believe, E'Lyn, we will be moving away from the forest and into more open, albeit undulating, land after we cross the Yorn."

"That is correct."

"Then I am of the belief that two is sufficient until we close in on the frontline, and then we'll likely double that up. As before that point we are due to meet back up with the main section of our force, that will not be a problem."

"And if they are not there?" he asked, leaning forward.

"We'll wait. For a time. And then we'll continue without them if we need to. People are dying everyday fighting in this war. Every moment we delay, the situation worsens."

"Very good," E'Lyn said, drumming his fingers on the arm of his chair. A chair I hadn't even see arrive in the main procession. "I suppose you'll want to know the latest news first?"

"That would be very much appreciated. We have heard very little since we departed the academy."

"Right. Well, your griffin riders decimated their forces, unfortunately perishing in the process."

I nodded. I knew this much.

"The number of drakes and basilisks is low, and one perhaps two wyverns are all that have been seen in the area since that fateful day. The wyrm soldiers spoke of has not been seen again. However, a large orcish war band arrived to the front lines recently. The word is it's the Kre'Hrez clan, with Ugrea at their head. The situation is... dire."

"When can we leave?" I asked. I meant what I said about delaying our journey costing lives, and this news meant the risk had risen again.

"Immediately," he replied. "My men are rested sufficiently. Get them across the Yorn and then set up camp. You will then have time to make the border area camp by tomorrow evening."

He went on to describe some of the more intricate details with regard to bridge strength and the approach we'd need to cross safely. I found myself wishing I'd brough Sars' notebook with me.

"Understood, my lord," I said, when he finished. I stood, passing my untouched drink back to the young elf by my side, then excused myself with a small bow to Lord E'lyn and pushed through the tent's flaps.

Hestia hadn't moved while I'd been inside and rose to her feet, chirping softly. I hopped on her, and we joined back up with my squad.

"Circle up," I ordered.

They noticed my tone, bringing their griffins around until we waited in a circle, beaks in the center.

I paused, working through the words in my mind before addressing them.

"We're heading out now," I started. "The bridge is only an hour north from here, but we'll need to cross carefully. It's an old wooden structure and might not be able to bear the weight of the entire column."

I scanned my friends' faces. Serious faces looked back at me.

"We'll divide the forces into fifths, and then as pairs," I continued, "we'll take to the air, watching their surroundings as they traverse. Once the first group is safely over, the second group will begin."

"How long is the bridge?" Mallen asked.

"Just fifty yards or so where we'll cross, but the bridge is old, and we need to be sure we do this safely."

"Understood," Mallen replied.

"You really think we'll have any trouble?" Sienna asked.

"Maybe a particularly angry trout?" Brom added, and a couple of the others chuckled at the stocky shadow mage.

"Better to be safe," I said, and the seriousness returned. "Let's form up, split their warriors into twenty on horseback and sixty on foot for each party, and then we'll move out."

With that, our circle disbanded. We spent the next fifteen minutes dividing up the elven forces. Before departing, Lord E'Lyn trotted over to inform me that he would be returning to Birchvale with his guards. To assist in our journey, Nerimyn and Ella had been chosen to accompany us onward, knowing the land better than anyone else.

With an hour's travel, an hour's crossing, and only three hours or so until dusk, we moved out, Brom and Fitmigar taking to the skies on Gren and Shadowtail as we headed north again.

As the afternoon moved on, the temperature dropped, and I found myself wishing I had a certain pair of girls wrapped around me to keep me warm. Elandra rode alongside me now, and I struggled to find a balance between orderly and serious and the urge to flirt a little.

I knew that they were aware of how serious this all was, but I hated the thought of them thinking I wasn't serious about them. I'd never been more serious about anything in my life.

Elandra seemed to sense my internal struggle. She alternated between questions about our approaching plans and leaning over to offer a view down her shirt. This was why she was an absolute keeper.

Soon, Elandra was called away to take her turn scouting on Veo, and Rammy joined me.

I didn't think I'd ever tire of listening to my friends. We all held that belief, with our bonded griffins at our side, that we could conquer the world. No, conquer wasn't the right word. Protect. We could protect the world.

I was still smiling, lost in thought a short time later, when the bridge came into view. I happened to be in the air at the time, and it struck me just how fragile the structure appeared over the tumultuous waters below. The river moved at a fair speed down from the mountains of Urg-frei, and it was still rapid here.

I signaled for Rammy to remain in the air and took Hestia down, joining up with Brom and Fitmigar. The bridge was just coming into view on land.

"OK," I said. "Rammy is circling above, and I'm going to send Syl up to join him. You've both got the first group. Spread out the horses and get them all across safely."

"Right on it," Brom replied.

I offered him a smile. "There shouldn't be any danger here, other than a potentially collapsing old bridge, but keep alert regardless."

"Understood," Fitmigar said, and I gestured for them to begin.

They took off. I remained behind to watch, flicking my gaze between the two griffins circling overhead and the procession of elves slowly making their way across the bridge.

Half of the horses trotted ahead, giving some distance between them and the foot soldiers. Remaining cavalry brought up the rear, spreading the weight as they went. Creaks and groans of the bridge gave me some anxiety, but somehow it held. The first group of eighty reached the other side and began to spread out on the grassland past the bank.

One down, four to go.

Brom and Fitmigar flew higher, allowing Rammy and Syl to descend. The next lot of elven soldiers started their trek across the rickety bridge. The first group's successful crossing had mollified everyone's worries somewhat, and the soldiers looked more at ease, joking and laughing as they went. The second eighty also passed without issue, and as we swapped out our watch above, I allowed myself to relaxed, too. I noticed Mirek had joined this second group to travel over. Not brave enough to travel with the first group but clearly now keen to be across.

When the third group was halfway across, I caught movement under the frothing waters. Something big and dark.

"Sea drake!" Mallen shouted from above. "Get off the bridge! Now!"

Fuck. It was heading for the bridge, and it was traveling fast.

Chapter Seventeen

"Move now!" I roared.

The elves on the bridge hastened their pace immediately, racing for the closest end.

A fin broke the water as the beast approached the bridge. It was big. Sixty feet long big.

I shouted them to run faster but already knew that some wouldn't make it. The next time the fin broke the water, two huge scaly arms emerged, smashing the bridge like it was matchsticks. The screams of twenty or so falling elves were drowned out by the churning waters. One tried to hang on to the ruined bridge, only to be caught by a gigantic claw and crushed to a pulp.

It was amazing how quickly military training kicked in when lives were on the line.

"Get airborne, and save those soldiers!" I said to Sars and Elandra. "Men and women before horses!"

The great wings of Ralartis and Veo powered past me, the wind buffeting me almost off my feet.

With the fallen men and women covered as best we could, I turned to focus on eliminating the threat.

Think, Jadyn, think...

Sea drakes, from the stories Wendia told me, were notoriously hard to kill. Wind and water didn't work so well on an underwater attacker, and fire tended to snuff out when it hit the water.

Great. Even with extra spells I was going to struggle. I tried to work through potential mergers in my mind, even going so far as to try and work out what a three-way merge would resemble. I deduced there was nothing suitable.

There was only one real option here: stick it full of holes.

I looked down at Orcgrinder and Dragonkiller—what could I say, maybe Tad was right about naming them? I whistled Hestia into the air.

Hovering above the others, I shouted, "Mallen, Sienna, get Rammy and Helstrom and bombard it with spells. Any will do, just try and get it confused. We need to get up close and personal with this one. Everyone else, up with me. We fly in close and let our griffins rake the beast's body. If you have a weapon that you think will help, use it!"

I'd like to say they all nodded in agreement here, but the truth is I didn't wait to find out. A few strong beats of Hestia's wings and we were up, heading for the river.

I now appreciated those martial lessons with Galen. These were the moments when magic would at best serve as a distraction. It was just us and the beast. Up close and personal. A watery god and an orphaned magic-wielder and his friends, only now we were young men and women flying in on whirling vortexes of beak and claw. The main challenge here was that the sea drake could simply dive under and get rid of us. We tried a couple of fly-bys first, gauging the intelligence of the beast. It knew enough to dodge, to deflect, and to dive.

The beast's head emerged from underneath, its snout thinning, cheeks and neck ballooning. A jet of water shot from its mouth like a lance, slicing through a group of elves on the northern bank.

It needed to end now.

As we closed in, a barrage of spells flew at the beast, and I looked across to see Helstrom, Rammy, and Sienna throwing [Fireball] after [Fireball], the few that made contact forcing screeches of pain from the beast below. Sienna had clearly been practicing with her newest spell. Mallen joined them launching a series of [Lightning Bolt]s.

We continued our dive, taking the chance while the beast was distracted, and Hestia's knife-long claws ripped through its back, blood spurting into the churning river. The others dived after us, claws rending flesh from the creature's body as it struggled to evade our attacks.

As we turned to fly by again, I was forced to pull Hestia into an evasive spin, a jet of water powering toward us from the mouth of the enraged sea drake.

So, it needs a cooldown before it can use that skill again.

Good to know.

Hestia screeched in defiance, lowered her head, and we swept in again. [Lightning Bolt]s and [Fireball]s flew down from behind us, singing the beast and driving it back underwater. It resurfaced a moment later, and I knew what was coming. I counted down in my head, ready to evade the next attack.

I cycled through my ten spells, dismissing all until I reached [Fire Elemental]. After mentally locking it in place, I pulled hard on my mana, feeling it flood from my core and rapidly fill my body.

As we closed in, I released the spell. The fiery elemental burst into life on my hand as an eight-inch-tall griffin of pure flame. It leapt from my hand, tucked its wings in, and dived for the beast below.

The sea drake's neck swelled with another jet of water. But when its mouth opened, the elemental slipped in past yellowing fangs and down its throat.

A muted explosion rocked the drake. It's eyes ballooned. Steam billowed out from its mouth and nostrils as the sea drake roared in agony, its massive body writhing above the surface.

"Let's do this!" I roared, and we dove.

Griffins tore into the floundering beast with beak and claw, pulling huge chunks of its body free as the river turned red. The riders plunged their lances and weapons into the wounds, opening them further.

It let out a pained bellow. The massive body turned to flee, its mass sliding under the foaming rapid. "Finish it! Before it flees!" I roared.

Hestia's claws dug into its scales, and my scimitars pierced deep into flesh, seeking arteries beneath muscle. I hacked away with abandon, but still, the beast refused to go down.

Then, I was beneath roiling waters.

Behind me, the other riders let go as the drake dove deeper in the riverbed. Plumes of blood trailed it from numerous wounds, darkening the water.

You're not getting away. Not after the lives you've taken, I promised, swallowing as my lungs asked for air.

But we wouldn't kill it from down here. Its back had layers upon layers of protective muscle to hack through.

Hestia sensed my intentions after I reversed my grip on a scimitar and sank it into the hide as a climbing spike. We only had several feet of drake to climb, but against the current, underwater, it felt like a mountain.

Still, the beast tried to shrug us off. It thrashed around, banging it body against the riverbed. Hestia surged forth, squishing me between herself and the drake as it slammed into the rocks.

I screamed into the water as her claws lost their grip and my beloved griffin floated up. Had she been hurt? I didn't know, but I would avenge her all the same.

Two more stabs and I reached a spot in its neck where the others had gouged out a large chunk and exposed a pulsing jugular. Lungs burning now, I plunged Atanian-steel into the beast's neck.

A cloud of blood blinded me.

The mass of drake beneath my feet coiled. Afraid of being squished in its death throes, and completely out of air, I kicked up and scrambled for the surface.

My head broke the surface. I drew in the deepest breath and was plucked from the currents and into the air by a familiar pair of claws. "Hestia! You're alright!"

She chirped affectionately, clutching me closer.

"Good girl. Now help me climb up."

She did, and Hestia turned in the air, scanning for further threat and survivors in the water below. Unfortunately, most of those pulled under had already been torn apart.

I gestured for Sienna and Helstrom to stay airborne and took Hestia down. We landed on the southern bank, immediately greeted by Nerimyn and Ella.

Both rangers looked on, speechless.

"You ever seen… any of these… in the rivers… before?" I asked, taking deep, gulping breaths.

Nerimyn shook his head. "Never. Not in these rivers, though we have stories from sailors."

"That's similar to us, then." I paused, checking my body for bruises. "There's a chance it came in from the Eilerin Sea, but I'd be much more inclined to believe that it's from the north, sent from beyond the border."

"Drakes, basilisks, a wyrm, and now a sea drake?" Ella shook her head.

"That's about the size of it," I confirmed. "Everything else has been kept closer to the battle lines before. Is this desperation?"

"Intelligence, I would say," Nerimyn replied.

"If it had arrived a moment sooner it could have just taken out the bridge completely," I said.

"It may have done that to the other bridge to the west already," Nerimyn noted.

Fuck. I thought of the main party, potentially stuck on this side of the river, unable to bring the wagons north. They could fly over the river, so that wasn't an issue, but transporting the wagons across would likely delay them further, having to fashion harnesses of some description for the griffins to carry.

If that was the case, we'd be lucky to meet them on the track north in time.

Although, right now, we had our own problems.

Half of our elven army was on the northern bank, and the other half stuck here with us. I looked around our squad and asked, "So, how are we going to do this?" I asked. "Any ideas?"

Somewhat surprisingly, Brom spoke first, "Can we use the griffins to carry the elves across on their backs?"

I considered the numbers. "We could," I admitted, "but there's no way we'd carry the horses over, too. That's then thirty to forty cavalry turned into footmen. A big loss."

"Any way to fashion a bridge?" Rammy asked. "With Ice magic? Something like that?"

"That's a little beyond our capabilities right now, Rammy, but I like your thinking."

"Maybe the ice doesn't need to reach all the way to the other side," Elandra said, and something clicked.

"You're right," I said. "Nerimyn, do you have any rope?"

The ranger nodded.

"We're good then," I said, a smile growing on my lips. "Actually, Sars, do you have [Ice Blast]?"

A realization dawned on his face.

"That's three of us then. So, Sars, Elandra, and I will use [Ice Blast] to create some large blocks of ice. We'll rope them to the griffins, load elves and horses on, and drag them across the river like rafts."

Sounds of understanding spread throughout the group. "Clever," said Brom.

"One large block or several smaller ones?" Sars asked.

"You're the scholar," I replied. "I've only just come into water magic. What do you think?"

Sars and Elandra discussed matters for a moment before Sars announced, "One large block. It will melt slower in the currents."

"Okay, one large block it is then," I said. "Brom, can you organize the ropes while we get this cast?"

"On it," my stocky friend confirmed, lacking his usual humor.

With that part underway, I looked at Sars and Elandra. "We ready?"

"Soon as you are," Elandra replied.

"Yes," Sars confirmed. "Just aim it down and relatively close by, and then we will move out as it grows."

I guessed that kind of made sense. I hadn't used it yet, so this was going to be one hell of a learning curve.

"Drawing mana now," Sars said, and I nodded toward Elandra to start.

I'd used quite a bit of mana today, and the extra I'd received from my surges was starting to dip. Although I pulled more mana than I could have dreamed of before that late-night shower with Sienna, it wasn't nearly as much as I'd wished.

We worked together, three [Ice Blasts] joining to fashion an ice raft of sorts. Brom did as requested and organized the ropes and griffins, and before too long passed, we had all the rangers, warriors, and horses on the northern bank, ready to join the camp that had sprung up in our absence.

While ferrying the elves across, my mind wandered to the dead, whose friends were now fishing their bodies out of the river. I felt responsible, guilty even.

This had happened under my watch. Under our patrol. Though a few elves commended me for how I'd slain the sea drake, thanking me for avenging their comrades, I couldn't feel pride. All I could think of was that people had died. War was fucking awful. The sooner we took care of this mess, the better.

Chapter Eighteen

I walked into camp absolutely shattered. My core ached from depletion, and my legs felt like lead.

The elven army worked as efficiently as I'd expected. They had set up tents and perimeter, with traps and palisades, in quick time. They would take care of the night patrol, letting us rest and worry about the daytime scouting. My steps dragging like an old man's, I led Hestia across the makeshift pen area they had set up, and then collapsed to a seat by a fire, warming my hands from the chill of the evening and letting my body rest. Soon, Brom and Fitmigar sat next to me with steaming bowls of food. Brom had come prepared and passed one to me.

"Oh, that's perfect. Thanks, man," I said.

"Least I can do after the shit you had to deal with before."

"We lost a few—" I started.

Fitmigar cut me off, "We lost some, aye. But won't be losing any more thanks to you taking down that snake. We'll lose more, too. Everyone knows the risks, Jadyn, but don't make it your fault."

"Yeah, seriously," Brom added. "We did our best. You did your best. Don't whip yourself over what you couldn't have done."

"I know…" I shook my head, clearing away any morose thoughts, "and I'm sure the elves will honor them accordingly. Our job is just to keep the rest as safe as possible tomorrow."

"No more rivers, handsome," Brom said, a small smile appearing.

"That's true," I agreed, picking up some bread and taking a bite. After today, even the ration bread and simple soup tasted divine. The rest of our squad trickled in to join us by the fire, except for Mirek.

"Where's Mirek?" I asked, glancing around the camp.

"Already in one of the tents. They'd barely driven in the final peg before he shoved past them and dropped to the ground to sleep," Sars answered.

"Bit rude," Mallen added, shaking his head.

"I think he's just struggling a bit," I said. "He's got no magic, and other than the lance, he's not much of a fighter. Probably feels less prepared than those around him."

"Still no excuse," Mallen said.

I'm not sure I agreed, but I'd best catch-up with him in the morning. Let him know we had to stay sharp with the elves. Besides, we would soon be heading to fights much tougher than today's. Everyone would have to toughen up and figure out a way to deal with it, rather than wandering off and isolating themselves. Trying to handle the stress of combat alone was a losing battle, we'd all been taught that much.

"What's the plan for the rest of the night?" Syl asked.

"We've got an early start," I began, noticing Fitmigar taking a swig from a hip flask. Alcohol was another not-so-great way to deal with combat. "So best not to drink too much."

Fitmigar's shot me a look of defiance but then acquiesced and put the flask away. It might not be for long, but it was a start.

I'd noticed Syl looking apprehensive before, and Helstrom, too. I'd need to lift them up somehow. Most of us looked resolute, not upbeat per se. More than anything, the battle today had proven we had the strength to step up and protect our nation, and despite all the darkness and death, that knowledge had lit something inside many of us. Not everyone, though.

I wouldn't speak to them tonight, but I'd pull alongside them in the line tomorrow and talk through things. Hopefully, I could give them the boost they needed to be at their best when we met the challenge ahead.

Tonight, I had only one plan in mind. I'd depleted my mana with the ice raft stunt. But lucky me, it just so happened that there was a way I could relieve stress, enjoy my time with Sienna and Elandra, and prepare us for the upcoming war all in one blow. Or however many blows it took.

No one seemed up for much conversation, not after the sea drake, which made slipping away an easy decision. Sienna rested her head on my shoulder, and Elandra's hand had been homing in on my crotch for the last few minutes, so when I suggested we made a move, they quickly agreed.

"We're going to head off now, everyone. Make sure you're rested and fresh for tomorrow. We'll hopefully be joining up with the others again, so be your best selves."

Rising to my feet, I took one last look around the fire, and then I took both girls by the hand and eased them up. Sienna's eyes sparkled with excitement.

Elandra leaned into me and whispered, "About time."

We'd had tents set up by the elven forces. I'd had a discrete word to make sure mine was large enough for three but not to be shared with the others in our group. Leader responsibility cometh with leader privileges—something I was in dire need of right now.

As I pushed my way through the flaps of the tent, I pulled the girls in behind me. Both giggled softly at my urgency.

"We've been waiting for this all evening," Elandra said.

Sienna leaned in and pressed her lips against mine.

I felt the softness of her lips and pulled her closer, increasing the intensity of our kiss. As I slipped my hand around the back of her head, I felt hands move to my hips, tugging at the waist of my pants.

Sienna moaned and arched her back as I probed with my tongue, eager for release and the chance to forget the troubles of our day. Below, Elandra gasped as she pulled at my waist, my cock springing free as my pants lowered to the ground.

I kept Sienna close, our lips entwined. A tongue flicked the head of my cock, teasing me.

Hands cupped my balls, lips tensed around my shaft, and soft moans came from Elandra as the slow rhythm gradually picked up speed. Sienna pulled away, glanced at what was going on below, and smiled. She knelt beside Elandra.

Two gorgeous girls below me, pleasuring me, loving me. Both girls I loved. The view was intoxicating.

Fucking hells...

I set a hand on the back of each of my girls' heads, encouraging them closer. Elandra remained locked to my shaft, while Sienna took over the massaging of my balls, sliding her tongue across them. She took one into her mouth, sucking gently.

My knees tensed. I struggled to focus. Elandra's head bobbed back and forth, faster and faster. Sienna moaned beneath her.

It felt great, and I would've been glad if it had lasted hours, but a primal need arose within me. I knew the girls could feel it, too.

I growled, pulling both to their feet. "I need you both, now, tonight."

Elandra licked her lips. "Fuck yeah, Jadyn!"

I lowered myself to the blanket laid on the ground and pulled Sienna down. She placed a leg either side and lowered herself onto my cock, gasping as I entered her. Our hips touched. Hers went into motion immediately, rising and falling, grinding against my thrusts to push me deep inside her.

Elandra crawled over toward me a huge grin on her face, cheeks dark with a flush of arousal. "Gosh, you two look hot," she whispered.

Sienna moaned in answer.

I grunted.

While I thrust into Sienna's tightening pussy, Elandra placed her lips against mine. My tongue probed, eliciting a growl of delight from the girl. She then pulled away and smiled mischievously.

"None of that," I said and I grabbed the back of her legs, pulling her forward.

With a yelp, she fell on me. Her thighs squished the sides of my face, while her soaking hot sex sat on my lips. My tongue flicked out, running between her folds, tasting her excitement as Sienna cried out.

I'd been with both before, and there'd been others before that meant nothing, but I wasn't superhuman. Her pleasure cries did something funny to my brain and cock. Sienna's hump grew in desperation, her moans turning ecstatic, and all the while Elandra gyrated her gorgeous dark pussy against my mouth, whimpering out her own soft cries of pleasure as I sampled her lips.

Sienna came first, rocking back and screaming as she tensed up. Her insides tightened, shuddering against my shaft. I joined her, hot spurts streaming with my release.

Through the bliss and moans, for the first time, I actually felt the surge in my mana.

Sienna stayed frozen for a while as she came down, her breath catching in short bursts. Above my face, Elandra grew louder, pressing herself down harder against my mouth.

A minute or so after, Sienna slid off me, falling next to me, exhausted. I pushed myself up on my elbows, lowering Elandra down my chest.

"Already?" she asked, a huge grin appearing on her dark flushed face.

I didn't reply. I just eased her farther down my body, until she reached my waist, and my cock touched her lips. I then eased her up slightly and slid inside her soaking pussy, already rock hard and raging to go again sooner than I'd ever felt before. Perhaps it was the mana surge at work.

I could get used to this.

Elandra gasped, tensing around me as I rocked my hips upward, sinking into her and then out again, first slowly, then faster. Her gaze never left mine as we moved together.

Her breaths hitched with moans and gasps of ecstasy as I took her hard. Her fingers dug into my thighs.

Elandra bounced on my cock, her juicy wet ass and thighs making wet slaps against my hips. Her perfect dark breasts danced with sex, mesmerizing to watch.

Sienna, still breathless, slid fingers between her thighs as she watched us. "Take her, Jadyn. Fuck her senseless," she whispered, humping her own hand.

Girly moans built in volume as Elandra lost herself in the euphoria, as we connected in a way that made it feel like the mana flowed between us with every thrust.

I felt another orgasm building up and knew that Elandra was almost there, so I pushed faster, deeper, harder. Each thrust, I drove in until the hilt and squished her thighs to hug her against me, filling her with cock until her moans broke into a climaxing cry. Then, I let go and joined her, grunting as I shot my load inside her.

As we rocked, catching our breath, our chests pounding, Sienna moaned out beside us. Her legs and hips clenched as she joined us in orgasming.

We lay there for some moments, breathless, sweaty, relishing the glow.

As our bodies started to cook, Elandra gently slid herself off my body and snuggled to my left, with Sienna claiming my right. A warm glow ran through my body. I could sense my core was larger and denser than ever before.

I didn't yet understand how it was all happening, but I was damn thankful to land on an advantage like this. We needed every edge in the upcoming battles.

The fact the girls felt it, too, was equally as important to me. They were badass and strong in their own right. The enemy wouldn't know what hit them. Sienna had received [Fireball] and Elandra [Fire Elemental] from our union. Together, we would destroy anything that opposed us.

"That was perfect," Sienna murmured, running soft kisses across my chest. "I feel so full of life and energy."

"And warm, dripping cum," Elandra added, laughing softly and pressing her lips against me.

I smiled and lay back. "Wouldn't know what I'd do without you two."

"Plowing some random farmgirl? Or an elf?" Elandra chuckled.

I replied with an amused grin. "I meant to say, I'm glad you two are here. Glad we're doing this, despite the circumstances."

"The cum in my pussy circumstances?" Elandra asked, playing dumb. "I don't mind."

"We know, Jadyn," Sienna replied, running a hand across my chest, her fingers curling in the hair.

"Yeah yea, we're totally glad to have you, too, and would be aimless and aching if we didn't," Elandra added. "Going to need that cock of yours for the rest of our days, now that you've got us addicted."

"Happy to oblige," I said, smiling.

Some kisses and a bit of goofing off later, both girls were breathing softly next to me, sound asleep. I trailed my hand over their naked curves, lost in thought.

I remained that way, unable to sleep until a call of nature got my attention, pulling me from thoughts of companionship and war. All I had to gain. All I had to lose.

I hated disturbing them, but I needed to piss, so I slid my arms from under them, pulled on a shirt and pants, and crept out the front of the tent. Scanning the camp in the gloom, I took in how peaceful it all looked. A few fires burned low across the camp, and several elves sat in low discussion, or in some case dozing, perhaps due up next on watch.

I padded quietly around the side of my tent, fully intent on releasing there, when something caught my eye. Was that a figure hurrying through camp, a flaming torch in hand? They walked hunched over and avoided crowded areas, head swiveling left and right to keep an eye on the night watch.

Yeah, that's not right.

I turned and followed, stepping quietly on the balls of my feet like Brom had taught me. He would be so proud.

It wouldn't do to spook the suspicious sneak now. I needed to know if they were up to something, or just weirdly nervous.

The rest of the camp remained oblivious as I weaved stealthily between the tents, following the vaguely familiar silhouette. I avoided guide ropes and smoldering embers, keeping to the shadows. Must be what it felt like to my friend. A feeling of being invisible. Untraceable.

I paused when the figure did. They looked around, face shrouded in shadow, then bent down and put the flame to the bottom of a large tent. It was the one Harnell and Ryal had set up as a command tent, but it doubled as their sleeping quarters. Harnell and Ryal were the two most senior elves in the reinforcements Lord E'Lyn had sent.

The saboteur!

I gave up stealth and sprinted at them. The figure remained oblivious as I raced through the camp, focused on their task. I threw myself forward, tackling them to the ground.

We rolled across the grass. They swung out, the flaming torch swooshing past my face. I grabbed their wrists and found myself overpowering them.

Still, they struggled, bucking beneath me, growls coming from under the hood.

I pulled them up, and then forced them down, bouncing their head off the hard ground. The tent now caught light, flames starting to climb the sides, smoke seeping into the night sky.

"Fire!" I shouted. "Damn, bastard. You're in for one hell of a beating for..."

Their face appeared in the light of the fire, their eyes as pitch-black as the night.

I froze. "Mirek?"

Chapter Nineteen

Mirek snarled, tossing his head from side to side, his eyes as black as the void. The flaming torch slipped from his grip as he flailed, landing on another tent.

What the hells?

Shouts of alarm and commotion broke out. People dashed out of tents. Someone hurled water over the flaming tents.

I was still dumbstruck. Mirek was being controlled? How? As I stared at crazed boy beneath me, I noticed him curling in, arms crossing his chest, fingers protectively clasping over□—

The chain!

He was protecting the chain.

I pulled his arms away, forcing them to the side. Kneeling on his arms, I grabbed the chain. He screamed in defiance as I yanked it off.

The blackness left his eyes. The scream stopped. He went still under me, a bemused look on his face.

"Jadyn?"

"Just stay where you are, Mirek," I told him. "We need to work out what's going on."

His eyes flicked left and right, wide and afraid. He looked confused.

I ran a hand through my hair, taking it all in. All those incidents... the potions at the stores, the axle, the attack on Syl...

Mirek had access to Ralartis, too, which explained the injury. The griffin was fine with him after, though. She must have known he wasn't himself when he did what he did.

"Mirek," I said, getting his attention, "Where did you get the chain?"

He looked confused. "What chain?"

"The one you've been wearing, fidgeting with." I held it up before his eyes.

It took a moment, but then his mind seemed to clear. He must have been controlled in a way to make him unaware of its presence, or at least not to dwell on it.

"I got it from Rivers," he said.

"Rivers?" I asked, checking I hadn't misheard. "Beastkin Rivers?"

Mirek nodded. "Told me to wear it on our travels. Said it would keep me safe. What's happened, Jadyn? Why am I here? What have I done?"

He looked genuinely afraid.

"You've been controlled, Mirek. You've done some things. All those acts of the saboteur... that was you."

"Me? I don't understand."

"The chain, Mirek. It allowed someone to possess you. Make you do things. If my hunch is correct, it also allowed them to track our movements. It would explain the wolves, the bison, even the sea drake turning up just as we were crossing."

"I'm..." He looked down, head shaking. "I'm so sorry..."

I lifted myself from him, helping him to his feet. "It wasn't your fault."

"It doesn't change what's happened. I-I hurt Tordlum, I might've even killed him back in the stores."

"Well, you didn't. No lasting damage that we know off." I was as certain as I could be that the young man before me was innocent, but I had a whole group of friends that would help me make sure.

"Now, Mirek. I'm going to have to tie your wrists and ankles. We need to make sure everything adds up, OK?"

He nodded solemnly, accepting that this was the way we'd have to do things. I took the rope from Sars who now stood at my side and proceeded to do just that.

Now, I just needed to work out how to dispose of the chain.

By this point, the entire camp was up and alert, dawn still a couple of hours away. I sent most back to bed. We had a long day ahead of us, and this wasn't something that could be solved with numbers.

With my recent mana surge, I felt wide awake, so I took Mirek to an empty tent to question him further. Sienna and Elandra joined me, both feeling great after our recent tryst.

Satisfied that Mirek was innocent of any crimes, and forced to act by forces alien to him, I untied him. We'd be departing soon, and he could help break the camp with the others.

I pulled back the tent flaps and we exited to the early dawn light. The chill lingered, and I found myself wishing I'd questioned the young jousting tutor around a fire instead.

My worries about us being delayed were proven unfounded as I gazed upon a field devoid of tents and enclosures. The elven warriors were already lined up in orderly ranks, faultless in their positioning, and my squad waited off to the side. Hestia, Dawnquill, and Veo pawed impatiently at the ground, claws gouging the mud.

Only covered fire pits remained as proof of our presence. These elves had been taught well. Having met the imposing Lord E'Lyn, I could understand their high levels.

I walked over to the others, Sienna and Elandra at my side. Mirek followed a few steps behind, his head bowed.

"We good?" Fitmigar asked, and I nodded.

"Mirek was never at fault here. Everyone understand?" I said, looking around the group. "The matter was dealt with and doesn't go beyond us."

The affirmative responses came swiftly, accompanied by more than a tinge of relief. Although we'd all hoped we weren't being sabotaged from within, we'd all considered the possibility. It felt good to know someone else had been at fault.

Now, we just needed to find out who.

I took a moment to stroke Hestia's neck feathers before climbing up. She was itching to depart and so was I.

"OK. Form up around the main column of elves, and I'll confirm with Nerimyn, Harnell, and Ryal that everyone's ready to go."

"Certainly fuckin' looks like they are," Brom said.

I smiled. "Gonna check anyway, buddy."

With that, I nudged Hestia forward. We approached the front of the elven line.

The three elves were waiting with Ella, and all four looked up as I approached.

"We good to go?" I asked.

"Just been waiting on you, Jadyn. All good with the fire situation?" Nerimyn asked.

"I'll fill you in more on the way, but essentially, one of ours was possessed by the enemy."

"How?" Ryal inquired from his horse.

"Through a chain, a necklace. A cursed item of some kind? Not sure how it worked. Part of me wants to explore it further, see how it worked, but without the expertise to hand, it might be best to just destroy it." A thought struck me. "You don't have anyone here that can inspect magical items at all, do you?"

Harnell spoke up, his turn to respond it seemed. "Not here in the column. We could send someone back to Birchvale with it?"

I sighed. "With the bridge out that won't work. Plus, they'd run the risk of being possessed or being tracked back to your city and putting everyone in danger." I thought for a moment. "I think I have a better idea."

Without giving them a chance to question me further, I threw the chain to the ground and formed [Fireball] in my hand.

Nerimyn coughed. "Before you do that. What if destroying it alerts whoever it is that their magic has been discovered?"

"Is there a better way?" I asked, happy to take suggestions from the ranger who I'd quickly come to trust.

"This might sound silly, but can't we just throw it in the river? It will likely still show as working, and perhaps it might give us the chance to get farther in our journey before they discover we are on to them?"

"If it gives us the chance to gain an advantage, no matter how small, I'm willing to try it," I said, dropping off Hestia. "Bear with me a moment."

I walked across the field and reached the riverbank. There, I brought my arm back and hurled the chain out into the fast-flowing waters of the River Yorn.

With that taken care of, I nodded to Nerimyn and pulled myself back onto Hestia.

"We're going to need to send a message to the academy somehow, too. There are people there that may have nefarious motives."

Nerimyn nodded. "That's something we can arrange for you."

I nodded in thanks, and we took off northwest, toward the rest of the fourth-year Griffin Knights.

If what Galen had told me came to pass, we would meet up with the main column sometime after lunch. If they'd encountered similar issues as the sea drake, they might be running behind. But assuming only Mirek wore a chain, maybe they'd escaped unscathed.

As we rode, I pulled my overshirt tighter around myself. This cold made my very bones ache. I wasn't sure I'd ever understand how the dwarven population of Atania survived in these climes. Then again, from what Fitmigar had told me, they dug deep into the mountains, heading underground to find warmth.

The constant cold did explain, at least, why they always seemed so grumpy.

We switched to a four-up scouting cycle on the march, to put more eyes in the sky. Our surroundings were only slightly hillier than before, but the proximity to front-lines warranted extra caution. The ground was growing hardier, and the plains were broken up by hills and rock formations. The area was perfect for ambushes, but everything looked clear from up high. I suspected part of it was thanks to us putting a stop to whoever had been controlling Mirek's actions.

Still, we remained alert. We were approaching the war. People were going to start dying soon. Those elves at the river already had. I couldn't afford to let the same to happen to my friends. I couldn't relax now. With the general mood growing tense, we rode past lunch and ate on saddleback, seeing no point in delaying our reunion with the main column any longer. Syl and Helstrom appeared troubled, so I dropped back between them.

"How are you both doing?" I asked.

"I'm scared," Syl admitted, his honesty taking me by surprise. "Not sure how Father will cope if I don't make it through this."

"Aye," Helstrom added, "only the thought of carrying on the Ironmantle name keeps me going."

Hold on…

Ironmantle?

How did I not know this?

"Helstrom, are you only telling me now that you and Fitmigar are family?"

"Aye, Jadyn, but only first cousins."

"Only," I scoffed. "Better to find out now than never, I suppose."

I'd never seen a sheepish look on a dwarven face before, but Helstrom did a good job of creating one now. Bloody hells.

"But we'll be fine," Helstrom said, patting his friend on the shoulder. "Got each other's backs, aye?"

"Ah. Aye." Syl grinned back. "And together, we've got Atania's."

"Damn right we do!"

I looked both over, seeing their determination blossom before my eyes. We'd all been taught well. We all knew the risks. Some might have more to lose than others, but we all approached this as an opportunity to save lives. To protect those who couldn't protect themselves.

I didn't need to bring Syl and Helstrom up. No, we all brought each other up. Every conversation. Every word. It intertwined, tying us into a knot that no enemy could untie. We were Griffin Knights, and no matter how many monsters they sent our way, we would prevail.

Of that, I had no doubt.

It felt kind of expected that the first voice I heard once we'd spotted the others was Lana's, boasting about the way she'd guided the rest of the main column over a bridge that her story painted as even more perilous than a collapsed one.

Typical…

I immediately sought out Galen. Upon realizing that both groups had missed lunch, we found a spot to recuperate and take in some much-needed food and fluids. The brief stop also was a good moment to compare journeys and also introduce Galen and Algernon to Nerimyn, Ella, Harnell, and Ryal.

It turned out that the others had had it easy. After Glymavor had used replaced the broken axle, they made rather serene progress. One of the triplets, Oscar, had reported spotting something swimming under the bridge and on downstream as they crossed. However, no one else reported the same and so they had carried on.

It soon came to my turn to fill in my instructors.

"Where should I begin?" I asked. "The bison charge, the attack on Syl, meeting Lord E'Lyn and the elven army, the sea drake attack and subsequent loss of lives, or the discovery of the saboteur?"

The elven instructor's mouth dropped open, and Algernon shook his head beside him, seemingly in disbelief. Galen shook his head, eyes wide. "Start from the moment you left us and run through it from there."

We spent the next half-hour going over our journey. Galen and Algernon remained silent for the most part. The pair only interjected with the odd question when they wanted more information, be it the black eyes of the bison or the exact timeline of events from when we first spied the sea drake to its consequent expiration.

By the time we had finished our catch-up, lunch was over and we were ready to move again. Due to our proximity now to the border, and the fact we had a larger force, all forty griffins and mages present, we sent up large patrols, scanning the area for marauding orcs or scouting wyverns.

The ground was becoming more uneven every step we took. The wagons bounced around on the rocks and the horses grew wary with their steps. The griffins weren't bothered. Their paws and talons found sure grip effortlessly on any terrain.

I pulled in alongside Enallo for a bit. I wanted to speak with each of the other squad leaders briefly. Although their journey had sounded relatively straightforward, I still thought it might be beneficial to run through it with them, also passing on our own journey details. Yes, Galen would likely share what he thought relevant, but I wanted to ensure they were all as up to date and knew what to watch out for.

Bernolir came next, and the dwarf was keen to hear of our adventures. He chuckled when asked that he wasn't related to Fitmigar and Helstrom, but I had to check, right?

Last was the unenviable task of delivering the news to Lana.

I approached her from behind, admiring her form as she rode. Her tight ass and muscular thighs hugged the back of her griffin, wrapped up in those skintight pants of the female Knights. Her red braids bounced against her slender back, drawing my eye to her narrow waist.

I flicked my gaze away, admonishing myself. It wouldn't do for her to catch me ogling her form. Was fucking Sienna and Elandra turning my brain hornier than normal?

"Lana?" I started, pulling up alongside the earth mage squad leader who boasted twelve spells of her own. Boasted. Repeatedly.

"Jadyn."

I mulled over how to pass on the details of our travels without the redhead trying to turn it into some kind of competition. It turned out I needn't have worried. I went first, describing our travails, and perhaps for the first time, Lana realized she couldn't top something.

Or maybe she didn't want to turn a story about twenty dead elves into a competition. Either way, I appreciated her tact for once.

That didn't stop her from being aloof with me, dismissing me out of hand with a quick: "Good to know."

Her tone may have been dismissive, but I could sense her mind working overtime. It was a lot to pass on, and with the confirmation of mind control at work, it gave an extra level of threat.

I'd just dropped back into line and discussion with Brom and Fitmigar when a shout came from above.

"Hawk!"

"That be a tunnel hawk," Fitmigar noted with delight as the bird approached. "Could be news from me dad. Maybe he's had a change of heart and sending assistance!"

"Let's hope so," I said. With the loss of the elves, any unexpected help would be welcome.

Interlude 4

Warchief Ugrea's second vision had arrived the night previous. Now, rather than heading directly to the battle, joining in the fight against the pitiful specimens from south of the border, they had been routed towards the southerners' mountain range.

The dwarven mountain range paled in comparison to the Grikk mountains of the Kre'Hrez clan's home. But then again, everything south of their home was weak and lesser, wasn't it?

Ugrea's vision had shown him leading his clan against the mountain dwarves in a fortress set deep in a mountain pass, once again three thick stripes of blue warpaint running across his face. The route ahead was perilous, through a huge labyrinthine stone quarry.

Not one they wouldn't overcome, though. Nothing compared to the challenges of home.

Useless, scheming thoughts didn't really cloud Ugrea's head, but somehow he knew that to take this fortress would help to win the war.

The fortress was a choke point. The only way dwarven reinforcements could reach the battles lines. Unlike the weak Dreiz, warchief of the Kre'Speiw clan, Ugrea would do something meaningful to thank his new master for guiding visions.

He would kill the dwarves and collapse the fort on the passageways below, defeating a third of the enemy in one blow.

No more dwarves would reach the battle. Ugrea knew his master would be pleased.

The orcs streamed from the surrounding mountains and through the labyrinth like a black tsunami, led by a huge orcish warchief, blue warpaint across his ferocious features. They caught the dwarven reinforcements unawares. Axe met spear, roar met defiant roar. Blood and death painted the quarry.

Realizing their peril before the overwhelming numbers, Thrargud called for a retreat. The dwarves formed up ranks, retreating into the tunnels of the towering quarry fortress.

Only, it hadn't been enough.

Now, with barely a third of his forces remaining, Thrargud Ironmantle backed up toward the imposing stone doors of the fort. He hurled boulders with his magic and crushed skulls with his twirling war hammer from the front, standing together with his battle brothers and sisters.

He crushed an orc into pulp as he backed up, blood and brain spattering against the dark stone walls of the approach.

"Everyone inside!" he roared as he pulled the ground apart in another section, the orcs chasing them down falling into the newly created chasm below.

Thrargud wobbled on his feet, feeling the ache of mana depletion in his core. The last few dwarven stragglers limped past, bleeding from cuts as they held others on their feet.

Then, no more dwarves came.

Sighing deeply, he pulled on his dwindling mana and collapsed the archway behind them. It would hold off the attackers, at least for a moment.

There would still be dwarves out in the quarry, fighting for their lives, but they could not be helped. Hard decisions had to be made. With grim determination, Thrargud entered the fort and the huge, stone doors were slid closed and barred. They were trapped. To retreat farther out the rear of the fort would allow the orcs to follow, potentially reaching their homes, their families, in the mountains. That wouldn't do. No, they would hold them here until assistance arrived.

Whatever it took.

Chapter Twenty

The tunnel hawk drifted down, landing on Fitmigar's outstretched arm. The whole column had paused. News from the frontline could very well change the course of our reinforcements. Fitmigar ran a hand down the bird's head and back in perhaps the gentlest manner I'd ever seen from her. She untied the message from the bird's leg, slid off the ribbon, and unrolled it. As her eyes scanned down, the furrows in her forehead deepened.

"Gah! Orcish scum!" she roared.

Gasps and uproar broke out from the entire column.

"What is it, Fitmigar?" I asked. This didn't sound at all like the good news we'd hoped for. She clenched her fists and gritted her teeth into a scowl. "Damn orc warband taken the passageways 'round Brickblade Fort. Killed hundreds of reinforcements heading to assist in the war, trapping Father and others in the fort."

"We will help them," I assured her. "We need all the help we can get in this war. Does your father say anything else?"

"After being trapped, they discovered smaller wyrms in the tunnels beneath the fort. Worried more will arrive. Bigger ones. They be trapped inside fighting monsters they can't hope to compete with."

I whistled, alerting the entire column that we needed to take a break. We would need to put our heads together to work out the best plan going forward. It looked like we'd have to split our forces again to deal with this.

While the column rested, a fire was lit and the squad leaders, instructors, and elven leadership gathered around it. Galen spoke first, "So, we have quite the situation to deal with here. We are close to the war now, but it appears again that other needs have arisen. And we have no time to delay our actions."

"How many can we spare?" I asked.

"From the numbers expressed in Fitmigar's letter, I am inclined to believe we may have to halve our griffin rider forces. Two squadrons to the fort, the remaining two to continue to the front."

"Which two?" Lana asked.

"I'd like to put us forward, sir," I said.

Galen nodded. "Makes sense with your pair of Ironmantles."

"Anyone else?"

Bernolir stood. "Aye, sir. My squad, too. I might not be a Ironmantle, but those are still my mountains. My people. And I have strong magic that should assist."

"That OK with you both?" Galen asked Enallo and Lana. Both nodded in agreement, though Lana now seemed a little despondent. Perhaps she was disappointed she wouldn't get the chance to outshine me. Ridiculous.

Harnell rose to his feet to address us all, "We cannot, in good grace, allow you all to take on this task alone. Ryal here will lead fifty of our elven reinforcements with you. Due to the urgency of your mission, and the fact that whoever remains can travel no faster than the wagons here, all that go with you will be on horseback."

Galen nodded. "That seems sensible enough. And thank you."

Nerimyn spoke next, "Ella here will also accompany you. I am aware that you have those amongst you with the knowledge needed to get you there quickly, but she has skills you may find beneficial. I'm sure she will be happy to fill you in on the way?" Nerimyn looked to his compatriot, and she smiled and nodded.

"Absolutely." She looked as serious as ever.

"Then organize yourselves and head out immediately." Galen said. "You can discuss the plan as you go." Our two squads pulled our armor from the wagon Thom had been dragging along. We'd traveled light previously to make the travel more comfortable and speedy, but now we donned the traditional griffin knight armor.

As Griffin Knights of Atania we wore light gray steel with a gleaming matte finish. On top of our reinforced clothes and mail, we donned chest plates, vambraces, poleyns, greaves, and our open-faced helmets decorated with griffin wings on the side.

"You think twenty of us is enough?" Sienna asked from alongside me as she pulled her chest plate down.

"It's all we can afford to send," I said, frowning. "It's going to have to be."

"I'll kill 'em all myself," Fitmigar fumed from alongside us.

"We're right with you," I promised.

The dwarf nodded aggressively and pulled herself back onto Gren. She was serious at the best of times, but this was something more. I made a mental note to keep an eye on her. I didn't want her to get blinded by lust for vengeance. Soon, twenty griffins bearing twenty mages stood ready for war, all armored and armed with lances and secondary weapons. Fifty-one elven warriors sat on horseback, all armed with bows and blades.

"OK," Bernolir called at my side, "let's move out."

I saluted the rest of the party, wishing them good luck as they traveled on toward the border. They too would face harder odds than we'd bargained for, with fewer elves and griffins. I took a good long look at the faces of my peers, trying to etch and every one into memory, just in case.

Some hugged in departure. Others spoke quiet words. The mood was different than when we'd split off to fetch the elves. Graver.

An hour into the ride, we took a left-hand fork in the track and headed westward, crossing the Yorn again soon after, this bridge far sturdier than the one destroyed earlier. We headed towards the looming wall of snow-capped peaks. The ground immediately became rockier, and the temperature dropped as we ascended a slowly steepening incline.

Bloody cold.

I rubbed my hands, glancing around. The mood was solemn, anxious. Something had to be done, so I made an effort to travel up and down the line, talking to all.

Syl seemed a little nervous, so I did my best to lift his spirits. Fitmigar was focused, determined, but I took the chance to remind her again that we were there with her.

Sars joined me as I spoke to Fitmigar, pulling his notebook out as I questioned her on what we could expect to find when we arrived.

"Brickblade Fort be located in a narrow pass near the end of the mountain range," she started, and Sars began noting everything down.

"Reinforcements would have traveled there, resting overnight, would have continued onward through the quarry beyond. Normally well-guarded, so how these orcs got the drop on them..."

"What's the actual fort like?" I asked. That was where most if not all surviving dwarves would be located.

"As wi' most dwarven buildings, there's as much below ground, cut into the rock, as there is above. Floors of tight tunnels lead to surface, and then towers rise into sky, four stories up."

"And is there a way of us getting into those tunnels unnoticed?" I asked. It sounded like a preferable way to cutting our way through an orcish horde.

"Aye. But they be not large enough for our griffins to enter."

Fuck.

"Okay. So, we'll need to split up. We can bombard the quarry first, rescuing any dwarves holed up there, but then we'll likely need to leave our griffins and take to the tunnels. Especially if the orcish forces have entered the fort, which I hope to hells that they haven't."

"Guess we'll find out soon enough," Sars said, putting his notebook back in his pocket.

Fitmigar growled and headed back to join Brom, a crazed smile crossing her face as I noticed him greet her.

"Sars, can you head over and talk to Mallen. He'll hopefully have some ideas on how best to utilize the elves. I'll talk to Ryal in the meantime and see if he suggests the same."

"Right on it, Jadyn." Sars joined his elven friend's side.

I rode to the rear of the column, encouraging Hestia along as we approached the leader of our elven allies. Along the way, I gestured to Bernolir, and my fellow squad leader joined me.

"Jadyn," the elf greeted, nodding as we pulled up. "Bernolir."

"Ryal. We just wanted to see how best we can use your assistance," I said.

He nodded. "All of the elves you see before you have been trained in both swordfighting and ranged weaponry. It is up to you to see how best they fit your plans."

"The quarry not be easy. Not with the way it forces fights into narrow corridors," Bernolir said. "Best half, at least, remain outside, pick off attackers from distance."

"And the other half?" Ryal asked.

"Led by meself, Fitmigar, and Helstrom. We'd be best understanding how walkways be followed."

"That works," I said. "We don't know exactly what we'll find, so be ready to adapt as required, but that is a good starting point."

Sienna and Elandra were my final stop on the column. The pair greeted me with firm, resolute looks.

"How are you both doing?" I asked.

"Determined—" Sienna started.

"And ready to fuck up some orcs," Elandra finished.

I beamed. "Too, right."

I paused for a moment, running a hand through my hair.

"I'm sorry, we haven't had the chance to practice your new magics as much as I'd hoped," I said.

"We wanted to talk to you about that, actually," Sienna said, and I leaned closer.

"Yeah, we took the chance to practice together before while you were filling in the others before we split from the main group," Elandra continued.

Sienna smiled and twirled her fingers, the ball of fire on her palm gradually increasing in size. "Seems our latest mana surge is really something."

My mouth dropped open in awe.

She smiled as she dismissed the casting, the mana returning into her body.

"And check this out," Elandra added, bouncing on Veo's back, full of energy. She concentrated for a moment, and then an elemental in the form of a fire-born mouse appeared on her hand before running up her arm and sitting on her shoulder.

"Oh, that's amazing," I said as Elandra pulled the casting, only a small amount of mana dissipating into the air.

"I'd better up my game," I said, "otherwise, I won't be needed anymore."

"Hah!" Elandra grinned. "There's plenty of you we need." I didn't miss the way she looked me up and down.

"The connection's increasing, too," Sienna added. "We could feel you approach."

"I could sense you in the line, too," I told them. "I feel like I always know where you are."

"Good. You can't lose us then," Elandra said, giggling.

"No fear of that happening, girls," I said, smiling at both as I pulled farther up the line.

Content after having checked on everyone, I rode on with my own thoughts, until Ella pulled up alongside me. "How's it going?" I asked.

She seemed a little reserved, hesitant to broach whatever topic she had come to discuss. "OK, thank you."

I decided to save time and be forthright.

"Nerimyn said you had something you wanted to talk about?"

"That's true," she replied.

"And that is?" I pressed.

"I suppose you'd like to know about my magic?"

"If you feel up to talking about it," I replied.

"I'd prefer to show you, but time won't allow currently."

OK? That got my interest piqued. "That rules out most of what I'd consider the norm."

Ella took a deep breath. "I can shapeshift."

Holy fuck.

"Wow. That's amazing!" Of all the students currently enrolled at Griffin Academy, there was no one there with that branch of magic. "Into what? If you don't mind me asking?"

She smiled. Maybe the change of subject was doing her good.

"No people as of yet, if that's what you want to know. I started with small animals – birds, voles, fieldmice – but then as I learned to control the magic, practicing and increasing my core and pathways, I learned larger ones."

"Such as?" I asked, intrigued.

"First, it was rabbits, foxes… then a wolf."

"And now?" I asked.

"A jaguar," she told me, a soft smile appearing.

"That's amazing!"

"It is," she admitted, blushing a bit at my enthusiasm. "I can only hold it for around five minutes currently, but as I grow and increase my mana, longer changes and bigger animals will come easier."

"So, your future could be one of bears or larger?"

She smiled and shrugged. "Who knows. Dragons maybe."

Fuck…

This was mind-blowing. Shapeshifting. That would be an amazing asset against our enemies.

It was a lot to think about, so I thanked the elf ranger and moved on to have some thinking time alone. We were making good time without walkers or wagons to slow us, so I needed to figure out a plan for when we arrived. More accurately *when* we'd arrive. It was all well and good thinking we'd immediately spring into action, but if we arrived after nightfall, plans would have to change. When my thoughts inevitably started running to dead-ends, I located Helstrom and Fitmigar.

"How much longer until we arrive?" I asked. The ground had grown steeper over the preceding hours, the temperature colder, but the mountains still appeared a good distance away.

"A few hours yet," the dwarf replied, shaking his head. Fitmigar still had that antsy, battle-lusty fire in her eyes alongside him.

"Means we'll arrive after dusk," I noted, grimacing. "And if we pick up the pace too much, we'll be nigh on useless when we get there."

"True," Helstrom acknowledged.

"OK. So, we keep our current pace, camp close enough to the fort that we arrive early in the morning and rest as best we can before the battle. No fires."

My face fell. Dwarves were going to die because we couldn't get there quickly enough.

Fitmigar seemed to read my thoughts. "It won't make much difference," she said, seemingly trying to reassure me. "Those dwarves caught in the quarry will either have expired by now or found one of the hidden tunnels that take you back under the fort."

"So, unless the orcs break into the fort during the night, nothing will change?"

The dwarf nodded.

OK, so was a little reassuring. With a better idea now of what we'd need to do, I spoke with Bernolir, then Ryal and Ella, before I passed on the latest plans to the entire party of griffin knights, Ryal filling in the elves.

Over the hours that followed, Bernolir and I made the decision to pull the aerial watch. We might already be too late, but we didn't want orcish forces knowing of our imminent approach.

The light was dwindling now, and by the time we made camp, the light was barely enough to set everything up. Any firelight would light the skies and stand out to anyone watching, so we ate dry rations and wrapped up as warm as we could. Blankets were shared between the groups, and several griffin knights chose to sleep leaning against their griffins, wings wrapped around them to keep the cold at bay.

I did the same as midnight rolled around. However, I found my mana still surged high, and my adrenaline pumped at the upcoming battle. Sleep didn't come. I remined at Hestia's side, however, feeling her powerful heart beating against her chest, trying to relax.

"We've got our biggest battle yet coming up later today, girl."

She nuzzled against me, chuffing sympathetically. She understood my sentiment if not the words directly.

"We'll have to part ways at some point," I warned, "but I trust you to continue to fight in my absence."

I'd spoken with Bernolir earlier in the day, and we'd decided that both squads entering the tunnels beneath the fort was too much. Bernolir's squad would instead remain outside, fighting in the quarry and the surrounding mountains, while we entered the underground to rescue the trapped dwarves.

As I lay there, contemplating tomorrow, a loud boom shook the air.

I jumped to my feet.

What the hells?

I rushed through our makeshift camp, trying to locate my stocky friend. Seeing Brom appear from a tent, Fitmigar at his side, I jogged across the uneven ground.

"[Shadow Cloak] up, buddy. We need you to find out what's going on. Just a quick fly-by. Can't have you using up all your mana on that and [Night Vision]."

Brom nodded. "On it, Jadyn." No humor, no relaxed stature. Brom meant business.

The shadow mage was there one moment and gone the next. The soft sound of flapping wings was the only sign of his departure. The rest of us settled down to wait, pulling blankets tighter to keep the chill at bay.

Another boom sounded twenty minutes later or so, this accompanied by a soft glow in the sky. Fitmigar stood next to me.

"I fear I know what they be tryin' to do," she whispered.

I turned to look at her, waiting for her to finish.

"They mean to bring down the fort."

Chapter Twenty-One

"They want to do what now?" I asked, eyes wide in shock.

"The fort," Fitmigar repeated, shaking her head. "They mean to bring it down."

"So, they don't want to take it?"

"If they can't get inside, they'll try to blow it. Block the whole route from the mountains. Cut the dwarves off from rest of country."

"So, it'll stop any dwarves joining in with the war efforts," I realized. Damn. That could be devastating. Before Fitmigar could continue, a brief breeze passed my face, and I turned to my left. "Brom."

[Shadow Cloak] dispersed, and my friend appeared on Shadowtail, panting, urgency etched on his face.

"Jadyn, they're□—"

"Trying to bring down the fort?" I finished.

"How did you"—he shook his head—"never mind. They've got an orc shaman, and he's using spells to try and bring down the walls of the quarry."

"Not the fort?" I asked.

Brom shook his head. "Looks like they're trying to bring the walls down on top of the fort, so far without much luck. There's plenty of magic being thrown but the fort stands."

"They be magically strengthened walls," Fitmigar said.

"So, they'll not fall to the shaman's spells?" I asked.

"Aye. They'll need to be coercing a dwarf earth mage to do it for them."

"Then we really have no time to waste," I said.

"Aye, we need to leave now," Fitmigar stressed.

"Agreed," I said. "Round everyone up. Pack the things. We move out now. It will have to be relatively slowly until the light improves. We don't want anyone tumbling down the mountainside. Brom, we'll need you at the front leading. You still have [Night Vision] going?"

He nodded.

"Good. Then keep it so. Going to need you to lead us close."

"Understood," he said, turning in the low moonlight and heading over to join the others.

The entire group was ready within moments. We set out, climbing ever closer in the darkness.

The sun began to lighten the rocky cliffs and slopes. The tops of the fortress' towers came into view beyond the next hill.

I dropped off Hestia as we neared the edge. Crouching low, I crawled to the lip of the quarry. Bernolir, Fitmigar, Brom, and Helstrom joined me.

"The shaman is going to be our biggest problem here," I began. "The orcs have spears, but we're relatively safe at range. The shaman, however…"

"Aye," Bernolir replied. "He be firing off spells at us as soon as we show our faces."

"We take him first then," Helstrom added simply.

I paused to contemplate the best way to play this out. "OK. So, our first problem is locating him. The second is how we deal with him."

"He be there." Fitmigar pointed.

There, on the opposite side of the quarry, a staff-wielding orc in a flowing red robe directed the other orcs around to sections in the rock face. "OK, so☐—"

That was as far as I got. I heard a groaning grunt. Then a huge section of the rock face collapsed, crushing the orc shaman to a pulp. Several other orcs unfortunate enough to be near were caught in the rock fall.

Aah… [Rock Fall].

I turned to Bernolir at my side, and he panted, looking weary. "Problem solved."

I gaped at him, about to admonish him for costing us the advantage of stealth.

But my worries were proven wrong. Orcs near to the devastation seemed to be of the opinion that an accident had transpired, rather than assuming assistance had arrived for the trapped dwarves.

"OK, so with that taken care of—thanks, again, Bernolir—we move onto our next issue. This labyrinth that leads to the fort doors. The main orcish force is based at those doors, but we can see from here that there are plenty in the walkways that lead there."

My three dwarven companions and Brom nodded in agreement.

"OK. So, we have the option of approaching at ground level, sneaking up from the labyrinth and catching the orc main force unawares, flying in on griffinback and laying waste, or a mixture of the two."

"We have elves, too," Bernolir reminded me.

"That we do," I acknowledged. "So, elven archers lining the side, perhaps half of the fifty, shooting down into the labyrinth, the other half approaching through those passageways, and then half of our griffin knights attacking the main force at the fort entrance."

"And the other half?" Helstrom asked.

"Well, we'll be taking to the tunnels underneath." We'd be split four ways, but it was our greatest chance of success. The elves could secure the approach, should the orcs receive reinforcements mid-battle, and we could deal with the main threat.

"Who'll lead the elves through the labyrinth if we otherwise occupied?" Bernolir asked, scratching at his beard.

Luckily, I had already considered this. "Ella. She was recommended by Nerimyn after all. Helstrom, if you can go and fill her in, detailing the route required, I am sure she will be fine."

The dwarf disappeared to detail the approach to the elven ranger.

While the messages were delivered and orders spread, we spent a few moments scanning the battleground, trying to calculate enemy's numbers.

"Time's up, everyone," I called, when everyone was ready. "Let's go!"

I felt a huge sense of pride in my squad as they lined up before me, griffins majestic, their armor pristine, their eyes determined. Without a sound, we separated into four distinct groups, ready to attack.

"We have to get into the tunnels and up into the fort. We just removed a single shaman threat, but we fear there will be more, and without the ability to bring the fort down themselves, they are going to need to control the dwarves trapped inside to do their bidding," I explained.

"We have a dwindling amount of time to do all this. So, squad, we'll fly by once, hitting the main force by the fort's entrance, and then, Bernolir, if your squad can continue to harry them, we'll land around the side while they're distracted, and Fitmigar will lead us into the tunnels."

"Griffins will return to assist us, right?" Bernolir asked, and I nodded at the dwarf.

"That they will, Bernolir." I turned and addressed the griffin knights again. "Now, select your first casting, hold it in place, and let's move out!"

Twenty griffins started to run downhill, gaining speed. Their wings spread, catching the wind and lifted us up. We turned toward the orcish forces.

As Hestia pulled us up into the golden dawnlit sky, I watched the elven forces split below us. Half of the horses rode to the lip of the quarry, while the half led by Ella galloped into the labyrinthine passages of the quarry.

I returned my attention to the fortress looming above the narrow mountain passage. Cold winds streamed past my face, forcing me to squint. Still, I could make out the fort's huge stone doors, surrounded by a swarming horde of orcs that tried to slam battering rams and hammers against them.

I pulled hard on my mana, selecting [Fire Wall*]. I didn't know how much mana I'd need inside the fort, but it was important to hit these forces hard to soften them up for the others.

"Spells ready!" I shouted.

Magic bloomed in the hands of two squads of Griffin Knights, ice, fire, lightning, stone, and air.

Orcish faces turned our direction. Fingers pointed up. Several threw spears into the sky.

A [Wind Wall] blasted out, throwing them all off course. The rest of us released our barrage.

Earth split beneath the orcs' feet. A firewall swept through the disoriented forces. Lightning boomed amongst the ranks, sending warriors flying. Fireballs detonated, clearing out large swathes of the force. Ice and earth engulfed those on the outskirts of the burnt forces, herding them into the pen of destruction.

Black plumes rose from the inferno, filling the sky with the stench of burnt fur and skin.

With our opening barrage released, we swept in to secure the area. Brom dove in low enough that Shadowtail could eviscerate orcs with claw and talon, tearing heads from shoulders in showers of dark blood. Mallen released [Lightning Bolt]s up close that blasted apart orcish heads and chests, and Elandra and Sars followed up with [Water Burst] sweeping them off their feet to be picked off by Sienna and Syl's [Gale Force]-imbued arrows.

As Rammy and Helstrom flew by and released roaring [Fireball]s, we turned and followed Gren and Fitmigar to the tunnels. The sounds of battle filled the air behind us. I hoped we had done enough and hadn't just left them to die, but we had to hurry. Now that the orcs knew we had arrived, they too would no doubt take desperate measures to win.

Fitmigar guided us back down the mountain and around the left-hand side of the fort. Gren's wings slowly eased, and we lowered to the ground near a copse of trees near the base of the mountains.

My dwarven friend slid off Gren's back and walked across to a huge stone slab. A pile of sticks and autumn leaves lay to the side, recently swept off the stone. I prayed it had been the dwarves who had survived the initial orcish attack.

I hopped off Hestia and joined Fitmigar's side. Together with Rammy's assistance, we pushed the slab aside. Crude steps led into impenetrable darkness beyond. I turned and patted Hestia's cheek. "I'll be back in a bit. Go get them, girl!"

Hestia screeched. Leading the other griffins, she tore off into the low light of the morning, heading back to the battle above.

"Is there any way to get some light inside?" I asked.

"Magically linked," Fitmigar explained. "[Fireball] the first, and then the rest will light up in response as that magic-wielder moves on."

I went to pull on my mana, but Sienna moved past me, placing a hand on my arm. "I've got this."

She tensed a little, formed a ball of roiling flame in her palm, and tossed it onto the first sconce. A soft glow bloomed, lighting up the first thirty or so feet of the rough stone tunnel. "Weapons out, magic ready, let's move," I said.

We formed up, Sienna and I leading the way. The cavernous rocky tunnels were easy to follow and gently sloped, gradually rose back toward the surface. They branched off every now and then, but Fitmigar knew the way and kept us on track. At the first crossroads, we encountered our first dead dwarf.

I placed a hand on Fitmigar's arm to stay there, then headed over to inspect the body. Fitmigar turned away momentarily before turning back, her face resolute.

The dwarf's left leg was missing, bitten off by something. He had battled hard, though. Dark ichor of something inhuman coated his mace.

I looked at the others as they gathered around in the low light.

"Something is in here with us, and it's no orc. Keep your eyes on a swivel as we continue."

We quickened our pace and soon passed another pair of deceased dwarves, lying in death, back-to-back, their final act taking a ten-foot-long wyrm with them on their journey to the dwarven afterlife. Helstrom growled as he dropped to a knee and said a swift prayer for the fallen.

"The blood isn't dried," said Brom. "This had to be recent."

"These may be our survivors," I said.

We hastened our pace, ears and eyes open for any signs of struggle or life. I hoped we weren't too late, but considering the corpses so far, it didn't look good. "Cavern up ahead," Fitmigar called as we crested another incline.

I couldn't be certain, but I estimated that we had to be over halfway to the surface by now. One tunnel admittedly felt like the next, but the air seemed to be getting a little less dusty and easier to breathe.

As the tunnel widened, multiple sconces burst into light. A wide cavern lit up before us, easily a hundred feet across, though the ceiling couldn't have been more than twenty-five feet up. *Perfect. Wide and low...*

Shouts echoed from up ahead, from the gloom beyond the light. We broke into a run and raced towards the sound. A sudden scream from behind me halted my step.

I spun to see Sars on his knees, acid sizzling through the armor and clothes of his left arm, burning into his skin.

"Wyrm!" I shouted.

The beast that had ambushed Sars now charged him. Mallen dashed in to save him, too slow.

I sprinted in to help but knew I wouldn't make it.

Arrows flew overhead, striking the wyrm in the head and body. Another volley rained in right after. The wyrm recoiled, its charge stopped.

I glanced back and gave Sienna and Syl a thumbs-up. Those were some clutch arrows.

"Elandra!" I called, still running to Mallen's side. "[Ice Blast] this bastard!"

Shards of frost coalesced on Elandra's hand as she pooled her mana. She hurled it like a spear and the blast struck the wyrm head-on. A cold frost outlined the wyrm's body. Ice cracked and bits of its body shattered off as it writhed, slowed.

Brom, Fitmigar, and Rammy charged in to finish it.

Its tail swung out, slamming Brom and Fitmigar against the side of the tunnel. Then another sweeping strike knocked Rammy to the ground.

"Elandra! Keep up the ice!" I shouted.

She gathered another [Ice Blast]. "But it's not doing anything?"

"It's helping," I said. It slowed the wyrm enough to let Mallen and Sars retreat.

With Sars out of its range, the wyrm immediately turned to open its wide tooth-lined maw and engulf Rammy in a single bite as the redhead lay on the floor, dazed. Ice, arrows, and my own fireball flew out, knocking the creature's head off target. Its teeth instead bit into the damned bedrock.

Rammy growled in pain as Helstrom helped him clear. His leg was bleeding, and it had only grazed him. The wyrm lifted its head, letting out a series of deep undulating clicks and slamming its body against the tunnel. Its head reoriented and locked on the closest mage.

It must have some kind of tremor sense, I realized as I watched it writhe and attack.

"Fitmigar, wait for my signal and then throw up a [Rock Wall]!" I shouted.

The dwarf nodded as another spray of acid spurted out of the wyrm's maw.

A gust of wind ruffled our cloaks and hair as Sienna's [Wind Burst] breezed through the room. Acid that had been about to rain on Brom changed directions mid-flight, splattering instead on the stony wall, which it melted into gooey slag. Brom stared at the splatter, eyes wide.

I faked a fall and the beast twisted and turned, fangs and gum sizzling from its own acid. It lumbered towards me, mouth opening wide.

"Now!" I screamed.

Two pillars of stone struck out from the cavern floor, smashing into the wyrm. As it jerked, momentarily stunned in agony, broken fangs littering the tunnel floor, I pulled mana into a huge [Fireball] and hurled it straight into the beast's maw. An explosion of fire detonated within its bulbous body, lighting up the chitinous scales and skeleton for a split-second before its top half burst open.

We all ducked into cover as acid and fleshy bits rained down. The rest of the wyrm collapsed with a heavy thud, shaking the cavern floor.

I hastily brushed some acidy-flesh off my armor before it could eat through and rose to my feet.

"Everyone alive?"

A round of affirmatives returned.

Others tended to the wounded, mainly Sars' arm and Rammy's leg, while I inspected the remains. One of the eyes had survived the explosion. *Black.*

Deep-fucking-black.

More of that fucking mind control.

Dwarven shouts sounded out from the other side of the cavern. I looked across to see another twenty-foot-long wyrm closing in on the captives.

Damn. "Another wyrm!" I shouted and hurried to help. I pulled on my still-abundant mana and threw an [Ice Blast] at the beast. Two more flew from beside me, thrown by Elandra and Sars. His left arm hung limp, his face red with exertion as he hobbled at my side.

"Take it easy, Sars."

"I'm not done after the first fight," he insisted.

"Then stay back as artillery. I'm going in," I said and began towards the other end of the cave.

Frost covered, the beast's movements slowed. The dwarves scrambled upright and formed up into a defensive formation behind their axes and shields. As I approached, magic-empowered arrows flew in over me, puncturing the wyrm's scaly hide and rocking it with their force. Still, it refused to go down. Closing in, I shouted "Halt arrows!"

The wyrm turned to slowly inspect me with its black eyes. I stepped on its tail and ran up its body to reach the neck. Scimitars twirling, I laid slashes and stabs into the frozen scales. Blood stained the frost.

But the wyrm writhed, flicking its tail out. I had to roll off and away to avoid being crushed.

Mallen dove past me while I regained my footing. His war hammer met the beast's face. Ice shattered and ichor burst. Teeth flew off. The beast shook its head, dismissing the strike.

How strong was this thing?

Helstrom and Brom reached its body, axes and [Shadow Blade] stabbing into the scales. It writhed, attempting to slam and bite us off, but with so many coming at it and the frost slowing it down, there was always an opening for one or two of us to take advantage of. Rammy's greatsword bit into its body. He roared and hacked again with an overhead cleave that I swore I could hear his sword move through the air as the powerful swing cut deep the wyrm's body. The muscular redhead bellowed and continued to chop away as if he didn't have a blood-soaked rag tied around his leg.

As I joined in, Fitmigar came flying past me, mace in hand, screaming in dwarven. Her weapon met the creature's skull with a wet crack.

Still, the wyrm defied death. Its maw reared back. Acid bubbled and frothed on its gums.

As one, we buried it in a blender of steel.

Flesh was cleaved off in chunks. Bones were pulverized. Organs smashed. That acid breath never came.

The wyrm flopped on the ground. Its tail twitched one last time, before all life faded from its dark eyes.

We stepped back. A few of us stumbled against their weapons and friends, breathing heavily.

"Still alive?" I asked.

Another round of affirmatives came in reply.

I wiped my scimitars from ichor and cleaned off the acid as best I could. With the current threat now destroyed, the dwarves lowered their shields and edged forward. As they came into the light, a look of recognition appeared across one of their weathered faces.

"Fitmigar?"

She looked across at the dwarf who had spoken. "Brother!"

The dwarf limped forward, blood running down his left leg, and clasped arms with his sister. He grinned fiercely. "You have our thanks. All of you."

"No need for thanks," Fitmigar stressed, giving him a small hug. "Talk as we move, Frenell. We be in a hurry."

Her brother nodded, and as we left the butchered wyrms behind, he filled us in on the situation.

"We didn't see them coming," he started. "Was all we could do to try and get to the tunnels. Stragglers we be. All the other dwarves are inside."

I nodded beside him. "What of their plans?"

"Larne here overheard the orcs. They have shaman here. Plan to use some kind of mind control to force dwarven earth mages to pull the whole thing down if they can't do so themselves. The dwarves they'll be after will likely be locked away toward the top of the tower by now."

Just as we'd feared.

We stepped up our pace as much as the wounds allowed. The dwarves we left behind for now, for their safety and so we wouldn't need to protect them in combat.

Thankfully, we passed no more bodies as we made our way up. Nor were we ambushed by any more wyrms. We reached the door that Frenell had said led into the main entrance hall and took up defensive positions. When everyone had a spell or weapon prepared, I took a deep breath, slid the slab aside, and stepped out into bright sunlight.

Hang on… Sunlight?

Interlude 5

As the low light of dawn broke, Lana and Enallo paced before their squads. Today, they would meet the orcish forces head-on. Today, they would face drakes, basilisks, wyverns, and wyrms. Galen had already delivered his grand speech, and now all that remained for the pair of squad leaders was to lead their griffin knights into war. Harnell had taken all three hundred-odd elves a couple of hours previous in an effort to time their arrival with the griffin knights for a bigger boost in ally morale and more devastating initial charge.

A sound plan, but the waiting was stressful. Lana's guts were in a knot. She was nauseous. Her hands were damp with sweat. She didn't let it show though. No. Lana was the ace student, the most proficient mage, and the best leader. She would not be the first one to show fear.

"Worried?" Enallo asked.

"No." Lana scoffed, offended he would even ask. "You?"

"Not in the slightest." He swallowed. "I think it's time."

"So it is." The pair nodded toward each other, turned on their griffins, and lifted an arm into the air.

"For Atania!" they roared, their cry echoed by the eighteen knights and joined by the defiant screeches of twenty griffins. Lana nudges her knees, and her griffin galloped forward, picking up speed down the grassy slope, churning the turf, aiming for the end of the tree line near the fast-flowing river below. A rumble of paws and talons followed right behind her.

A step from the edge, a single beat of the wings lifted them off. They quickly climbed altitude on the powerful wings, up into the cloudless sky. Wind streamed past her face and howled against her winged helmet. The ground raced beneath them in a blur.

Lana turned on her griffin's back, signaling for the others to follow her lead. Turning to the north, her griffin screeched. Nineteen others cried out in response, surging forward.

It felt like barely a moment had passed before they arrived on the front line. Chaotic battlelines snaked across the rocky landscape. Scores of individual battles raged around the tiniest of environmental advantages—small valleys, flat areas, and high grounds. Steel and green of human and elven uniforms held back the surging tide of mis-matched orcish forces. Arrows flew in volleys, felling dozens. Spears and javelins of the orcish forces thunked against a shield-wall of humans, some piercing through shield and armor both. Charn's voice sang loud, his [Ballad Boost] imbuing the knights with a mana boost to strengthen their assault. Some heads both ally and enemy turned skyward, pointing.

Lana hovered in place and took it all in, Enallo beside her. Wind changed directions as eighteen griffin knights soared past them and flew into battle.

[Fireball]s and [Ice Blast]s mixed with [Lightning Bolt]s and ruptured earth. Over a hundred orcs fell in the opening salvo.

Something seemed to have lit within the allied forces. Their tide threw itself to match the orcs with renewed ferocity. Slowly, the orcs started to fall back. Further magical bombardments only speeded up the allied advance.

It was working. They were turning the tide. Lana looked to Enallo. The knot in her guts had not come undone. If anything, it was tightening. The orcs were now put to the slaughter, their forces crippled under overwhelming aerial support.

But where were the drakes, the basilisks, and the wyverns?

Where was the draconic army?

Chapter Twenty-Two

Sunlight?

I gasped as I realized the great stone gate of the fortress had been utterly destroyed. Huge granite slabs lay in shattered pieces. A couple of dark green dwarven banners fluttered on the wall. Broken tables and benches lay scattered across the ruined fine carpets of the fortified entrance hall floor.

On the upper floors above, murder holes for archers and mages to rain down death appeared empty, unmanned. The dwarves must've retreated much higher up.

I scanned the surroundings warily, keeping myself hidden to the side. The doors leading farther into the fortress were ajar as well. Something big had smashed through every door and seal. I needed to make sure it wasn't poised to strike us down the moment we stepped into the open.

Battle raged outside still, huge beasts wrestling with griffin knights over the labyrinthine quarry. Claw meeting talon. Beak meeting maw. Spell meeting draconic skin. Something had changed since we entered the tunnels, turning the tide of the battle back in our enemy's favor.

I ducked in as a massive shape crashed into the hall. Glymavor, the lightning mage griffin knight, backed off from a drake. The beast had him cornered near the bottom of the staircase leading to the floors above, and the elf was staggering, injured. He flung out weak [Lightning Bolt]s, barely keeping it at bay.

I had to act. Charging out across the hall, I pulled on my mana and threw out my right hand, launching a [Fireball]. A bloom of flames engulfed the drake's head. The beast crumpled, its head a sizzling mess of char.

I slid to a stop beside Glymavor. "What's happening?"

"We had them!" he shouted back. "The orcs mostly defeated! Then the beasts arrived..." He wobbled and dropped to his knees, his hands flying to his face.

"What? How many?" I crouched beside him. *What the hells were we facing?*

"More than we could meet," he said. "Drakes, basilisks, a couple of wyverns swooping down, even a giant wyrm, fifty feet long at least. Tamar, Rylundur, Aernon... they never saw them coming..."

A rose to my feet aghast, mouth wide. We'd lost riders...

I shook it off. This was no time to let emotions take me. We always knew there would be casualties. This was war.

"It was the giant wyrm that broke down the doors," he explained just as a soul-rending cry split the air.

I spun around to see a griffin cry out outside, nudging a fallen knight with her beak. His body was bent double, a huge gash opening up the side of his chest.

There was too much blood around him for there to be any hope.

This was brutal, but we had to continue. I tossed a health potion from my pocket to Glymavor, and he nodded in thanks. The others had climbed up from the tunnels now and looked at the battle outside warily.

I shook my head, clearing my thoughts. The pair of wyverns Glymavor mentioned still flew outside, meeting griffin knights in battle in the lightening sky, and basilisks roamed the grounds battling mounted elves and griffins alike. "Where's the giant wyrm?" I asked.

Glymavor looked up. "It went up the stairs, joined by a couple of those shaman, a handful of orcs, and a few drakes."

"And the other dwarves?" I pressed.

He nodded. "Up. Apparently, one is a powerful earth mage. The one they intend to capture to bring this whole place down."

"Me dad," came from beside me, and I turned to see Fitmigar, eyes wide.

"He's the mage they need?" I asked.

"Aye. It was he who strengthened the walls in the first place," she confirmed, her gaze focused on the staircase.

"Fuck," said Brom from beside us.

"Fuck," Fitmigar agreed.

"Yep," I said. "We better hurry. Glymavor, I don't know where Bernolir is, but we need you to hold this space. Nothing else comes up after us. Syl, help them hold it. Helstrom, see if you can locate the main dwarven survivors holed up down here. They can't have all gone to the top of the tower, and you know the layout."

I continued, "You need to get everyone out of the fort. Fitmigar showed us tunnels you can use to evacuate them all through back towards the mountain villages. They don't need to remain to defend the fort anymore. That option's gone. Get them out in case this all comes crashing down."

The three nodded in confirmation, immediately falling into defensive positions at the base of the staircase.

"Everyone else, we go up."

We rushed up the stairs, taking the steps two at a time. The footsteps of my friends followed right behind me, pounding against the stone.

We reached the first floor to find our way blocked by a group of drakes, massive lizard beasts larger than griffins with winged forelimbs and taloned hindlegs. Spittle dripped from their fanged maws as they prowled toward us. The spikes on their spines stood up and their long whip-like tails flicked from side to side. The first lowered on its back legs, tensed up, and then sprang forward, hissing as it charged.

I reacted instantly, sending a [Fireball] at it. It exploded in the beast's chest and the impact sent it cracking against the stone wall. Chest smoldering like old coals, it slid limp onto the floor, singed, smoking, and very, very dead.

Holy fuck...

The others formed up around me, all well-drilled enough to not stare open-mouthed at the power I'd just shown.

Sienna stood at my side, bow out, [Gale force]-imbued arrows already protruding from three drakes. Her mana surge was not only increasing the power of her shots but also seemingly allow her to fire faster than ever.

Mallen threw out two [Lightning Bolt]s. The arcs of thunder seared into the drake's chest, making it seize up with silent cries of pain. He didn't pause to admire his aim, though. Charging in with his war hammer raised, he swung it down on the drake's head before it could recover, rattling its skull.

Fitmigar's mace joined in, meeting the side of the second drake's head. Broken fangs and blood flew from the beast's maw. Rammy followed up, forcing his greatsword through the beast's long neck to confirm the kill.

On my other side, Elandra strode toward the two remaining drakes, her sword ready and back straight in a fencer's pose. Sars stood beside her, a little unsteady on his feet. He'd taken a health potion, but the acid still crippled the movements of his left arm.

Scimitars swirling, I joined the pair in facing down the remaining beasts.

Snarls from behind drew my attention. I glanced back to see three more drakes closing in.

"Change of plans," I said, nudging Elandra to turn. "We'll take these three. Mallen, Fitmigar, Sienna, Rammy, finish the two in the corner! Brom, you're with us."

"On it!" came back from the others.

"Already here," said Brom's disembodied voice. The first sign of his presence was announced by a [Shadow Blade] appearing above one of the new drakes. It dropped down before the creature even saw it, staking it through the head. The body dropped to the ground, blood and brain spurting against the stony floor.

The other two drakes began snapping and snarling at empty air, and I could hear Brom yelp as he retreated.

"Elandra, you take the right one, I'll take the left. Swift and brutal. Sars, cover us. We have to get moving," I urged. This fort could come down any moment, with us in it.

My girl nodded once, slid her sword away, and threw out a hand. The drake before her froze in place. She hurled another ice spell, and another. Pain contorted the drake's features as its blood froze in its veins and it stilled. The accidental tail-swipe of its kin shattered it into a million icy fragments.

Elandra turned and winked, a soft smile on her face. "You may praise me now."

Whoa... No wonder both girls loved the mana surge being with me provided.

No sooner did her enemy drop than I was carving through the remaining beast, chopping sections of its body away with each swing of my scimitars, the ground soon a bloody mess of butchered drake.

I turned, wiping blood from my face. I heard another drake corpse drop.

The others stood over it proudly, Fitmigar kicking the head of a deceased drake, Mallen smiling in grim determination.

Movement in the skies outside caught my eye through the narrow window. I smiled as I saw the outline of twenty griffin knights flying in over the mountains to join us. The battle must be under control at the border if they were able to reinforce us. A welcome sight. Every spell, every sword, every claw and talon mattered.

"Up we go!" I roared and led the charge. Others formed up at my sides and rear. Brom remained cloaked, reminding me of his presence with a tap on the shoulder.

We were halfway up the next flight when the tower shook, sending us to our knees.

It was starting. The tower was going to fall.

I pushed myself back to my feet and charged onward.

I heard the snarl before I even saw the drake that prowled the second-floor landing. Still racing up the stairs, I threw out a [Wind Wall] as I reached the top step, the spell flying out and sending the beast skidding forcefully into the back wall.

I took one further step before a bright crackle of lightning filled my vision. I dove into a panicked roll. A huge crack sounded behind me. Static electricity zapped through me, raising all my hairs.

Shaman…

"Fitmigar, [Earth Wall]!" I shouted, while hugging myself against a pillar for cover. "Push it forward! Elandra, Rammy, Sars, fire spells over and around the walls, any you can manage, force the shamans out into the open!"

The trio peeked out around the earthen wall, peppering the shamans with fire and ice. All the while, Fitmigar strode purposely forward, arms outstretched, pushing the wall toward our assailants.

Methodically they closed in, forcing the shamans out of hiding, out into my line of sight. I hit the first shaman in the face with an [Ice Blast], instantly encasing him above shoulders. The shaman clutched at his frozen face, flailing. The second shaman evaded my spell, throwing up some kind of magical wind shield and charged me. His face was red with fury and his staff raised high.

He made it five steps before a [Gale Force]-imbued arrow exploded, nailing him through an eye. His body collapsed, skidding across the floor.

Bones and armor crunched where Fitmigar's earth wall pressed orcish warriors against the wall, crushing them to death.

"The shaman is mine!" I shouted as I ran to meet the first shaman. He had shattered the ice around his head and was struggling onto his knees, balancing against his staff.

I kicked the staff from his hand. He dropped with a grunt.

"Your mind control tricks end now, Shaman," I whispered, bringing my arm back for the fatal strike.

"Foooolllllssss… we do not control the weak-minded. Geilazar has the dwarf now as we sssspppeeaakk. It is our master who will bring this feeble fort crasssshhing down." He laughed. "You've already llllllost."

Who the fuck is Geilazar?

The shaman reverted to the orcish tongue, trying to prepare another lightning spell. In one movement, I drove both blades down into his skull, stopping the casting before he had a chance to release his attack.

The others had finished up too. Elandra smiled grimly as she wiped dark blood from her blade. Fitmigar paced next to her, ichor still dripping from her mace.

A loud bang sounded from a door the orcs had guarded.

I ran over and pulled the door open. Several elderly dwarves tumbled out, falling before struggling back to their feet.

"Thrargud," one wheezed. "The shapeshifter has Thrargud."

I looked to Fitmigar, and she nodded. Her father.

"The shapeshifter? Geilazar?" I asked.

"Aye," the dwarf replied, bent double, struggling.

"So... the huge wyrm?"

"Aye, and if what Thrargud feared is true, he also be able to turn into a dragon."

Holy fuck...

Sars stepped up beside me, still looking a little woozy from his mana exertion and acid attack. "Jadyn, Galen spoke of this Geilazar once, and his name has cropped up in my reading. He was kicked out the academy decades ago for learning a forbidden spell. Disappeared north."

The tower rocked again. Dust fell from the ceiling.

"Great time to learn this now," I muttered. "Right, we need to run." I looked at the elderly dwarves. "Get out of the tower and save yourselves. This thing is about to come down."

As we pressed on towards the top of the tower, I shouted back, "This is going to be the most dangerous thing we'll likely ever attempt. We've got no time to plan, we just have to blast our way in and take this fucker down!"

A small group of orcish warriors blocked our path to the third-floor landing. Flashing swords separated orcish skin from bone. Arrows found chests and heads alike, and Fitmigar's swirling mace ended up dripping in orcish brain matter.

We cut them down before they got a strike in. Brom was the only one to take any kind of blow, but it bounced cleanly off his chest plate as we burst through. Another thunderous boom shook the tower, forcing us to brace against the walls. We hurried upright and ran. However, a few steps from the top floor, a growl from behind caught me mid-step. I almost fell as I twisted on the stairs.

Then, relief flooded me when I saw a charging jaguar, teeth dripping with dark ichor.

Ella...

Chapter Twenty-Three

"She's Ella," I said, sensing Brom was about to jump her.

Nodding once to the shapeshifting ranger, I turned and continued upwards, quickly reaching a short stone-walled corridor that led to a single wooden door at the end.

A wooden door that was guarded by the largest fucking orc I'd ever seen, eight foot tall and rippling with tensing muscle. Three blue stripes had been painted across his grizzled face. He tossed a huge double-edged axe from hand to hand so effortlessly I would've thought it made entirely of wood, if not for the blood-soaked metal edges. A large feral grin split his tusk-filled mouth. He took a step toward me.

"Fighhhhttt…"

I didn't have time to melee this bastard now. Fitmigar's father was the other side of that door, and the tower might come crashing down any second now.

"Figghhhhhttttt!" the orc roared again, stepping closer, swishing the axe through the air with one hand, beckoning me on with the other, spittle flying from his mouth.

Yeah, fuck that.

I poured a good chunk of mana into a [Fireball] and hurled it straight at the prick's face. Flames exploded around his upper half. The orc fell backwards, its head a smoking ruin of charcoal. Shaking my head at the precious seconds wasted, I stepped over his smoldering corpse and kicked in the door.

We barged into a dome-roofed room. The space was bathed in blue-purple light by runes that coated every available surface.

An elderly dwarf lay prostrate on the ground, leather restraints binding him to the wooden floor. Cuts and bruises marred his face, and his left arm lay at an awkward angle. It was clear he'd struggled before Geilazar got into his mind.

Now, the shapeshifter towered over Thrargud in wyrm form, his titanic bulk rising until his head brushed the underside of the room's domed ceiling.

Immediately, he slammed his massive body in our direction, before I'd even taken two steps into the room. I rushed back and shoved the people back into the hallway as a gigantic tail swept past us, cracking stone.

"In! In! Distract him to disrupt his control spell!" I shouted, and we streamed into the room.

The others followed as I dashed in left, trying to circle around him. Sienna immediately threw up a mana-dense [Wind Wall] to deflect a huge acid breath, which splashed into the far wall and began to eat through the already shaky stone. Thrargud groaned, the elderly dwarf's arm flicking out as the runes lit up again. Another thunderous boom rocked the tower. Fissures spiderwebbed between and through the boulders and bedrock the fortress was made of. The dwarf had black eyes. It seemed like Geilazar didn't even need to focus to maintain his control. *Damn.*

"Change of plans!" I shouted. "We end him here!"

Roars of approval and wrath agreed with me. Arrows peppered Geilazar around his eyes and weak-spots, forcing him to coil and guard his face with his bulk. Ella pounced in, her razor-sharp teeth and claws ripping into his skin. Ice blasts rained down on the tail to try glue it to the floor. Electricity arced to zap it.

However, nothing slowed down the great wyrm. He shrugged Ella from his writhing body. Her jaguar form twisted in the air to land on all four paws and skidded to a stop across from our current position. He had her cornered.

Geilazar's tail whipped out at Ella, and I threw out a [Wind Wall]. Wind blasted against its bulk, slowing the blow just enough to allow her to vault off the wall and jump over the tail, then sprint to our side. The tower creaked again. Gravity began to tilt a little sideways. Wind whistled through the cracks. Sounds of battle outside now reached us clearly.

Time was almost up. Thrargud looked like a withered husk. The tower had mere moments before it crumbled.

Fitmigar crept toward the middle of the room to try reach her father, but a whip of Geilazar's tail struck her back into the wall. She slumped to the floor, barely breathing, her chest plate dented. Brom disappeared, reappearing at her side to press a potion to her lips.

Mallen threw [Lightning Bolt]s and Sars tried [Ice Blast]s, but their mana was running low. Geilazar batted the spells away with his tail as his body changed before our eyes. Legs, small and stubby, sprouted from his lower body, and wings burst from his back, growing larger by the second, a thin pink membrane darkening between them.

Fuck…

I needed to hit him with all I had before he became a dragon. If he changed completely, one breath of fire and we were all done for. The heat would blow out a wind wall, melt rock and ice, and overpower any flames I could call forth.

I pulled deeply on my core. Mana rushed through my body. I screamed defiantly as I poured as much I could into a[Fire Wall*].

A huge, towering wall of flame roared across the room, flying at the twisted creature.

Geilazar's mouth split into a feral grin. Then, a single strike of his wings turned the [Fire Wall*] around, buffeting it back toward our party.

Elandra and I threw out protective [Ice Blast]s, slowing the wall of flame some. Sienna joined our side, hurling out a [Water Burst] that extinguished it into tiny flickers.

Sienna had her bow already out again. Her arrows peppered the wyrm-dragon hybrid, catching it in half-transformed joints, delaying its transformation.

"Joints and half-formed parts! Hit them before it can change!" I called out.

The others joined in, copying Sienna's tactic.

Geilazar shook his huge head and roared, and the runes in the room glowed again. Thrargud's back arched, though the dwarf looked half-dead by now. Already, stones were falling from the outer wall to the quarry floor below.

We had to finish this here. If he fully transformed, there was no telling how dangerous he would be in the open skies.

Ella came in again, tearing through the webbing of his right wing. A [Shadow Blade] then appeared from the left, slicing into the left wing.

Nice work, Brom!

Still, Geilazar continued to transform. Our spells were bouncing off him, seemingly without dealing any harm. I looked around the group. Everyone was on their last dregs, mana almost depleted and vigor nearly spent. Our physical blows felt like ants wrath against a giant's toe, but we didn't falter. We couldn't.

We had to do this. We had to kill Geilazar now. If he escaped and lived to hurt others, every one of those lives lost would be on us.

I gestured Fitmigar, Mallen, and Sars to the left, encouraging them to wait on my signal to give everything they had, and then I did the same with Sienna, Elandra, and Rammy, moving them to the right.

"Now!" I screamed, launching the largest [Fireball] I could conjure at the wyrm's face.

[Lightning Bolt]s and [Ice Blast]s hit the beast from the left, arrows, [Ice Blast]s, and [Fireball]s from the right.

Fitmigar, meanwhile, directed her earth magic to move the very stones in the wall behind Geilazar, opening his back to the sky.

And with one final boom, the tower started to fall.

I sprinted across the room, heading straight for the shapeshifter. Something invisible cut through Thrargud's bonds as I passed him by, then dove headfirst toward Geilazar, powering my fall with [Wind Boost].

Scimitars first, I landed onto his chest. My knees and spine rattled with the impact, and I tasted blood. It had also been just enough to topple his massive frame off balance.

We fell, and I rode his body out the side of the collapsing tower and towards the ground and certain death.

My heart racing, eyes lock on the approaching ground, I wrenched Orcgrinder and Dragonkiller free and whistled hard.

Wind pulled me off the hybrid's body and into a helpless tumble. For a moment, I spun, the wind rushing past my face.

A screech called out from above.

Then a clawed paw arrested my fall, tossed me up, and Hestia flew down to catch me on her back.

"Good girl!" I laughed, giddy with the near-death adrenaline.

Hestia screeched back with cheery determination. We circled to help our friends.

But as the tower fell behind me, griffins of varying hues powered past us, grabbing their riders from the air. Fitmigar held her unconscious father in her arms as she leapt, and Gren caught them both.

As the stone and wood tower collapsed to the ground on the fort below, a single falcon swirled in the air above, and I breathed a sigh of relief to know that Ella was safe.

I also noticed that Geilazar had somehow stopped his fall and was airborne. His battered half-dragon form retreated from the fort with feeble, wing-strikes keeping him aloft in an erratic, jerky flight.

No, you fucking don't!

I nudged Hestia, and she immediately tucked her wings into a dive. We landed on the shapeshifter's back talons first. She dug into his right wing and pulled him into a spinning descent. He was still flailing when Dawnquill streamed by, raking her talons down his back to spill more dark ichor.

Shadowtail and Veo came next, claw, talon, and beak ripping flesh off the bones. Svendale and Mossrik joined in the fray with the other griffins.

Several griffins tore at Geilazar from every angle, with us riders adding steel to the bloodthirsty storm of talons and beaks. We worked as one, somehow perfectly in sync, each rider and griffin cognizant of their place in the butchery without a word or screech exchanged between us. All riding that perfect flow of violence like a pack of wolves descending on a wounded deer.

Geilazar's roar became a pitiful mewl. Chunks of his body tore off to splatter the ground below. It was working.

Geilazar was losing power. With no ability to retaliate, drained of all mana, life literally flowing from his body, he was heading for the ground.

We paused to let him fall.

Bones of the titanic beast cracked rocks with the impact. Dark blood pooled on the stony ground of the quarry.

Breathless, still dazed from with a strange bloodlust, I gave Hestia a pat.

Beneath us, the body of the wyrm-dragon lay twisted on the stones below. However, it still breathed weakly, and I prepared myself to end this threat once and for all.

As we hovered there, Geilazar's wings shriveled up, and the tail split, shrinking and forming a pair of mangled human legs. Before our eyes, the true form of Geilazar, the human, appeared, broken and beaten, wheezing for breath, blood pouring from every orifice and dozens of new holes.

Nudging Hestia to the ground, I alighted from her back, running a hand through her feathers, and strode over to finish Geilazar where he lay.

I lifted my scimitars high and drove them down, piercing the man's heart. With one final gasp, his eyes flew open, and deepest, darkest black stared back at me.

What?

Geilazar had been controlled all along…

This wasn't over.

Not by a long shot.

Chapter Twenty-Four

We'd done it. We stopped the shapeshifting dark mage and the ruthless draconic beasts and orcish horde that followed his orders. The fact that it turned out that Geilazar had been controlled all along was troubling, but with nothing to go on, we had done all we could. The battle at the border was won. The threat had been vanquished.

For now.

We sat now in the main border camp. A whole village of tents spread out over the dusk-darkened hills like a small sea of campfires. The buzz of celebration could be heard from every fire.

I was surrounded by my squad, my friends. We had lost four griffin knights -- Tamar, Rylundur, Aernon, and Oscar, one of the triplets – but we would not forget them. We would soon head back to the academy and honor them there.

Oscar's griffin, Kelia, still pined after the young knight, but we hoped, in time, she might find another rider to bond with. The other griffins had lost their lives with their riders.

Excusing myself from one of Fitmigar's stories, I rose and headed over to speak briefly with those I considered my seniors, passing several groups clustered around roaring fires as I weaved my way across camp. Galen looked up from around the fire he was seated at. The blond-haired elf rose to his feet and beckoned for me to join them.

"Good evening, sir—" I started.

"Now, Jadyn, I think you can drop the 'sir' after your recent accomplishments. At least, until we are back within academy grounds."

I nodded and acquiesced. "Galen."

As I took a seat, I gazed around the fire, noting all present, the flickering flames casting them all in shadow.

Harnell, but no Ryal. The brave young elf had not made it through the quarry labyrinth with his life. I'd been told he'd taken multiple orcs down with him, dying as a hero. Proud as they were of his sacrifice, his friends still looked to have eyes red from dried tears.

Algernon and Mirek. Mirek still seemed quiet, and I didn't have the energy to think about why. Guilt? Confusion? We wouldn't know more until we got back and had the chance to speak to the dean about Rivers, the beastkin.

They were joined by Embar, the nervous young potion maker looking a lot calmer since the threat level was reduced.

"Good evening," said Galen in return. "It isn't a time for serious talk, you all deserve to relax this evening, gods knows you've earned it, but we'll all need to get together in the coming days."

"Absolutely," I said. "There is still a threat out there. This isn't over."

"Indeed it isn't," Galen replied. "I suppose you'd like to know about Geilazar?"

"Please. Whatever you can tell me."

"I'll tell you all I know, Jadyn, though, admittedly, it isn't much. From what I understand, he was a very troubled young man who turned to dark, forbidden magic after his girlfriend died on academy grounds under what he had considered to be mysterious circumstances."

"He was a student at the academy?" I asked, aghast.

"He was, yes. It was before my time, but I believe it was Dean Hallow himself who banished him."

"Is there anything else you can tell me about him?" I asked.

"Unfortunately not," he admitted. "If you want to know more, I suggest you speak to the dean."

I made a mental note to do just that. "And what of going forward? Someone must have been controlling him."

"We will discuss that very threat this evening, in fact, going over our best plan for the future defense of Atania."

"Would you like me to join you all?" I asked. I'd have preferred to enjoy the festivities, but if duty called I would answer. Nothing mattered more than keeping the people of Atania safe.

"That won't be necessary," the elf said, and I felt myself relax. "You've done enough. Now, take young Ella off with you, and you all go and enjoy your evening. I fear we are boring her senseless."

The young elf smiled politely and leapt to her feet to follow me as we headed back across camp.

As we passed the first group, I overheard Lana telling all who would listen about how she had utilized all twelve of her earth spells in rapidly defeating the orcish forces that had remained at the border. She looked over and I nodded slightly, appreciating her actions if not her lack of modesty.

She nodded back, and I was almost caught off guard. Maybe I imagined it. It was likely just the flickering fire playing with her shadow.

I took a seat around my squad's fire. Ella walked around a little farther to sit in a space between Mallen and Sars. Sienna immediately leaned over, kissed me, and handed me a cup of ale.

I smiled in thanks and brought the drink to my lips. The soothing liquid ran down my throat, quenching a thirst I didn't realize I had. I made a sound of satisfaction and pulled Elandra in from my other side into a deep kiss. A murmur of delight left her lips as she arched her back.

"Mister Handsome's at it again already I see," Brom said, and a few chuckles broke out.

Fitmigar yanked him by the collar into a deep kiss of their own.

"Not just me it seems, buddy," I replied laughing.

He smiled back at me, a goofy look on his face.

"Shall we get this party started then?" Sars asked politely.

I smiled as roars of approval sounded out.

"As long as you keep that notebook safely away," Mallen added.

"You have my word," Sars replied, a smile cracking his otherwise serious expression.

"I'll be getting more ale then. Tonight's a proper drinking night," Fitmigar said, dragging Brom along by the hem of his shirt.

Brom stumbled to his feet, and the pair disappeared off to find Thom, who acted as the night's bartender. We were a little light on ale, but the spirits were plentiful, and he knew how to mix them good.

Most of it was sourced from the semi-destroyed stores of a dwarven fort. We'd at first worried the supplies were gone, but it was amazing what a stocky shadow mage could achieve when he was thirsting for alcohol.

"Bear with me a moment," I told the others, rising to my feet again.

Thinking about it again, it wouldn't do to have us divided into three groups. We were one group. All fourth-year academy students, all Griffin Knights of Atania. We should be hanging out together on a night like this. Heading over to the two other fires, I soon returned with twenty more griffin knights in tow. My friends had already backed away from our fire, creating room for everyone.

I looked at a certain sandy-haired bard. "Care to officially start this party?" I asked, smiling broadly.

"You've got it, Jadyn," Charn replied. I could sense him pulling on his mana stores. This would do us all the world of good, helping boost of our mana levels — if only it also helped with the hangovers that would surely arrive tomorrow.

Enallo joined me at my side. "Jadyn, you know that it's a Darlish Coast tradition to join in a round of blue lightning to celebrate any great battle victory, right?"

He was likely messing with me, but if so I didn't mind it. A little silliness would bring us all together as one in celebration and remembrance of the fallen, so I nodded and smiled.

"Get it sorted then, Enallo. Blue Lightnings all around. I'm pretty parched here."

He nodded respectfully, barely suppressing a smirk. "Harlee! Let's get them sorted!"

I laughed as I saw Enallo's friend start to collect cups. This was going to be a night of epic proportions.

Charn burst into song, and Brom cheered loudly as he returned, arms full of ales. "Finally! The venereal tales of the farmer's daughter!"

Charn winked and [Ballad Boost]ed his voice even higher, the more well-oiled of the group immediately joining in with the bawdy tune.

I laughed and sat back down, wrapping an arm around Sienna and Elandra, pulling my girls close. I was feeling drained. The battle had cost me more mana than I ever thought my body capable of holding, but I hoped that my girls and I would all be feeling much, much better before the night was over.

Sienna leaned her head on my shoulder, softly sighing as she raised her drink to her lips. Elandra, on the other hand, was boisterously accompanying Charn from my side, taking special delight in the farmer's daughter's nocturnal adventures.

"So, what happens next?" Sienna asked.

I stared at the others dance and sing for a bit before answering, "From what Commander Flint told me, we head back to the academy. We've done well these past few days, but we still have much to learn."

"And if they need us again?" Mallen asked from a couple of logs down.

"Then we go," I told him. "We learn when we can, and then we fight when we have to. There's a larger threat out there than Geilazar, so we need to improve, be stronger, learn to better work together in the skies."

"And then next time we head to the border, maybe it'll only take half the time to get there," Brom said having found his seat and chugged back another ale.

"That's the dream, buddy," I said.

I couldn't wait to be able to travel longer distances on Hestia's back, covering great spans in a single day. Maybe one day we'd even be able to cover the distance to Eilerin Island, home of the beastkin, just out across the Eilerin Sea or farther over the raging seas. It might be a dream to most, but something, deep down, told me there was more out there to discover.

More to threaten us.

"Blue lightning!" came the roar, and several of the Darlish Coast students, led by Harlee, started passing out their concoctions as they moved around the group.

I glanced around the fireside to see Ella looking back at me, a hesitant look on her face as she sat there with a blue drink in her hand.

I gestured for her to copy me, and then I threw my own drink back, gasping as the heat of the various spirits hit my throat.

Ella did the same and then laughed as she coughed, her eyes watering.

We traded knowing grins.

She wiped a sleeve across her mouth and then fell into conversation with a couple of girls at her side. They all giggled at something.

Another drink soon appeared in my hand, and I felt warmth suffuse my body as the songs got louder, the laughter increased, and the worries of the day drifted away into drink and night.

We continued to sing and dance around the fire for hours, letting ourselves be just fourth year students again, if only for a night.

After a sweat-inducing dance with Elandra, I took a moment to excuse myself and wandered across camp. I found Hestia where she roamed in the temporary paddock they had created.

"How are you doing, girl?" I asked, running my hand through her feathers as she lowered her head, chuffing gently at my ear.

I tapped her once on the side of the neck, gently, and she lowered herself to the ground. I sat next to her and lay back against her side for a while, gazing up at the sky above, feeling her powerful heart beating against her chest as I pondered life.

My gaze rested on the stars above. Some part of my drunken brain remembered learning that each light up there was a potential other world, drifting through the cosmos. Considering the sheer scale of it all made me feel small. Here we were battling hard to keep our people safe, and there was so much more potential danger out there.

Or perhaps wonder. Who knows what you might find in the stars?

We laughed and joked when students spoke of potential other land masses on our world, out across the raging seas, but what if there was life up there, too, in the stars. Would we ever feel truly safe? Sars spoke occasionally of stories of griffins and riders traveling between worlds, but we couldn't even travel off our own coastline. It couldn't be true, right?

I shook my head and brought myself back to the now. Laughter and song still sounded across the night, and I was likely going to be missed soon.

As I pushed myself to my feet, gently patted Hestia's neck, and wandered back toward the fireside, I noticed Ella had also made her way across camp and now sat with Kelia, soothing the distressed griffin with elven words I couldn't hope to understand.

Returning to the fire, I seamlessly slid in again at Sienna's side.

She turned and smiled at me, and I whispered, "You want to get out of here?"

"Elandra, too, right?"

"Of course," I replied, leading her across to the dark-skinned beauty's side.

Elandra looked up, the flames dancing in her eyes. "Ooh, is it time?"

I laughed. "It's time." I leant down and offered my hand, pulling her to her feet.

"Where are you taking us?" she asked before kissing me and running her hands through my hair.

"You'll see," I told her, leading my girls through the trees, heading toward the sound of running water.

We walked for a few minutes, the sound of crashing water growing ever louder, before I pulled back a branch and revealed a cascading waterfall beyond.

"Ooh…" Sienna's mouth dropped open. "It's so beautiful."

"It's missing something," Elandra added, looking me up and down.

I smiled and pulled them closer, revealing a blanket I'd laid out on a rock near the water's edge earlier in the evening.

Elandra growled, and I realized there was a whole lot of pent-up frustration about to come tumbling out. I pulled her in and pressed my lips against hers, forcing them apart as she moaned against me. Her hands flew to my top, lifting my shirt as I felt Sienna's hands come around my waist from behind, tugging at the waistband.

I dropped my hands and lifted Elandra's shirt over her head, releasing her breasts, losing myself in the beauty before me. I paused for a moment as I felt Sienna's bare chest press up against my back, and I smiled.

I turned and grabbed her hands. "Nu-uh… you first." She smiled in that way that made me think she was still shy and lowered her pants to the ground, standing naked before me.

"Hells yeah," Elandra said, and I turned to see she had done likewise, both my girls naked at my side.

"Where do you want us?" Sienna asked, her sultry tone stretching my control to the limit.

The scenery was beautiful, picturesque, but our need for each other was primal, raw. I needed them both. Now.

"Both of you, on the blanket, on your hands and knees. Now…"

My girls giggled, swaying their hips as they seductively walked over, dropping to their knees before leaning over, perfect asses wiggling in the air as they placed their elbows on the ground and moaned in wanting.

"What are you going to do to us, Jadyn?" Elandra asked, looking back over her shoulder and running her tongue over her lips.

I wasn't here to talk. I pushed my pants down to the ground and off. I strolled over to them, dropping down behind them both and running a finger up between their thighs, feeling how wet they were, already begging for me.

I slipped a single finger inside each, before teasing and slipping in a second. Both girls moaned, bucking against my hands as I teased them, backs arching, legs trembling slightly.

Keeping my fingers inside Elandra's pussy, I took my hardened cock and slipped it inside Sienna. A gasp slipped from her as I pushed it in deep, thrusting against her, chasing release. She bucked against me, and I moved faster, the spray of the waterfall glistening off her perfect skin.

Feeling her tighten against me, her breathing quickening, I slid out and moved across. My fingers slipped between her thighs again as I knelt behind Elandra and pushed my cock into the dark-skinned beauty's soaking pussy.

"Oh, Jadyn..." she murmured, tightening around my shaft. Sienna's breathing quickened against my fingers.

Two girls bent over, trembling under my touch, but I needed release. I needed to spurt hot streams inside them both.

Sienna bucked against my hand, her body tensing. I continued to plow into Elandra, her whimpers and cries growing in volume as I gave her everything I had, every inch, every breath.

Sienna came first. Her juices ran between my fingers as she cried out in ecstasy. Elandra soon joined her as I pushed deep. Her legs trembled as she lost all control. She was still climaxing against me as I released into her, stream after stream shooting inside her.

"Fuck..." Elandra cried out, dropping to the ground, arms splayed out, breath hitching.

I slid out of her and moved back to Sienna. This mana surge was instant now, and it seemed to be able to keep me going, so I wasn't going to refuse the chance.

I grabbed Sienna by the hips, lifted her ass, and slid my cock back inside her. Tense from her recent orgasm, her sex hugged me with a vise-like grip.

She whimpered, looking back at me, her cheeks flushed. "Already?"

"You bet," I told her, pushing in slowly at first but quickly thrusting harder, pulling her against me.

"Give it to her, Jadyn. All of it!" Elandra cried from beside us, her hand already working its way between her legs, teasing her folds as she watched me fucking Sienna.

Our cries increased, and the tension drained out of us all as we all came together, collapsing into a heap on the stony floor. Moments of bliss passed, where the only thing I heard was my girls' labored pants and moans.

"Hells yeah, Jadyn," murmured Sienna. "I needed that."

"I think we all did," I told her.

"We're not done yet are we?" Elandra whispered from my side.

I pushed myself up onto my elbows. "Not by a long shot," I told them both. We had all night.

"Jadyn?"

I sat up, immediately alert, full of energy.

"Jadyn. We have received a message from the academy."

I looked at Sars as he leant over me, doing his best to not stare at the two semi-naked girls curled up next to where I had been lying.

"Where is it?" I asked, rubbing the sleep from my eyes.

Sars passed me the rolled-up parchment, pausing as he waited on me to open it.

I slipped the ribbon off and unrolled the missive, my eyes widening as I ran through its contents.

"Well?" he asked, shifting from side to side.

"Dean Hallow says they've made a discovery while we've been away."

"What kind of discovery?"

"They captured someone uncovering a door under the arena floor made of some unknown stone. Covered in some script that no one can interpret. Apparently, it's reinforced with strong magic. Too strong for the dean, even."

"Anything on who they captured?" Sars asked.

"Nothing," I admitted. "Makes sense given the precarious nature of these messages."

"Holy fuck…" came from the tent flaps, and I looked up to see Brom stood there, mouth wide open, Fitmigar stood at his side.

"Holy fuck indeed, buddy. We best get packed. We're due back at the academy with upmost haste."

End of Book One.

About the Author

Travis Dean is an author of progression fantasy with more than a touch of spice. Griffin Academy: Knights of War is his debut novel.

Travis hopes you've enjoyed meeting Jadyn and the griffin knights of Atania and are as excited to follow his journey as he is to bring it to you.

Amongst other places, you can find Travis on Facebook and X (@TravisDeanGA), so do come by and say hello.

Check This Out !

Thank you for reading!
If you enjoyed this book, please leave a review.
Reviews are so important to authors.

Join the Royal Guard Publishing Discord to participate in tons of giveaways, extra content, and chat with all our authors and narrators.

Check out

For more Harem Lit / LitRPG Adventures:

www.royalguardpublishing.com

https://www.facebook.com/RoyalGuard2020

https://www.facebook.com/groups/dukesofharem

https://www.facebook.com/groups/haremlitbooks

https://www.reddit.com/r/haremfantasynovels/

https://www.facebook.com/groups/LitRPG.books

https://www.facebook.com/groups/litrpgforum

https://www.facebook.com/groups/LitRPGReleases

https://www.reddit.com/r/litrpg/

https://www.facebook.com/groups/LitRPGsociety

Printed in Great Britain
by Amazon